KILL
switch

KILL switch

CHOOSE A SIDE

GORDON bonnet

FLEET PRESS

AN IMPRINT OF
OGHMA CREATIVE MEDIA

Fleet Press
Oghma Creative Media
Fayetteville, Arkansas

www.oghmacreative.com

The characters and events in this book are fictitious. Any similarity to real persons, living or dead, is entirely coincidental and not intended by the author.

ISBN: 978-1-63373-057-1

Interior Design by Casey W. Cowan
Editing by George "Clay" Mitchell

ACKNOWLEDGEMENTS

I am deeply grateful to Casey Cowan and George Clay Mitchell of Oghma Creative Media, Inc. for making this book possible, and for the invaluable assistance they provided in editing and preparing the manuscript for publication. Their insight and expertise, not to mention their dedication to seeing *Kill Switch* in print, have been incomparable.

Thank you also to Jess Nelson and Staci Troilo for their wonderful assistance in marketing and promotion.

I would also like to make three other acknowledgements of a more personal nature. My writing partner, Cly Boehs, has followed this story from its very beginnings, and her advice and creative input have never failed to help me. The online group Writers Without Borders has been a wellspring of encouragement and support through this entire process, and I'd like to give a shout-out to my friends the Bordies. And to my lovely wife, Carol Bloomgarden, a heartfelt thanks for her continual encouragement of my rather quixotic personality.

To my dear friend K. D. McCrite,
without whom Chris's story would never have been told.

CHAPTER 1

Chris Franzia expected to have only a few items on his to-do list after closing up his classroom on the last day of school. A nap in the hammock, a cold bottle of celebratory beer, some time playing with his dog, maybe a movie in the evening. He hadn't thought much beyond that. Summer still stretched before him, an endless expanse of leisure, sunshine, and few responsibilities.

This happy, far-from-September mental fog is why he didn't notice the white four-door sedan parked in his driveway until he had nearly rear-ended it.

Chris shut off his car, heart pounding, and got out. Two men, dressed in tailored suits, exited the sedan. As they approached Chris, they reached for their wallets, flipping out badges and ID cards.

His heart rate accelerated.

Police? This can't be good news. Did someone in my family die? Would they send plainclothes detectives for something like that?

"Christopher Franzia?" said the one who had gotten out of the driver's side. He was an older man, silver at the temples, with dark eyes and an angular, weather-beaten face. He carried an elegant dark leather briefcase.

Chris nodded, trying not to let the alarm show in his face. "That's me."

"I'm Special Agent Jim Hargis," he said. "This is my partner, Special Agent Mark Drolezki. We're from the Federal Bureau of Investigation. Can we have a few moments of your time?"

Chris, his mouth open a little, nodded again. He swallowed. "Let's go inside. I... um, I just have to get my chinchilla out of the car."

He went around the back of his car, opened the hatch, and pulled out a spacious cage that contained the biology classroom pet, an irritable chinchilla named Jabberwock. Jim followed Chris, watching from a few feet away.

He's making sure I'm not getting out a weapon.

Even Chris's mental voice sounded incredulous. He set the cage down briefly to close the hatch, then headed off toward the house.

FBI? What can the FBI want with me?

At least they didn't look like they were ready to accuse him of something and arrest him on the spot.

"Those little guys are so damn cute. My niece has one," said Drolezki, tall and blond with a linebacker's build and an incongruous little boy's face. The two agents followed Chris up the sidewalk toward his house.

"He lives in my classroom, usually," Chris said. He balanced the cage on one knee and turned the doorknob with the other. "I take him home on vacations."

"You don't lock your door?" Hargis said.

"Around here?" Chris asked. His face relaxed into a smile. "No need. Besides…" As he opened the door, a large, furry form pushed its way out, giving Chris no heed at all, and barreled right into Hargis, nearly knocking him to the ground. Then it ran into the yard, barking merrily, turned, and cannoned into Drolezki. Strafing complete, he trotted over and peed on a bush before returning to Chris, tongue hanging out, tail wagging furiously.

"… I have a dog," Chris finished. "C'mon, Baxter, get in here." He pushed the door open, and the dog went inside, followed by Chris and the two FBI men. Hargis brushed the dog hair off his immaculately-pressed trouser leg.

Chris set Jabberwock's cage on the top of a bookshelf, and gestured for the two men to sit down on his disreputable-looking sofa. Chris sat in a rocking chair on the other side of a coffee table strewn with magazines, papers, and three unwashed coffee cups. Baxter, now that the excitement was over, decided that his master didn't need to be defended from the two strangers, loped over to his dog bed and flopped down with a heavy sigh.

"We have a few questions for you," Hargis said. "It should not take much of your time."

"Yeah, no problem," Chris said. "But I don't see why you could want me…" He trailed off.

"We're not here to accuse you of anything," Hargis said, as if he'd read Chris's thoughts. "Like I said, just a few questions."

"Okay." Chris took a deep breath. "Shoot."

"Do you know two men named Glen Cederstrom and Gavin McCormick?"

Now *that* was a blast from the past.

"Yes, years ago," he said. Chris leaned back in his chair. "I knew them in college."

"At the University of Washington," Hargis said.

Chris nodded.

"Have you had any contact with either of them recently?"

"No. None. I haven't seen or heard from them since college."

Hargis opened his briefcase, pulled out a folder, and extracted one sheet from it. He handed Chris the sheet. "Would you happen to know what this is about?"

Chris took the reading glasses from his shirt pocket, and put them on. The page was a printout of an email, dated May 28, 2013.

Glen:

I know we haven't seen each other in years, and I wonder if you even remember me. We were in a Field Biology class together back in the mid-80s at UW, and maybe a couple of other classes, too. Cellular, I think? Not sure about that. Anyway, it's been a while, and I'm hoping that you'll remember me well enough to take what I'm about to say seriously.

Your life is in danger. So is mine, but I knew about it ahead of time, and I'm taking precautions. I know this will seem to make no sense, but it has to do with that field work we did up in the Cascades. I'm not sure I completely understand it myself, yet, but I'm figuring out more and more. Most of it I wouldn't put in an email, or in print at all, because you never know who's reading. I found you through a Google search, and if I can, anyone can.

You're the only one I've contacted yet, mostly because I remember you as being the most level-headed of all of our circle of friends. I'm going to try to find the others — Mary, Deirdre, Chris, Elisa, and Lewis — and I'd like your help. Reply to me and we can discuss it more. I'm in Vancouver, Washington, so we're only an hour or so's drive apart. At least a couple of the others, I think, scattered further afield. But we need to let everyone know, soon, about the danger.

Please take this seriously. It's important.

Your old friend,

Gavin McCormick

Chris finished reading, and looked up. The two FBI agents regarded him questioningly.

"Well?" Hargis said. "Do you have any idea what this is about?"

Chris shook his head. "I have no idea. What possible reason could there be that we're in danger? We were in class together almost thirty years ago, and as far as I know, haven't seen each other since."

"We were hoping you'd tell us. You see, Mr. Cederstrom never responded to this email, because he was already dead."

Chris gaped.

"He was struck by a car while riding his bicycle on May 26. Killed instantly," Drolezki said. "The driver was never caught."

"It was assumed to be a simple hit-and-run," Hargis said. "It would have been a matter for local police if Cederstrom's wife hadn't found this email when she was taking care of his personal things after he died. She informed the police, who tracked down Gavin McCormick, who worked as a pharmacist in Vancouver, Washington."

A light sweat break out on his forehead. "Worked? As in past tense?"

Hargis nodded. "McCormick didn't show up at work on the morning of June 2. His assistant was concerned, and called his house, and received no answer. That afternoon, the assistant and another store employee, who were personal friends of McCormick's, went over to his house, and found him dead."

"Murdered?" Chris said, his voice thin in his own ears.

Hargis shook his head. "No. Apparent heart failure. An autopsy showed nothing that allowed the authorities to claim foul play. He seems to have simply died quietly in his sleep."

"Good lord," Chris said.

"At that point, we were called in, and started to try to track down the others mentioned in the email. We got access to UW records for the Field Biology class that Cederstrom and McCormick had taken in 1983, and looked for the first names he mentioned. They seemed to correspond to Lewis Corelli, Mary Michaels, Deirdre Ross, Elisa Howard, and you."

Chris nodded. "Yes," he said. "They were in the class."

"Three of them, Corelli, Michaels, and Ross, were still in the Pacific Northwest, and were fairly easy to track down. We were worried about the women, because of names changing at marriage, but Ross never married and Michaels kept her maiden name."

"Well?" Chris said. "Are they all right?"

For the first time, Hargis looked ill at ease; everything else he had said had been delivered with a clinical lack of emotion. "Corelli was an EPA lawyer, working in Seattle. He had a stroke on June 11 while walking to work and was dead before the ambulance arrived.

Michaels was a jazz pianist in Eugene, Oregon. She fell from a bridge on the fourteenth. She apparently had a history of mental health problems, and her death was ruled a suicide, until our investigation tied her to the rest of you. Deirdre Ross went missing on a hiking trip in the Olympics, probably on either the fifteenth or sixteenth. Another hiker found her clothes on the morning of June 17, dry and neatly folded, on a rock near the shore of Lake Quinault, as if she had gone in for a swim and never returned. She is still missing and presumed drowned."

Chris stared at the two men. "All within a month's time?"

"Less," Hargis said. "Cederstrom was the first, on May 26. Ross disappeared before the seventeenth of June."

Chris swallowed and looked down, staring at the magazine he'd been reading the previous night.

It had already happened. I just didn't know about it. I was sitting there reading, and all five of them were dead.

Finally, he looked up. Hargis, sat patiently staring at him, as if he had all the time in the world. "What about Elisa?" Chris asked.

"We haven't been able to find her. We know from university records that she lived in Spokane for a while, where she worked as an artist. But she left Spokane in the early nineties and we haven't been able to trace her further. We think she may have changed her name." Hargis looked down at the folder he was holding. "In any case, we haven't found her yet."

"And that leaves you," Drolezki said.

"I can't believe they're all gone," Chris said. The horror in his voice was unmistakable.

Hargis' voice was calm, but insistent. "They were not the only ones in the Field Biology class that semester, were they?"

He leaned back in his chair, the faces of his long-ago classmates running through his head. He brought himself back to the present with an effort. "No. I'd guess that there were about twenty-five people in the class. Give or take."

"Twenty-three," Drolezki said.

"Do you have any idea why the seven of you were mentioned, and none of the others in the class?" Hargis asked.

"No. None at all."

"And those seven…" Hargis shifted slightly in his seat. "Do you know anything about their deaths, Mr. Franzia?"

"Me?" Chris asked. It came out in a squeak.

It's like in those murder mysteries, wait until the victims die one by one, and the survivor must be the murderer.

He got control of his voice, and said, as calmly as he could manage, "No. None at all. I haven't had any contact with any of them since graduate school. I got my master's degree in… let's see, it was 1984 or 1985…"

"1985," Drolezki said.

Chris turned and looked at him in astonishment, but the agent's boyish face showed no emotion other than mild interest. Chris realized there might well be more going on behind those guileless blue eyes than had appeared at first.

"Right," Chris said. "1985. Well, I lived in Seattle for another eight months or so, applying for jobs in the northwest. But the market for teaching jobs was pretty bad at that point. So I started looking further afield. I came out here at the end of summer of 1987 for a job at Guildford High School, and have been here ever since."

"What made you choose Guildford?" Hargis asked. "Family from this area?"

Chris looked over at him, trying to keep the suspicion from his own face.

They know when I got my master's degree. They know the answer to this.

"No," he said. "I came out here knowing no one."

"Really?" Hargis said.

The anger rose in Chris's chest. "I don't understand what my background has to do…"

Hargis raised one hand. "No need to get angry, Mr. Franzia. But we would appreciate it if you would answer the question."

Chris took a deep breath. "Look, why do I have the feeling that you already know the answers to all of these questions? If you know the answers, why are you asking them?"

The agent gave a chilly little smile. "We want to hear

what your answers are. You must understand, Mr. Franzia, it isn't always the facts that are important, but the connections between them. And the connections come from talking to people, not from researching the records in a university registrar's office."

Chris looked him directly in the eyes. But those eyes didn't give anything up; they were receivers of information, not transmitters, trained through years not to allow anyone to see what was going on in the brain behind them.

"Fine," he said, in a level voice.

If he's not going to give me anything more than the bare minimum, I won't give him any more than that, myself.

"I came out here knowing no one. I grew up in a rural area. Seattle was a great place to go to school, but I never had any intention of staying there. Upstate New York appealed to me because it was rural."

"And far away from Seattle," Drolezki observed.

"Look, I wasn't running away from anything," Chris snapped.

"I didn't say you were," Drolezki said blandly.

"Sorry," Chris said, not sounding particularly sorry, and not really caring. "I apologize if I seem testy. But I come home on the last day of school, and I find a couple of FBI agents on my doorstep, it's kind of off-putting."

"I understand," Hargis said. "But you have to understand we have some deaths to try to explain. Clearly

Cederstrom was a homicide; with Michaels we can't rule out suicide, but given her connection to the rest of you, you can see that we're considering that less and less likely. The others... well, with McCormick and Corelli, there was a ruling of natural causes, but you probably know that there are poisons that can mimic the effects of stroke and heart attack. And with Ross there's been no body found, but she left for her backpacking trip almost two weeks ago and hasn't been seen since. She was a doctor in Seattle, with a thriving practice she was apparently devoted to. She was gone for what was supposed to be a week's vacation. Her friends and coworkers describe her as a workaholic who had to be bullied into taking the vacation in the first place, and think it extraordinarily unlikely that she would simply not come home. So do we."

"Yes, that's Deirdre," Chris said. "Sounds like she didn't change much."

"Has anything unusual happened lately?" Drolezki asked. "Have you seen any strangers around? Any odd phone calls? Anything at all out of the ordinary?"

He shook his head. "Look, this is the quintessential small town. I know everyone, and everyone knows me. If anyone strange was hanging around, someone would notice, even if for some reason I didn't. There hasn't been anything at all." Chris looked from one of them to the other. "I'd tell you if there had been anything."

Hargis nodded. "I'm sure you would."

Chris tried to extract anything—reassurance, doubt, suspicion—from Hargis' words, but there was nothing there to grab on to. It left him feeling like he needed to defend himself from something. It took an effort not to.

"What about Elisa?" he said. "Do you have an idea if she's all right?"

Drolezki glanced at his partner. "You understand why we can't give you any information about her whereabouts."

"Yeah, because I'm a suspect," he said. "Sure. I'm not asking where she is. I'm asking if she's okay."

Neither man spoke.

So either they really did lose her trail, or else she was their prime suspect.

"Mr. Franzia—" Hargis began.

Chris interrupted him.

"I can tell you that Elisa wouldn't hurt anyone. The others..." He paused, swallowed, and then continued. "If you think Elisa somehow has gone off her rocker, and is going back and killing all of her college classmates, you're after the wrong person."

"But the others, you were going to say?" Drolezki said.

Chris just looked over at him.

"Mr. Franzia," Hargis said, "if you really don't know anything about what is happening here, you have every reason to help our investigation, not impede it. Remember, with the possible exception of Elisa Howard, you are the only one mentioned in that email who is still alive. Your life may be in danger. I urge you to tell us anything you remember about your classmates that might be help-ful. Even if it seems unimportant to you."

"All I was going to say," Chris said, fighting back the feeling of having been admonished by a superior, "was that of the seven of us, Elisa would be the last one who would ever hurt anyone. She was kind, gentle, and sweet."

Why am I talking about her in past tense? Does that sound suspicious?

"What do you recall about the others?" Hargis said. "Personalities? Goals? How did they interact with each other, and with you?"

So much for not giving anything up.

"I can tell you Gavin McCormick was an excitable guy, kind of a flake. He wanted to go into biological re-search, but I never thought he had the personality for it. The rest of us always thought he was a little weird. Glen Cederstrom was the quiet, solid, steady one. He was headed toward education, like me. The others..." He paused. "Okay, Lewis Corelli wasn't an especially nice guy. And I always thought that Deirdre Ross had a ruth-less streak, but we all knew she was thinking pre-med, and that kind of goes with the territory, doesn't it?"

"And Mary Michaels?" Hargis said.

"She was an odd one. She was taking biology classes purely because she thought it sounded interesting."

"There's a problem with that?"

"No, you misunderstand me. I was a Bio major; I loved that stuff. I don't mean interesting in that sense. Mary more loved the idea of biology. The actual work she found pretty distasteful, because, you know, biology leaves your hands dirty. But being able to tell people she was 'studying biological science' was somehow exciting and glamorous. Honestly, most of us thought Mary Michaels was a neurotic prima donna."

"Really?" Hargis said, his voice level.

Chris shook his head in frustration. "Look, none of us hated the others. It was the usual odd mix of people thrown together in college classes. I don't see why their personalities thirty years ago are important. We were young then. Who knows, maybe they all grew up to be perfectly nice, ordinary people."

"We don't know the answer to that ourselves," Drolezki said.

"I don't understand any of this," Chris said, a little desperately. "There was nothing special about this group. We weren't even all that close. We were classmates. We used to study together, sometimes with one or two others, sometimes not. We did field work together."

"So the email said," Drolezki said.

"But nothing happened," Chris said, his voice rising. "We did field work up in the Cascades. But it was nothing unusual, and it involved all the students in the class. I don't remember a single thing that happened up there that was out of the ordinary."

"How often did you go, and for how long?" the other G-man asked.

"I think for that class, we went three times, for about four days at a time. We camped up there, collected our data, came back. It was routine."

"McCormick didn't seem to think so," Drolezki said.

"I have no idea why," Chris said. "Do you know why he said that?"

"If we did, we wouldn't be asking you," Hargis said. He looked over at Drolezki, who gave a little nod.

Chris wondered if that was true.

"In any case," Hargis continued, closing up his brief-case, "we'll leave a card with you. If anything out of the ordinary happens, anything at all, call us. We can have someone out here in fifteen minutes. Don't discount what seems insignificant. We'd rather come out here for nothing than have a sixth murder to deal with."

Murder. First time he'd used that word.

Hargis and Drolezki stood up, and Chris rose to take the card that Hargis was handing to him. They walked toward the door, and Chris opened it for them. "I have to move my car," he said. "I boxed you in."

As they were walking across the lawn toward the cars, Drolezki nudged an old tennis ball lying in the grass with the toe of his shoe.

"Ankle breaker," he said, amiably. "Your dog leave this out here?"

Chris picked it up. "No, I can't give Baxter tennis balls," he said. "He eats them."

Someone put that there. Maybe it's booby trapped. Spring-loaded miniature hypodermic needles sticking poison into my hand right now. Maybe tonight I'll die in my sleep, like Gavin. Or collapse with a stroke, like Lewis.

Chris waited until Hargis and Drolezki climbed into their car, and he turned and winged the ball as hard as he could into the field across the street. Then he looked down at his hand, and felt the hairs on the back of his neck rise.

I shouldn't have touched it. Now it's too late.

Chris was awakened from a sound sleep by Baxter barking.

He sat up in bed in the pitch dark, groggy and disoriented, and squinted at the clock. Its red display stood at 2:42.

"Baxter, dammit, knock it off!" Chris shouted.

The barking continued, unabated. This probably meant that there was a deer in the yard, which was about the only thing that could really get Baxter going in the middle of the night.

Chris got out of bed, fumbled for his bathrobe, and pulled it on, then padded barefoot out into the living room. In the faint light from the streetlight down the road, Chris could see Baxter silhouetted, standing on the couch, nose pressed to the window. Now that Chris was up, the dog had subsided into woofs, but his tail was down, a sure sign that he wasn't happy.

"I am not letting you out," Chris said. "If that's a deer, you'll take off after it, and I'll spend the next hour chasing you down."

Baxter looked over at Chris and whined.

What if it's not a deer? What if it's someone lurking around, waiting for an opportunity to kill me?

Chris stood, staring at his dog and the dark window for a moment, then walked over to the door and switched on the outside lights.

The yard was suddenly illuminated with that yellow-ish, artificial glow that makes everything look strange and colorless and surreal. Chris went up to the window, reached out and put one hand on Baxter's furry shoulder, more for his own comfort than for the dog's.

The yard was empty.

Apparently satisfied that his job was done, Baxter turned and jumped down off the couch, went over to his dog bed and flopped into it with his usual heavy sigh. Chris watched him for a moment, then turned off the outside lights.

Before he went back to bed, he locked all of his doors and windows, something he never did unless he was going to be away overnight. Afterward, he lay there, trying to relax, but listening for any small noise that might tell him what had awakened Baxter earlier. There was nothing but the usual small night noises, and those weren't even enough to wake the dog again, who snored quietly in the living room, untroubled by the earlier disturbance, whatever it was.

Chris didn't fall asleep again until almost four.

· · · ·

Baxter was the one who woke Chris up again, this time at nine in the morning, with a cold nose pressed into the hand that hung limply off the edge of the bed. Chris came back to consciousness slowly, and he stumbled out of the bedroom, pulling his robe on, to let Baxter out into the back yard.

I made it through the night. No one killed me in my sleep.

So far, so good.

He was unable to sustain his sanguine mood, however. As he put the coffee on, shaved, showered, and prepared his breakfast, his mind kept going back to the visit from the FBI men. The details seemed foggy, and he tried to remember what they told him about how each of his classmates had died. And that started him thinking of each of them in turn, picturing their faces, remembering their voices, remembering funny incidents that they'd been involved in together.

One random connection and you're linked for life.

None of them had known the others prior to the class, or at least, that was the impression Chris had. Fate had put them all into a Field Biology class in 1984, and that connection was, one by one, killing them.

That's what the FBI men want me to think, anyway.

There was no proof of this, other than Gavin's email, and Gavin always had weird ideas.

What we really have is a bunch of dead fifty-somethings. Maybe it's all coincidence. After all, we're at the age where people start dying of strokes and heart attacks, and cycling and swimming accidents can happen to anyone.

The FBI was supposed to find connections. Maybe they were seeing them where there weren't any.

All morning he couldn't shake the feeling of being watched. He even went to the window twice, looking for a mysterious black car parked across the street, or someone hiding in the bushes with a pair of binoculars. Of course, there was never anything there, but he still couldn't relax into the book he was reading, and finally gave up and set it on the coffee table.

"I think I need to get out of Dodge," he said to Baxter, who responded with a thump of his tail against the floor. "Maybe we should go up to the Adirondacks and go canoeing, you think?"

But that's how they got Deirdre. Out in the wilderness, where there's no one to help you if you're in trouble.

He recalled Deirdre's cool competence, all during

their acquaintance, and allowed himself to feel a measure of reassurance.

Knowing Deirdre, she left information about her whereabouts with everyone but the state police. Her office staff would have known, and probably any friends, family, acquaintances, whatever. Anyone looking for her wouldn't have had to search hard. She isn't the type who takes chances.

Wasn't.

He shuddered at his own correction. Maybe Deirdre had left a broad trail for them to follow, but if they got her, what chance did he have? She'd been tough, smart, and even in college had been working her way up the belt ranks in karate. She wouldn't have been easy to catch off guard.

"Well, I'm damned if I'll stay home and fret over every noise I hear," he said, continuing his conversation with Baxter. "If I have a choice, which I do, I'd rather take my chances with meeting them out in the woods, than sitting at home waiting for them to show up on my doorstep one night."

He got up, and dialed a number on the telephone.

"Hello?" came a female voice.

"Hi, Joyce? It's Chris Franzia. Is Adam around?"

"Oh, hi, Chris. Sure, he's here. I'll get him."

There was a pause.

"Hello?" came a cheerful teenage voice.

"Hi, Adam? This is Mr. Franzia. Are you going to be around for a few days?"

"Sure, what's up?"

"I'm heading out to do some camping. I was wondering if you could do the usual. Feed Jabs, water the plants once or twice. I'll be gone for a week or so."

"Lucky you. Where are you going?"

Chris paused. "Away," he said, keeping his voice light. "School's over. I'm heading out where no one can find me."

Adam laughed. "Yeah, I know how you feel. No problem at all."

"Cool. I believe your mom still has a key."

"Yeah, she does. I think it's still hanging on the key rack in the kitchen from the last time you were gone."

"Great. You have my cell number if anything comes up. I'm leaving this afternoon, and I'll feed Jabs before I leave. You won't have to come by until tomorrow."

"Sounds good. Enjoy your trip."

"I will."

Chris hung up the phone and looked around.

I can be gone in an hour. After that, if there's someone after me, let 'em try to find me up in the High Peaks, and good luck to them.

•   •   •   •

Chris gathered his camping gear and hauled it to the car, feeling strangely conspicuous, each time he went outside, as if advertising where he was going to the entire world. While putting his backpack and sleeping bag in the back of the car, a blue BMW went by. He saw a hand give a little wave through tinted windows, but he didn't recognize the face hidden in the shadowed interior.

He didn't know anyone with a blue BMW.

Chris returned his attention to the task at hand, but his nerves were still on edge a few minutes later when, while struggling to get his canoe up onto the roof rack, a friendly voice behind him said, "Need some help with that?"

He half turned, lost his grip on the canoe, and saved it from sliding nose-first off the car at the last moment. Standing behind him was a tall, well-built teenager, with an unkempt mane of chestnut brown hair and a cheerful smile in a deeply tanned face.

"Sorry, didn't mean to startle you," the boy said sheepishly, getting underneath the canoe and giving it a gentle shove onto the top of the car.

"Dear God, Adam, you almost gave me a heart attack," Chris said, and immediately regretted having put it that way.

"Sorry, Mr. F.," Adam said again. "But I wanted to make sure that I knew where you were leaving the chinchilla chow. I called but no one answered. Mom said you most likely hadn't left yet, that you were probably out packing up your car, and so I decided to walk over."

"And here I am." Chris tossed a strap over the top of the canoe, and then walked around the other side of the car to hook it to the roof rack. "Glad you thought of it.

I think I left it in a plastic sack on my couch. You'd have found it, but better to leave it in an obvious spot."

Adam grinned, raising one eyebrow. "Yeah. You wouldn't want me to have to go through all your stuff, and find things no one's supposed to see."

Chris gave the kid a wry smile. "You have an unwarrantedly high opinion of the interest level of my private life."

"C'mon, Mr. F., you must have a girlfriend or two. Or three."

"Not even 'or one,' at the moment, Adam," he said, cinching down the strap.

"Too bad," Adam said, with feeling. "You coulda brought her along on your camping trip. Camping under the stars with your lady."

"Go home, Adam," Chris said, giving the boy a clap on the shoulder. "I'll leave the chinchilla chow on the top of Jab's cage. And I'll make sure to come to you if I need any advice in the romance department."

"Always happy to help," said Adam, undaunted by the sarcasm. "Have a good trip. See you when you get back."

• • • •

It was a relief when, a little over an hour later, Chris had the car packed. Baxter was happily ensconced in the front seat, his head already hanging out of the passenger side window, tail wagging non-stop. Chris climbed in behind the steering wheel, turned the key in the ignition, and backed out into the road.

He looked ahead, then into his rear-view mirror. No cars coming from either direction.

If they're going to follow me, they'd better get at it.

He drove off down the road toward the highway.

. . . .

The camping trip was brilliant fun. The first night he slept fitfully, convinced that every little noise was the stealthy footstep of someone with a knife or a gun, creeping up to his tent. As the days passed, he relaxed, the tension draining away as he absorbed himself in nothing more stressful than paddling, swimming, hiking, and relaxing by a campfire. He did have one momentary pang three days in, as he stripped his clothes off to go for a quick skinnydip in a mountain lake and remembered how Deirdre Ross' clothes were found, dry and neatly folded, on a rock by a lake on the other side of the country.

He stood naked on the rock, looking down at the still water. This is it. Will I go missing the same way? Will some passing hiker find my clothes, still being guarded by my faithful dog?

He looked over at Baxter, exhausted by their hike and snoozing under a tree.

I'm not going to wait here to find out.

The next thing he felt was the chilly water sliding across his skin as he dove in, leaving nothing but a trail of silvery bubbles behind him.

• • • •

He stayed out seven days. At that point, he began to long for the amenities of home. The ground, even through a foam pad, was not as kind to his body as it had been when he was twenty, and he found himself thinking about his bed, kitchen, and sofa more often than he liked to admit.

I'm getting to be a wuss. Look at Baxter. He could sleep on the bare ground every day, and he'd be as cheerful as ever.

Despite the pep talk, he was glad when he arrived back at the canoe put-in and saw his car waiting for him. He paddled to the shore, climbed out into the cold, calf-deep water, and dragged his canoe out onto the gravel. Chris was a quick and efficient packer, and had the car loaded up, Baxter in the front seat, and the canoe strapped to the roof rack within a half-hour. It was about three in the afternoon. Watertown, the nearest city of any size, was an hour-and-a-half away. With luck, he could find a restaurant that wouldn't mind a guy who was on his last clean t-shirt, saved carefully for the occasion.

He stopped for some food at a little Italian restaurant

that didn't seem too swanky. After eating his plate of lasagna, he pulled out his cell to call Adam and see how chinchilla-sitting had gone, and to let him know that he'd be back late that evening.

"Hello?" came a hoarse voice on the other end of the line.

"Joyce?" Chris said. "It's Chris Franzia."

"Chris," she said. "We've been trying to get a hold of you for days. No one knew where you were, and you must have been out of cell range."

"Yes, I was," he said, fighting down a rising wave of apprehension. The waiter came up to ask if he wanted a refill on his beer, and Chris waved him away. "Is everything okay?"

There was a pause. "No," Joyce said, and she gave an involuntary sob. "No, nothing's okay. Chris, Adam's dead."

C hris wasn't surprised to find the white sedan parked in his driveway when he arrived home.

I wonder how long they've been here, waiting for me? All afternoon? Or did they know exactly where I was and when I'd get here?

Hargis and Drolezki's doors opened as soon as he turned his motor off. Chris got out, held the door open for Baxter and said, without preamble, "You already know, I presume."

Hargis nodded. Chris turned and led them to the front door.

"Locking your door now, I see," he said as Chris fumbled with his keys.

"I was gone for a week. I may be trusting, but I'm not stupid." He turned on the lights in the living room, and gestured for the two men to sit down.

"Running away to the wilderness wasn't the smartest thing you could have done," Hargis commented, as he sat down on the couch.

"I figured that if anything, whoever it was that's behind this would come after me," Chris said heavily. "I didn't think they'd kill Adam."

"Well," Drolezki said, "they did go after you. Adam was collateral damage."

"Bloody horrible way to put it," Chris said. "Adam was a former student and a friend of mine. A really nice kid."

Drolezki looked over at Hargis for a moment, then reached into a folder he was carrying and pulled out a stack of typed forms, held together by a paper clip. "What it looks like is that they set a trap for you, and it got Adam, instead. Adam died four days ago. He was found dead on the couch, in his own home, by his mother."

"Poor Joyce," Chris said, staring at the floor.

"He was caring for your place while you were gone," Hargis said.

"Yes. Feeding the chinchilla and watering the plants. Keeping an eye on things."

Drolezki looked at the papers in his hand. "Autopsy and toxicology results came in yesterday. Looks like he came over, probably mid-afternoon on Tuesday, and while he was here, he pilfered a beer from your fridge."

Chris looked up. "He did?" He sighed. "Yeah, I can see him doing that."

"We believe he drank it here, and then went home. The speculation from there is that he began to feel drowsy, and laid down on the couch for a nap. He never woke up."

"Poison?"

"Looks that way. There was still a quantity of beer in his stomach, so it acted on him within fifteen to twenty minutes of consumption. The coroner's office did a complete work-up, tox screen of his stomach contents and blood, and came up empty-handed. Whatever it was didn't show up on any of the ordinary tox screens."

"Leading us to further speculate that it may have been the same chemical used to kill Gavin McCormick," Hargis said. "His tox results were also negative, and he was found dead in his sleep."

"Someone poisoned the beer in my fridge?" he asked, his voice incredulous.

"We believe so," Hargis said. "Do you remember when you last purchased beer?"

"Maybe two weeks ago," said Chris. "I'm not sure."

"And where did you purchase it from?"

"From the Save-a-Lot, right here in Guildford."

"Any left?"

"I think there were three bottles left." He shook his head. "Two now, I suppose."

"We'd like to take any remaining beer, and any empty bottles you have, for testing," Drolezki said. "We have more sophisticated tests we can run, see if we can pinpoint what chemical agent is being used."

"Of course,"

"And it would be advisable," Hargis added, "not to eat any food that's in your refrigerator or freezer. You might want to do a lot of eating out for a while."

"Jesus," Chris said. He shuddered and leaned back in his chair. "And you still have no idea why someone is after me? Or why Gavin, Glen, Deirdre, and the rest were killed?"

"Our only working hypothesis is that it has something to do with the field work you did in '84."

"Maybe if you could tell us a little more about what you did," Drolezki said. "What sort of work was it?"

His mind went back thirty years, searching for details lost in the haze of the past. "It was just a class," he said finally. "We went up into the Cascades. More than once. Sometimes only into the foothills, a few times into the high peaks, over Teanaway Pass, to Lake… Ingalls, I think it was. Little lake up near the tree line. The way Field Biology worked, each semester the class would learn some basics, the protocols and equipment and so on, and then spend the semester working on a specific project. The project varied from semester to semester. The term we took it, we worked on a study that involved tagging and monitoring bird populations. Mostly the residents, gray jays, Clark's nutcrackers, crows."

"Toward what end?" Hargis asked.

"The study was trying to see how much vertical migration the resident birds did. You see gray jays on Mt. Rainier in summer; you see them in winter. Are they the same individuals, or do the ones there in summer migrate down to lower altitudes in winter?"

"Interesting," Hargis said, not sounding interested.

Chris looked at him. "See what I mean? What on earth could that have to do with somebody trying to kill us?"

Instead of answering the question, Hargis asked a different one. "Was there anything on these trips that set the seven of you apart, that you did together that other members of the class didn't do?"

He shrugged. "I don't think so. I mean, we hung out together some outside of class, so I expect we probably spent more time socializing with each other than with the other members of the class, especially in the evenings when we weren't working. Sometimes in our free time, groups would go off on short hikes for fun, and we did a bit of that."

"But nothing unusual happened on any of those occasions."

"No!" Chris said. "Nothing! I've told you, it was just a class. One more hurdle to jump to get your master's degree. It was fun at times, and damned boring at times. Field work sounds a lot more exciting than it usually is. We did what was required of us and came home."

"I see."

He looked from one of the FBI men to the other, searching for some sign that they knew more than they were telling him.

And if that something might help him to understand this.

"Now what do I do? Sit here and wait to be killed?"

Hargis shook his head. "We'll have agents watching you and your house constantly. No one will get in or out without our knowing."

"Didn't exactly help Adam, did it?" Chris said bitterly.

"We didn't expect you to run," Hargis said. "You should have told us what you were considering."

"And then I'd have drank that beer one evening, and I'd be dead now," Chris said, his voice rising. "Forgive me for not having a lot of confidence in you clowns."

Neither man rose to the bait.

"It's possible that the beer was poisoned some time ago," Drolezki said. "Before we even located you. You said you purchased it two weeks ago, but you also told us that you don't lock your door. It could be that while you were at work, someone came in and somehow introduced the poison into one or more of the bottles. After that, all they had to do was sit back and wait. Only a matter of time."

"They'd have walked into my house? Right past my dog?"

Drolezki looked over at Baxter, who was asleep in his dog bed. "A couple of puppy biscuits in hand, and an intruder would be your dog's best friend. You don't exactly have a vicious animal, there."

"No, I guess not," Chris admitted. "I'm sorry, I'm having a hard time wrapping my brain around this."

"Easy to understand," Hargis said.

"Thinking this way doesn't come easily," Drolezki said. "Most people never have to. Which is a good thing."

"So, they might have laid out other traps in my house, right?" he asked. "Wouldn't I be safer going away, then?"

"Deirdre Ross wasn't," Drolezki said.

"I think the likelihood is that there was only the one bottle poisoned," Hargis said. "Not that you should chance it, but that's my gut feeling. From the other deaths, it appears that the killer, or killers, are clever opportunists, and always careful to raise as little suspicion as possible. As I said when we spoke last week, without McCormick's email, we never would have thought that the others' deaths were out of the ordinary. Even Adam's death probably wouldn't have generated an investigation, given the toxicology results. His case would almost certainly have been closed with the conclusion of cardiac arrest, reason unknown."

"That's reassuring."

"Mr. Franzia," Hargis said, "I'm not going to pretend we can guarantee your safety. Whoever is doing this isn't leaving a lot of footprints. But wouldn't you say that being here, under our surveillance, gives you a better chance than if you were in a strange town? Or out in the wilderness?"

"I suppose,"

"We can't make you stay here, of course," Hargis continued. "You're not under house arrest."

"And I'm not a suspect any more, I take it."

Hargis said, "Your story checked out. Unless you were in two places at once, you haven't taken a trip to the Pacific Northwest in the past few months."

"Glad to hear I'm off the hook," Chris said.

"This has nothing to do with suspicion, Mr. Franzia," Drolezki said. "It has to do with your own safety. We can't make you listen. All we can do is to urge you to stay home and relax."

"What happened to going out to restaurants to eat?" he asked pointedly. "Make up your mind."

Hargis sighed. It was the first emotional response Chris had seen. "All we're asking is that you exercise some caution, and let us do what we can to help you."

Looking at Hargis' unexpressive face, he stopped. Why exactly he was trying to antagonize the FBI men, anyway? Weren't they on his side?

Chris shivered. How did he know that? He let them into his house because they showed ID. An ID can be faked.

What if they were the ones who had killed his former classmates?

"Fine. I suppose you're right. I'm sorry I'm being a bastard about the whole thing. But finding out that all the others were dead, and now, Adam…" He swallowed before continuing. "It's kind of a lot to take in."

"No need to apologize. You're under a tremendous emotional strain. But we'd urge you… don't do anything foolish. Let us do our jobs. Take lots of naps. Catch up on your reading." There was a sudden glint in Hargis' dark eyes. "And if you suddenly… remember anything important about what went on during those expeditions into the mountains in 1984, please let us know."

The slight pause made Chris picture the word "remember" in quotations marks, and he wondered if they seriously thought he was hiding something.

Am I?

He said, "I will. But don't hold your breath. Nothing happened on those trips that would be of interest to anyone who wasn't fond of birds."

• • • •

Cops was on when Chris turned on the television that night. The second channel had a spy thriller, something about a guy being chased by bad guys even though he couldn't remember his identity and had no idea why they were after him.

He turned the TV off.

Those FBI guys are as in the dark about this as I am.

He looked over at the framed print on his living room wall—the blurry UFO photo with the caption "I Want to Believe." A replica of the one that had been hanging in Fox Mulder's office on *The X-Files*.

Mulder and Scully would be able to figure this out. They always did. They were FBI but weren't gonna sit on their hands and wait for the guy they were protecting to get killed.

But at least Mulder and Scully knew what the conspiracy was about. Aliens. It was always about aliens, plotting to take over the world.

But I have no idea why these people are trying to kill me.

He was a biology teacher, not someone with classified information about an alien invasion. None of them had been out of the ordinary. Just a regular assortment of kids you find in every college class in the United States.

That started him thinking about Elisa, who seemed to be the only survivor of the seven besides him. ...Unless they'd gotten her, too, and the FBI just hadn't found out about it yet.

Chris winced inwardly at that thought. He'd liked Elisa, a lot. A sweet, soft-spoken artist, intent on pursuing a career in biological illustration.

A wave of sadness washed over him. Maybe he and Elisa could have had something.

If he hadn't met Andrea.

Andrea Goldman had been everything Elisa wasn't—brash, outspoken, flashy, with a love for clubs and dancing and parties. Chris had been swept away. Compared to Andrea's bright colors, Elisa had seemed painted with shades of gray. Chris had met Andrea about halfway through the same semester he'd taken Field Biology. Five months later they were living together. A year after that they were married, and by that time, Elisa had slipped from his mind completely.

Unfortunately, Andrea hadn't been all she'd been cracked up to be, but it had taken five years before he'd discovered her darker side. There'd been a string of affairs, the first one just three weeks after they'd exchanged their wedding vows. He'd discovered it by mistake—an injudicious message left unerased on their answering machine. A confrontation elicited tears and self-recrimination, and what had seemed like genuine remorse. As a result they didn't split right away. Their marriage limped along for another three years before a second discovery of infidelity put the final note on the page.

Upon reflection, Chris realized that the marriage had ended the day he'd listened in stunned silence to a strange man's voice on his answering machine, wondering how he could have been so blind, so foolish?

The pain had been unbearable.

After that, there'd been periodic girlfriends, some serious enough to warrant a trip to the drug store for condoms... coupled with a silent prayer that there wouldn't be a former student staffing the checkout register. But nothing lasted very long. No noisy, angry breakups; just a gradual drifting apart, a realization by one or both parties that the relationship, while pleasant enough, was going nowhere.

Finally, Chris had more or less given up. He'd resigned

himself to being single, to living a comfortable life. And to avoiding pushing himself unless absolutely necessary.

Remembering Elisa brought back memories of what it had been like in his college years, before marriage and jobs and mortgages. He'd had some fire then, a willingness to take risks and wrestle with life rather than let it win the match by default. He wondered briefly if Elisa's romantic life had been luckier than his, but pushed the thought away. He was rapidly slipping into self-pity, an emotion he loathed. And if anything, the thought of Elisa in a happy marriage would only make the slide into maudlin depression faster and deeper.

Why hadn't the FBI been able to find her? She must have gotten married and changed her name, maybe moved away from Washington state. But she had to have left some records.

Chris went to his computer and turned it on.

He didn't know why he thought he could find her if the FBI couldn't, but a wild hope surged in him that maybe he had a shot. He knew her. They didn't. And if he found her, maybe he could warn her.

If it wasn't already too late.

What did he know about Elisa? She was from eastern Washington. Spokane, or one of the towns nearby. They had never really talked about their pasts that much, but if you're together long enough, things come out. It had always sounded as though she'd had a crappy home life.

Dad had died when she was young, mom had gone on to marry a real loser.

Something happened right before we met, Chris remembered. He strained to remember snatches of light conversation over coffee in the student union. Something… something about the holidays…

The mental circuitry finally connected. *Thanksgiving! That was it! It was Thanksgiving, and all of us were going home to family except her!*

It had been a casual chat during a Field Bio lab. They were looking at a collection of mammal skulls, identifying them using a key. Now that the floodgates of memory were opened, it all came back. He remembered the conversation as if it had just happened, and the awkward direction it had suddenly taken.

•   •   •   •

"My mom is the best cook," Mary Michaels said, running a hand across her frizzy dark hair with a self-conscious gesture. "She studied to be a cordon bleu chef. She'll be putting on a spread."

"It figures," Deirdre Ross had said quietly to Chris. She was sitting across from him, holding a skull in one hand and making notes in her lab notebook with the other. "And her father is probably the Duke of Norfolk."

Chris chuckled, and looked down so that Mary wouldn't see.

"I'm looking forward to some home cooking, too," Gavin Mc-

Cormick said. "I'm tired of cold canned ravioli, which is about the best I can manage most nights."

"It keeps body and soul together," Glen Cederstrom said, smiling in his quiet way. "But it's nothing like home-cooked. How 'bout you, Elisa? You going home?"

Elisa smiled. "No, I think I'll stick with the ravioli," she said.

"Wow, listen to you," Deirdre said. "I've never heard you be sarcastic before."

Elisa looked up. "It's not sarcasm. I'm not going home for Thanksgiving."

There was a brief, awkward silence.

"That's too bad," Glen said, sounding embarrassed.

"No, it's not," Elisa said, her voice steady. "I'd rather be here, that's all."

After class, Chris approached her. "Sorry if all that put you on the spot," he said.

Elisa gave him a grateful smile. "It's not a problem. I'm completely at peace with what I've got to do. It sounds worse than it is."

"If you want to talk about it…" Chris started, and then stopped.

Elisa reached out and touched his upper arm. "It's sweet of you. But I'll be fine. I wish I could get my brothers to come out here, that's the only problem. But they're strong, they can look after themselves."

"How many brothers do you have?"

"Two. They're half-brothers, actually. Jay and Dennis. Still in high school. They'll be free soon."

"Free from public school?"

"Free from my stepfather."

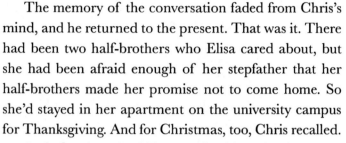

The memory of the conversation faded from Chris's mind, and he returned to the present. That was it. There had been two half-brothers who Elisa cared about, but she had been afraid enough of her stepfather that her half-brothers made her promise not to come home. So she'd stayed in her apartment on the university campus for Thanksgiving. And for Christmas, too, Chris recalled.

And after that, they'd lost touch with each other.

What was the last name of Elisa's stepfather and half-brothers? Had he ever known? She might have mentioned it, or might not. If she had, it was buried under thirty years' worth of memories. Who might know where she was? Of the seven, she'd been closest to Deirdre, but he doubted they'd kept contact after they graduated. Their paths had simply been too divergent. Deirdre was an upwardly mobile academic headed to medical school, Elisa an artist headed to—*where?*

That was the question, wasn't it? Who knew where she had gone?

They got Deirdre, though. If Deirdre knew where Elisa went, it was too late to ask her. But surely someone else has to know what happened to Elisa Howard.

Another memory was tripped in Chris's brain, and he remembered a different conversation. Elisa had had a roommate for a time. He'd met her once, when she'd come to meet Elisa after class. They were headed out together, to a party or dinner or something.

"This is my new roommate," Elisa said, gesturing at a diminutive Asian girl with a broad, cheerful smile.

Chris shook her hand. "Nice to meet you," he said. "I'm Chris Franzia."

"I'm Yee-Lin See," she said. "But my English name is Peggy See. Sort of like Peggy Sue, but not quite."

Chris laughed. "Nice to meet you, Peggy."

Peggy See, "sort of like Peggy Sue." He'd thought that was a really funny line, and wondered at the time if she always used it.

Where had that memory been lost, all these years? Chris looked at his computer screen, brought up a browser window, and entered "Peggy See" in a Google search.

Do you mean 'Peggy Sue'? came the inevitable response.

Chris sighed, and looked down the list of hits. The first three pages' worth were all of the type, *Will Peggy see her novel reach a broader market?* Nothing with See as a last name.

"I wonder if she stayed in Seattle?" he murmured to himself. "Maybe she got married, and has a different last name. He searched for "Peggy See Seattle."

The first page of hits was similar to the previous ones: *The personal side of Peggy, see photographs of her family in Seattle…* and the like. But on the second page, there was a listing for a Facebook page for Peggy See Liu in Seattle.

Chris clicked on it. The page popped up, with the usual

warning that Peggy only shared certain information with her friends, and did he want to become Peggy's friend? But there was a photograph. She was a lot older, standing next to a teenage boy and girl Chris guessed were her children. Older, but definitely Elisa's roommate. He looked to see if her location was listed. It was. Seattle, Washington.

Chris stared at the photo for a moment, then reached for his cellphone, dialed information.

"What city?"

"Seattle, Washington."

"What listing?"

"Peggy Liu. The last name is spelled l-i-u."

"One moment."

"We have a listing for a Peggy Liu in on 148th Street Northwest."

"That's it."

There was a pause, and the operator recited the number. "Would you like me to connect you, sir?"

"Yes, please."

Another pause, and then the sound of the number dialing, and a ring tone.

A male voice picked up. "Hello?"

"May I please speak with Peggy Liu?"

"Just a moment." Then, a muffled call of, "Mom! It's for you."

Chris swallowed. His heart pounded. Would this woman remember him, or would she be suspicious and hang up?

"Hello?" came a voice.

"Peggy?"

"Yes, this is Peggy."

"You probably won't remember me. My name is Chris Franzia. I was a friend, years ago, of Elisa Howard's. Elisa and I were in class together, and I met you once. I'm trying to get in touch with Elisa, and remembered you two had been roommates, so I thought I'd call and see if you'd kept up your friendship with her."

"I think I do remember you," she responded, with a smile in her voice. "Elisa talked about you a lot."

"Are you still in touch with her?"

"Not really," she said. "We send each other Christmas cards. That's about it."

"Do you have a current address for her?" Chris asked, and then added, "I mean, if you're comfortable telling me. I know this is out of the blue."

"No, it's no problem," Peggy said. "Like I said, I know you and Elisa were friends. Let's see…" there was the sound of rummaging, "I have it right here. Do you have a pen?"

"Yes."

"She isn't Elisa Howard anymore. She's Elisa Reed."

"She's married, then?"

"Was. She and her husband parted ways about a dozen years ago, but she never went back to Howard. Anyhow, she's Elisa Reed. She lives at 422 North Benton Street, St. Cloud, Minnesota, 56301."

"Thanks."

"No problem."

"Wow," Chris said. "Thanks so much. I really appreciate your giving me this information. It'll be nice to get in touch with her again."

"I'm sure," Peggy said warmly. "And it must be the season for renewing old acquaintance."

"Oh?"

"Yes," Peggy answered. "It's a weird coincidence, but this is the second time in a week one of Elisa's old college friends has called me asking about where she is these days. Is there a reunion happening, or something?"

CHAPTER 4

You've reached the home of Elisa Reed, and Orion's Belt Art Gallery. I'm sorry no one's here at the moment, but please leave your name and number after the tone and I'll return your call as soon as possible. Have a beautiful day."

Chris hung up before the beep came.

Could they track his cell? Was the mere fact of his making the call putting Elisa at risk? They'd found the others easily enough. It was all too easy to think of the killers as omniscient, as having no limits to their ability to strike. Once Chris knew where Elisa lived, finding her phone number had been child's play. If the killers were one step behind Chris, it was surely no more than that.

However they're doing this, they're still human. They can't do magic. Don't make them more powerful than they really are.

But that was the problem. An unknown enemy grows in the mind by virtue of being unknown. And Chris knew nothing about who he was facing—who they were, where they were, why they were picking off his college friends one by one.

He felt a sudden hatred of his own inactivity, his own complacency. Once again he considered how he'd changed since college. His current life seemed to him no more than treading out the steps toward retirement, spending off hours watching television and reading. Taking no chances, risking nothing.

"But what can I do?" he said out loud. "I don't even know where Elisa is." It was one in the morning—midnight, Minnesota time. It was possible she wasn't answering the phone, given the time, but he'd started calling her as soon as he'd found her number. If she had been home, trying to sleep, she undoubtedly would have picked up the phone the fifth time he called just to get it to stop ringing. So, there were only two possibilities.

Either she wasn't home, or else they'd gotten her, too.

Chris kept picturing Elisa, lying in her bed, curled up, her expression peaceful in death. Just as Adam and Gavin had been. In his mind, her face was still as young and fresh as he remembered it from thirty years ago, even though he knew she couldn't still look that way. None of them did. He'd looked up the others online. It was amazing how easy it was to find them.

Gavin's photo showed up on the webpage for the pharmacy he worked for. He was smiling, his round face rounder and his ruddy complexion pinker than it had been in college, and he'd lost most of his hair. But his expression still had the same buoyant good cheer Chris remembered so well.

Glen Cederstrom he found on the website for the community college where he taught. He was still slim and blond, with a gentle smile and wire-rim glasses, but now he had lots of laugh lines around his mouth and the corners of his eyes. Like most fifty-somethings.

Lewis was simple. He was a lawyer, worked for the EPA, and a search for his name generated hundreds of hits. The photograph Chris found was from *The Seattle Times*, showing Lewis speaking into a reporter's microphone, underneath a headline that said, "Landmark Settlement Reached in Toxic Spill Case." He hadn't changed much, his black hair was peppered with gray on the sides, but his square-jawed face still looked as belligerent as it had in college.

Deirdre showed up on the page for her medical practice, wearing the typical white lab jacket and stethoscope around her neck. Her brown hair cut in a no-nonsense way, her expression keen, penetrating, professional behind modern-looking square plastic-framed glasses. The website, like Gavin's and Glen's, hadn't been updated to reflect her disappearance and presumed death. There was no way to tell from looking at it that she was gone. That *any* of them were gone, erased because of some mysterious link in their past that only Gavin had somehow figured out.

Finding Mary Michaels took a little more digging, but he finally came across her on a website of musicians in western Oregon. He looked at her photograph, and smiled. Hers was the only one that clearly had "head shot" written all over it. Predictable, that. Her dark eyes were cast downward, not looking at the camera, a dramatic gesture that clearly said "I am a performer." She was in a low-cut dress, showing deep brown skin that still had a youthful glow. Not a wrinkle in sight. *The wonders of Photoshop.*

Chris chided himself for being cynical.

On a whim, he put his own name into Google, and his photograph came up instantly, along with plenty of links—the high school website, the page for the Guildford Amateur Astronomers' Club, for which he'd acted as nominal president for four years, a link to an educational workshop at which he'd given a presentation.

Traces all over the place. It's impossible to stay hidden.

Except that maybe Elisa had done it. Maybe. But now he was doubting even that, given the fact that she wasn't answering her phone. Maybe she was gone, too, hit by a car, poisoned in her sleep, drowned in a lake, or pushed off a bridge, and the news hadn't gotten out yet.

Chris rubbed his eyes, and shut off his computer. He dialed Elisa's number once again. This time, when the message came, he waited until the tone, and said, quickly, quietly, "Hi, Elisa? It's your old friend from college, Chris Franzia. Call me when you get this. It's important." He rattled off his phone number, and then hung up.

Shit. That probably was the wrong thing to do. What I should have done is told Hargis and Drolezki, and let them make sure she's okay. If the people who killed the others have my phone tapped, they now know Elisa's phone number, and it'll be simple for them to track her down.

"Too late now," he said out loud. Baxter lifted his head, gave him a quizzical look. Somehow, the phrase sounded like a death knell.

He tried to put it out of his mind, but the thought that perhaps in leaving a message on Elisa's voicemail, he'd doomed her to follow the rest of their friends stayed with him until he finally fell asleep at a little before four in the morning.

•   •   •   •

Chris was dragged upward into consciousness out of a deep, dreamless sleep by the his cell ringing.

He pushed back the sheet and stood up, then stumbled out into the living room, not even bothering to grab his bathrobe.

"Hello?" he asked, grabbing the phone at the last possible moment before it went to voicemail.

"Hi, Chris?" came a female voice.

Instantly, Chris was wide awake, heart pounding in his chest. "Elisa?"

He could hear the smile in her voice. "Yup! Did I call you too early?"

"No! No, it's fine. I'm so glad you called back."

"Of course I called back. I couldn't believe you called, though. And that you were able to track me down, after all these years. I'm glad, though. Really glad." She paused. "It's so good to hear your voice."

"Same. You have no idea."

"What on earth possessed you to get in touch? I mean, it's been, what, thirty years?"

"Just about." He sat down in his rocking chair. "How are you?"

"Me? Fine. I've got an art studio in St. Cloud. Maybe you already know that, though."

"Yeah. Combination of the internet and your old friend, Peggy See."

"You remembered Peggy?"

"Only with some difficulty, age and memory being what they are."

She laughed. "And you? What are you doing with yourself? You were headed into education, I think?"

"Yes. Still there. Just finished my twenty-sixth year in the public schools, and I'm still sane most days."

Another laugh. "That's probably pretty unusual."

"I don't know. I really love teaching. Not that I don't enjoy my summers."

"So, you're on break now? What are you planning on doing? Any travels planned?"

Chris's smile faded a little. "Well, no, actually. I called you because…" He fumbled, stopped.

"What's up, Chris? Is everything all right?"

"Do you remember our other friends, the ones who were in Field Bio with you and me, back at the University? Deirdre, Glen, Gavin, and the rest?"

"Of course."

"Elisa," Chris said, "they're all dead. All except for the two of us."

"What?" Her voice was thin, came out in a near whisper.

"There's something going on, I don't know what. The FBI is involved, and it has to do with the seven of us. Gavin figured out what was going on, and he left behind a cryptic email. Otherwise, no one would have been the wiser. I'm not sure I want to talk about this on the phone, though. It could be tapped."

"Seriously?" She gave a nervous laugh. "I… what could they want with us?"

"I honestly have no idea. But that's why I wanted to contact you."

"To make sure I wasn't dead, too."

"Yes. And to warn you if you were still alive."

"I see." She paused. "How did you find me?"

"Peggy told me your address and your married name. After that, it wasn't that hard."

"How did… how did the others die?"

"Gavin and Lewis were poisoned. Glen was a hit-and-run. Deirdre went missing on a hiking trip and is thought to have drowned. Mary jumped—or was pushed—off a bridge."

"Dear God."

"I know. I was as shocked as you are."

"How did you find out about all of this?"

"There are two FBI guys who are on the case. They filled me in."

When she spoke, her voice sounded heavy with doubt. "Are you sure it's not, you know, coincidence? I haven't… haven't seen anyone around here lately, no one that's unusual. I mean, there are people in the gallery, but they're tourists. At least, I think they are."

"I know it sounds crazy, but you need to believe me. For your own safety. You're better off not trusting anyone you don't know. I hate to put it that way."

"What should I do?"

"I'm not sure. But the first thing is, don't use any food or drinks in your fridge. They poisoned a bottle of beer in my fridge, and it killed a neighbor of mine. It was meant for me."

"That's horrible. Are you still at home? I don't know how you don't just pick up and run, if you think that stuff in your house could be booby-trapped."

"I did run. I went out camping after I first found out about it, and that's what got my neighbor killed. The FBI wants me to stay put. They say they can protect me."

"What else have they told you? About the murders?"

"That's it. They're still trying to find you. I should have tried to contact you sooner, but it didn't occur to me until last night to get a hold of Peggy."

"I wish I'd been home last night, and not missed your calls. But it all turned out for the best. I'm still alive, I was out with friends."

How does she know I called more than once?

But she was still talking.

"It's such a shock, I'm not even thinking straight," she said. "Finding out that all of our friends are gone, like that. And there's nothing more to explain it? To explain why someone is targeting us?"

"Not that I know of," Chris said, modulating his voice with an effort. "But I know it must be a shock. Especially finding out about Lewis. You two were pretty close, for a while. I thought at the time that you two were headed toward getting married."

"I know," she said. "I can't believe someone killed him. It doesn't seem possible."

And Chris said, through a throat that closed down around his very words, "Who is this?"

"What?" The voice still sounded light, friendly.

"Elisa and Lewis never dated," Chris said, and a shudder twanged its way up his backbone. "I don't even think they liked each other much. Who is this? And where is Elisa Howard?"

And the phone went dead in his hand.

• • • •

"Let's assume you've already given me the lecture about how I should have told you about finding out Elisa's address and phone number immediately, and move forward from there."

Chris was still sitting in his rocking chair, but fully clothed now. Hargis and Drolezki were sitting on the couch in his living room.

"You don't seem to understand the gravity of this situation," Hargis began.

"No, I think I understand it just fine. I thought it was more important to warn Elisa than it was to tell you people where she was."

"We could have had someone at her house within an hour of finding out her address," Drolezki said. "And we told you to call us at any time, day or night. You need to cooperate, Mr. Franzia."

"But what about Elisa? What are you going to do now?"

"We've already contacted our office in central Minnesota. They're going to send a couple of agents right out. They might be there already."

"Why don't you tell me exactly what the woman on the phone said," Hargis said.

"It was all vague. You know, not suspicious, at least not at first, just the generalities that you'd expect from someone you haven't seen in thirty years. How are you, I'm fine, that sort of thing."

"What did she ask you?"

"Well, I told her why I'd called. To warn her, because the others had died. She wanted to know about that, of course. How they'd all been killed."

"And you told her?"

"I summarized, but yes."

Hargis flashed a glance at Drolezki. "So now they're aware that we've pieced the whole thing together."

Drolezki gave a little shrug. "It probably doesn't matter. The fact that we're here means they almost certainly knew that much already."

"And the woman who claimed to be Elisa Howard," Hargis continued. "What else did she ask about?"

"She wanted to know how I found her. I mentioned her roommate, Peggy, the person that gave me her address. But they must have known that much, too, because when I talked to Peggy she said she'd been contacted by someone earlier in the week asking for Elisa's address."

"Did she give it to them?"

"I'd assume so. She gave it to me readily enough, and

asked me if there was some kind of reunion going on. She seemed to think it was completely innocent."

"And you didn't tell her what was happening."

Chris rolled his eyes. "Credit me with some intelligence, here. Why would I tell Peggy?"

"You haven't been acting very wisely thus far, Mr. Franzia," Hargis said. "But I hope that this will convince you that this is deadly serious."

"Adam's death was enough to do that. And I do take this seriously. I thought I was doing the right thing. But if they've gotten into her voicemail... she must be dead, right? They called me on her line. I checked my call history after I hung up. It was the same number. They must be in her house. They got her, too."

"It's possible," Hargis admitted. "They may have been trying to lure you to come to Minnesota. Or to give away what your plans were."

"I don't have any plans."

"They don't know that. And you caught on that it wasn't Elisa before they could reveal what exactly they were after, I think. That was clever of you."

"Something struck me wrong," Chris said. "I think it struck me wrong from the beginning, but I was tired, and I was so happy to talk to her, to find out she was alive. But her voice sounded... not different, exactly, but like a good imitation. Someone who knows what she sounds like, but can't quite get the feeling right. Elisa isn't a superficial person, and that's what the conversation was, right from the beginning. And then, she let slip that she knew I'd called more than once, which she had no way of knowing."

"Some voicemail systems will tell you that," Drolezki interjected.

"Oh. Well, even so. It jumped out at me. And then I asked her about how upset she must be about Lewis' death, since they were so close. I was waiting for her to laugh, and say, 'Lewis? Lewis and I couldn't stand each other,' or something like that, and she went along with it. That's when I knew it couldn't be her."

"It's good you caught on when you did," Hargis said.

"But what do you think they wanted from me?"

"We can only speculate. As I said, it could be that she was hoping to get you to come to Minnesota, be the Knight in Shining Armor. Or, perhaps, she simply wanted to continue asking questions, and find out what more you knew about the investigation. To reveal if you knew what the connection was between you, Ms. Howard, and the other five. You still have no further thoughts about that, do you?"

"No. None."

"I see. And your impromptu nocturnal research didn't turn up anything else you're not telling us, did it?"

Chris scowled at him. "Not unless you count my looking up pictures of all of my dead friends online."

"You found them all?"

"Photographs of everyone but Elisa, and I found her art gallery website once I knew her home town and married name. I even looked myself up. It's no wonder they found me so easily. We're all hiding in plain sight."

"One of the effects of the internet," Drolezki said. "No such thing as privacy any more."

"When you know more, will you…" Chris looked down. "I know you can't tell me anything, never mind."

"It wasn't Lewis Corelli who was interested in Elisa Howard, was it?" Drolezki said.

Chris looked up. "No," he admitted. "We were close. If circumstances had been different, we might have had something. But they weren't, and it's thirty years later, and I don't even know if she's alive or dead."

"Mr. Franzia," Hargis said, "when we know anything more about Ms. Howard's well-being—or, I should say, Mrs. Reed's—we'll let you know. I will personally contact you when we have further information, and tell you whatever I can, as long as it will not compromise this investigation."

"Thanks," Chris said. "I really appreciate it."

Hargis and Drolezki stood, Hargis brushing the dog hair off his pants.

"Sorry," Chris said. "Baxter sheds this time of year."

Hearing his name, Baxter looked up from his dog bed, where he'd been cuddled up with a plush toy monkey. He wagged twice, then put his chin back down and his eyelids drooped closed.

"Occupational hazard," Hargis said.

"And he's a good old boy," Drolezki said. "Not so much of a watchdog, but a good old boy."

Baxter wagged one more time without opening his eyes.

"We'll be in touch, Mr. Franzia," Hargis said.

•   •   •   •

Chris wasn't expecting a call from them any time soon, so it was a surprise when he was awakened from an afternoon nap by his cell ringing. Hargis was on the other end of the line.

"Mr. Franzia, I'm calling about what we discussed this morning,"

Chris frowned. "Mr. Hargis," he said, "what toy was my dog sleeping with this morning when you were here?"

There was a slight pause. "It was a stuffed monkey. Brown and white."

Chris let out a long breath.

"You're learning," Hargis said. "My compliments."

"I try not to make the same mistake twice."

"Yes. That's crucial." There was the rustle of paper from the other end of the line. "Agents were dispatched to Mrs. Reed's residence in Minnesota this morning. Her house was locked, and no one answered the door. A neighbor had been charged with taking care of her house plants and had a key. She let them in, but there was no one there, and the neighbor said she hadn't heard from Mrs. Reed since her departure, and that she didn't know where she'd gone, only that it was a 'family emergency.'" More pages rustling. "Her art gallery... Orion Gallery..."

"Orion's Belt."

"Yes. It was locked and dark, with a sign in the window saying that the gallery was closed for two weeks and would open again on Monday, July 8."

"That was yesterday."

"Yes." Hargis cleared his throat. "In your conversation with Mrs. Reed's former roommate, and your online research, did you come up with any further thoughts about where she might have gone?"

"No. I have no idea."

"And you don't know anything about her family that might be relevant?"

"I know she had two stepbrothers, both younger. Jay and Dennis. Her mother had remarried, so the last name would have been different. They lived out in eastern Washington somewhere. That's honestly all I know."

"I see. If you do find out more, or remember more..."

"Yes. I know. I'll call you."

"Thank you. We'll be in touch."

Chris ended the call.

He sat there for a moment, and then got up and went to his computer. He did a Google search for Orion's Belt

Art Gallery, St. Cloud, Minnesota. Seconds later he had the website in front of him that he'd been perusing the night before. On the home page were some images of Elisa's art work. Mostly they had mythological feel, and included a stylized raven against a backdrop of stars, a feathered lizard that had a Mayan look, and a stark painting of a Native American man with tattoos of spider's legs on his face, sending showers of silver sparks from his upturned hands into the night sky. There was no photograph of her, he noted, but there was the little box in the corner that said, "Contact Us."

He clicked on the link, and then on the email address that popped up. In the text box he wrote,

Elisa. Wherever you are. Don't go home. Stay away from St. Cloud. And don't tell anyone where you are. It's important. Whatever you do, if you answer this email, don't mention where you are.

Your old friend,

Chris Franzia

And he clicked send.

I t was just after dinner—a steak and some fresh broccoli bought that day at the Save-a-Lot—that Chris heard the familiar ping from his computer signaling a new email.

He got up, leaving part of his steak still uneaten on the plate. Baxter, who'd been watching him intently throughout dinner, responded with an enthusiastic woof and a furiously wagging tail, evidence that he had complete understanding of the concept of leftovers.

"Don't get your hopes up, buddy," Chris said, walking into the living room to his computer. "I'm not done with that yet."

He clicked the mouse to reactivate the monitor out of sleep mode, and saw a little message in the corner of the screen: *You have (1) new email.*

He opened his email browser. It was from ereed@orions-belt.com.

> *Chris,*
>
> *That was cryptic and scary, and I need to know if this is a prank. If it is, it's in very poor taste, but if it really is my old college friend, I can't imagine your finding it funny to freak me out for no reason. I almost didn't respond, but I have to know.*
>
> *Please tell me what this is about.*
>
> *Elisa*

Chris clicked *Reply,* sat staring at the blank page for several minutes, and finally began to type.

> *Elisa,*
>
> *It's not a prank. I wish like hell I could tell you it was. I don't think emails are easy to track, which is the only reason I'm taking the chance of writing to you. I hope I'm right about that.*
>
> *Remember all of the people we hung out with in Field Bio? Glen, Gavin, Deirdre, Mary, and Lewis? I hate to say it this bluntly, but I can't think of any way to be subtle about it—all five them have died, one after the other, in the last month, under what the police like to call "mysterious circumstances." You and I are the only ones left. The FBI*

is involved, and they think it has something to do with our field work back in 1984. I can't imagine how that can be relevant, but it seems to be the only commonality between us.

I'm relieved beyond words that you're okay. I am, too, for now, but whoever is doing this has already tried to kill me once, and a neighbor of mine died because of it. I think I'm not running around in circles screaming hysterically only because on some level I still can't really believe this is happening.

I won't ask where you are. If you're away from home, somewhere that people don't know you, you're safer. If you're in a place like that, then stay put, and don't trust anyone you don't know.

I hesitate to suggest this, but do you want me to give your email to the FBI men who are here? They gave me hell today because I tried to call you and left a message on your voicemail. I know they'd say that they want to contact you, for your own protection.

Take care and be safe.

Chris

Chris sat, thinking, as the computer made the whooshing noise that signified his email was off to its destination. Should he have told her about the impostor who had called him? After consideration, he came to the conclusion that it was probably better that he didn't.

She was already freaked out enough. That wouldn't be improved by the knowledge that there was someone in her hometown, possibly even in her house itself, intercepting her voicemail and calling people back pretending to be her.

He wasn't sure how long she'd take to respond. They'd known each other long before the time of email, so it was hard to know if she'd be the respond-instantly type, or the think-about-it-and-answer-later type. But he didn't have long to ponder the question, because five minutes afterwards her reply popped up on his screen.

Jesus. This is terrifying. I keep thinking, "Come on, this can't be true," but I looked up Gavin online and found his obituary. I think I read it four times before it finally sunk in. I'd look up the others, too, but I know what I'd find. One was enough to convince me.

I have often thought over the years that it would be awesome to get back in touch with you and some of the others, but I never dreamed that it would be in circumstances like these.

About the FBI… I don't know. Are you sure they're trustworthy? I mean, it sounds ridiculous, but you told me not to trust anyone. Are you sure they're for real?

I'm somewhere safe, and can stay here indefinitely, so don't worry about me. I'm really scared for you, however. Is there any way you can get away without anyone knowing?

Chris read her response in silence before responding.

Your question about the FBI is a good one, and I thought of the same thing. They had IDs, but how hard would that be to fake? They haven't given me any indication that they're not for real, though. So all I can say is that I'm trusting them for now.

I don't know how I could get away without them knowing. I get the feeling they're watching my house continuously, which is reassuring in one way and terrifying in another. And I don't really have anywhere I could go that I wouldn't be immediately findable. For example, I could go stay with my brother in San Diego for a while, sure, but I don't want to put him and his family at risk. If whoever is doing this found the others, they could figure out who I'm likely to run to just by hacking my Facebook.

And running off to the wilderness isn't much better. That's how they got Deirdre. Plus, I already tried that, and it got my neighbor killed. So I think I'm stuck here for now.

Her response came much more quickly this time.

How did they all die? I know that sounds morbid, but I want to know.

He wrote back:

Gavin and Lewis were apparently poisoned, but it was with something that wasn't detected in an autopsy, so it looked like natural causes. Same thing happened to my neighbor, Adam. It would have happened to me if I'd drunk a beer from my fridge that had been tampered with, but Adam got it before I did. Mary went off a bridge in Oregon, and the police thought it was suicide, especially given her temperament, but they now think she was pushed or thrown. Glen got hit by a car while riding his bike. Deirdre drowned in a lake while on a hiking trip in the Olympics.

The only way the FBI put all of this together was that Gavin sent Glen an email saying that there was something up, something dangerous, and he mentioned all of us by name. Just us seven. Glen's wife found the email when she was cleaning stuff up after Glen died, and reported it to the police. Unfortunately, Gavin wasn't specific about what was going on — only vague hints.

Her response, again, was immediate.

My God. There's a part of me that can't really believe this.

He thought for a while this time before writing back:

I know. I hate to be the one who has to tell you all of this. You mentioned having wanted to get back in touch. I've thought the same thing about you, many times. It isn't fair that this is the way it's happened. It isn't fair that all of our friends are gone. It's horrible, and there's no way around it.

The FBI men keep pressuring me to tell them what it was we were up to, back in Field Biology. It really does seem to be the only connection between the seven of us, so they're convinced that something happened during that class. I keep telling them that there was nothing to it but hiking in the Cascades while wearing packs that were way too heavy, and putting bands on birds' legs. Can you think of anything that might be the explanation for this? Something the seven of us did, that the rest of the class didn't do?

She responded with one line.

Could this have something to do with the cave Gavin found?

Chris stared at the single line in complete incomprehension for some time, and then wrote back only two words:

What cave?

There was a thunk from the dining room, and Chris looked up to see Baxter making off into the kitchen with the remains of his steak. He stood up, but the epithets he was considering shouting died on his lips as there was another ding from his computer, and Elisa's response popped up.

You don't remember that? It was up at Lake Ingalls. Not surprisingly, you and Gavin were the most gung-ho about it. Both Lewis and Mary took some convincing, I remember.

Chris wrote back immediately, ignoring the sounds of contented chewing coming from the kitchen.

I have no memory of that at all.

This time the response took a few minutes. Chris sat, staring at the computer, waiting, as if his rapt attention would somehow make her click *Send* faster. Finally there was another ding and her response appeared.

It was the last time we went up to Ingalls, right before the snows started. We'd spent the morning working, and after lunch Dr. Garcia gave us the afternoon to relax. We sat around for a while, and then Gavin suggested going further up the trail, past the lake. There were some really pretty alpine meadows, and it didn't look like it'd be too strenuous a hike. You wanted to go right away, I remember. You always hated hanging around doing nothing.

I think it was just the seven of us. I'm pretty certain about that. We did tend to hang out together more than we did with the others in the class. I remember that Mary didn't want to go, at first, but she was never very enthusiastic about anything, and someone—maybe Glen?—finally talked her

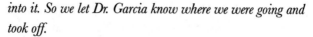

into it. So we let Dr. Garcia know where we were going and took off.

We'd been on the trail for maybe an hour, maybe a bit less, I can't remember for sure. It wasn't very long. There was a rocky hillside, and Gavin decided to climb it. He was showing off a little, I think, mostly for Deirdre. I always thought he had a crush on her. So he goes off up the hill, and in a moment, he says, "Hey, look! It's a cave!"

You climbed up. And I think Deirdre did, too. I remember you saying something like, "It's a big lava tube." Finally everyone had to come up and take a look. And it was this dark opening in the hillside, big enough to climb into. And then you and Gavin said you were going to go inside.

Gavin went first, and then you went in, and we could hear your voices. I recall one of you saying that once you got a few yards in, it was tall enough to stand up and seemed to go a long way in.

But then, Gavin's head popped out of the entrance, and he said, "It's big, but there's no light. It's too dangerous without flashlights, there could be a dropoff, and we wouldn't see it until we fell in." And a moment later, you came out.

By this time, it was getting time to get back to camp and make dinner, so we just climbed down the hill, and struck off back down the trail.

So it wasn't anything too exciting, but it's the only thing I can remember from the class that we seven did that didn't involve everyone else.

Chris read her email three times. He felt as if he was reading a description of something that someone else had done in a place he knew well. The setting was so familiar that he could picture every detail, but the events were entirely foreign.

He wrote back:

Why don't I remember this?

The response was almost instantaneous:

I have no idea.

Chris leaned back in his chair, and rubbed his face with one hand. Could this be another trap? Was this really Elisa Howard he was chatting with? Something about the way she wrote felt authentic, like the real Elisa he had known thirty years earlier. The quiet, friendly, determined young woman who had spoken so calmly about having promised her half-brothers to stay at school over Thanksgiving for her own safety. It was hard to be certain over the internet, but there was a tone in her writing that rang true. He scrolled back and read her email describing finding the cave for a fourth time, and then clicked *Reply*.

This is really freaking me out. It's like there's a hole in my memory. I remember the trip you're talking about — for one thing, it was really cold at night, and I recall being pretty uncomfortable trying to sleep. I can remember there being ice on the lake edge in the morning. That was the trip that Dr. Garcia said would be our last time there for the season, because there was no telling when snow would hit the passes.

But that day hike? Nothing. I don't remember anything about the hike past the lake that you describe, and nothing whatsoever about finding a cave. To me, that all feels like it never happened.

And there's one thing that strikes me, here, and I don't know if it's important, or if you're remembering wrong. Certainly, after all this time, it would be understandable if so. But you said we left right after lunch, hiked for less than an hour, and found the cave, and were down there for minutes, came out, and then "it was time to get back to camp and make dinner." Wouldn't it have only been about two in the afternoon?

Okay, maybe I'm grasping at straws?

There were crunching noises from the kitchen. Chris sighed, stood up, and went to take the denuded steak bone away from Baxter, who gave him an aggrieved look as he deposited it in the trash can.

"You should be thankful I don't yell at you for stealing it," he said. "Plate robber."

There was another ding from the computer, and he went back and sat down.

You're right, of course. I don't know why that didn't oc-
cur to me, because it seems obvious now that you've pointed
it out. I mean, it could be that I'm remembering wrong, but
that's the way I recall it. We were standing around the cave
entrance – you'd just come out, and were brushing dust off
your clothes – and someone, I think it was Deirdre, said,
"We'd better get back to camp. We'll get all kinds of grief
if they hold up dinner for us." And someone said, "Nobody
here on cooking duty tonight, I hope?" And nobody was.

I have this vivid picture of it all, like it happened yester-
day. We got back to camp, and it was dusk. But how could
that be? Maybe we left later than I thought. I don't know.

Aren't there all kinds of studies that show how unreli-
able memory is? Now I'm confused.

And Chris wrote back:

If I remembered this at all, I would be more likely to
shrug it off as your simply not remembering the details right.
To me, this feels more like we both have pieces we don't re-
member about this, but you remember more than I do. I'd bet
you cold hard cash that Gavin and I, and maybe some of the
others, were down in that cave for longer than five minutes.

This has to be significant.

Now, the million-dollar question: should I tell the FBI
about it?

She responded:

It'd mean telling them that you got in touch with me.

Chris wrote:

Not necessarily. I could tell them that I just recalled it myself. I won't tell them about you unless you explicitly give me permission to.

Her next response took a little longer:

I appreciate that, and it might make sense for you not to tell them about me, for the time being. I'm going on intuition, here. You probably will think this is silly. After all, you seem to think they're trustworthy. I have a sense, I'm not sure why, that it's better if they still think I'm MIA. You can always tell them later, but you can't untell them, you know?

As far as telling them about the cave; you need to make the call about that one. You'd have to make it convincing, or they'll think you're lying. I'm saying this because I'm a terrible liar, so it'd be really hard for me to pretend I'm re-membering something that I didn't. But it'd be interesting to see what they say about it.

The more I think about it, though, the more I wonder what on earth could have happened up there that would be worth killing all of us thirty years later? Even if I'm not remembering some of it, there doesn't seem to be anything that happened that could be a rationale for murder even then, much less three decades afterwards.

Chris responded:

That depends on what it is we're not remembering.

The remainder of their exchange gradually faded into small talk about their current lives, and from Chris's perspective, became awkward. It was as if neither of them knew how to draw the conversation to a close, and neither wanted it to end while focused on the deaths of their classmates and the terrible, omnipresent question of why it was all happening. But finally, after a clipped, self-conscious mutual goodbye, it was over.

Chris shut off his computer, retrieved his plate of cold broccoli from the dinner table and scraped it off into the trash can. His head still spinning, he went into his bedroom and flopped down on the bed.

He didn't expect them to be able to pick up where they'd left off. And in any case, these were bizarre circumstances to have to reconnect over. Part of Chris wanted to ask her where she was so he could rush in and protect her. Part of him wanted to have a friend who knew what was happening, who could hold his hand and make him less scared. The habit of complacency and ease was not so easily shucked.

But despite his fear, he knew he'd done the right thing in telling her not to mention where she was. Chris was a dinosaur, technology-wise, and something of a legend in that regard in his school. Still, he knew enough to know there was certainly a way to monitor the content of emails, so anything she told him about her where-abouts could lead them back to her. He hoped there was no way to trace where emails are coming from, but he had to take that risk. He had to warn her. Whatever happened now, she was better off knowing, and taking precautions, than she would have been simply unaware of what had happened.

But he'd promised Hargis and Drolezki to let them know if he remembered anything else. He'd held out on them once, and it had resulted in Adam being poisoned. Elisa asked a good question. Did he, or did he not, trust the two FBI men? He had responded that he did.

So he had to call them now. Maybe tell them that he had just remembered about the cave. He didn't have to mention Elisa's name. But he needed to either play by the rules and let them protect him or tell them to fuck off and take his chances. What he was doing right now was trying to play both sides and impeding their investigation for no particularly good reason.

The problem was, he had also promised to tell them if he got in touch with Elisa.

He climbed out of bed with a groan and went to living

room, where he'd left his cell. Hargis' card was still next to it. He dialed the number, and two rings later, a familiar voice said, "Hargis."

"Mr. Hargis, this is Chris Franzia. I've remembered something that I think might be relevant, and I wanted to let you know."

"Yes?"

"I was thinking about the field work the class did, and I remembered something that the seven of us did together. It might be the only thing that we all did together, with no one else involved, so if you're looking for something that links us, maybe this is it."

"What is it?"

"It was on one of our field trips, up in the Cascades. We had the afternoon off and went exploring. We found a cave in a hillside, probably an old lava tube. We spent a little while exploring it."

"And what did you find?"

That's the question, isn't it?

"Nothing, really," Chris said. "I mean, it was only a cave, and we didn't have flashlights on us. We didn't even bring day packs. We were just off for a walk, not even a serious hike, and weren't more than a mile or so from camp."

"What makes you think this is relevant?"

"I don't know. But you told me to let you know if I thought of something that connected the seven of us, and this is the only thing I can come up with."

"And you don't remember what happened, when you were inside the cave?"

Chris frowned. "That's a weird question to ask. What makes you think I can't remember? I said nothing happened." He shivered. It was like when he talked to the false Elisa. Something felt wrong.

Hargis didn't answer for a moment. "It seems odd that you had a sudden recollection of something that you all did together, and made a point of calling me, only to tell me nothing happened."

"Look," Chris said, "I'm doing what you told me to do. I'm being a good soldier, okay? You said to call you if I remembered anything. I remembered something, so I called you. It is the only thing I can bring to mind that connects the seven of us and excludes the rest of the class." He paused. "And by the way, are you sure that the rest of the class should be excluded? How did you narrow it down to the seven of us?"

"We've followed up on everyone on the class list, with the exception of one foreign student who was from South Korea. She left the country upon receiving her master's degree and returned home, and it seems far-fetched to connect her to this. Of the rest, one of your classmates died in an automobile accident in 1998. Other than that, they're all still alive. We also have Gavin McCormick's email, remember, which mentioned you seven by name, and no others."

"Oh. Right."

"And as far as your memory of finding the cave, I appreciate your letting me know. I apologize for sounding suspicious, but in this job, suspicion is more or less an occupational hazard. You did the right thing by calling."

"Okay. Keep me apprised of any further developments, all right?"

"I will."

Hargis hung up.

Chris stood there with the phone in his hand, looking down at Hargis' business card, for several minutes.

Elisa said that her intuition was not to let Hargis and Drolezki know she was alive, and he'd told her that he trusted them. So why, then, did he feel like he had put himself in further danger by telling Hargis about the cave?

He set the phone back into the charger, and headed back into his bedroom, trying to ignore the sick feeling in the pit of his stomach and the thought bouncing in his skull.

But after hearing Hargis's voice again, he was sure. He didn't trust the G-man at all. Maybe the whole ruse was a set up, and everything, including Adam's death, was part of a plan to get Elisa and find out what she knew.

And maybe by calling Hargis, he'd just signed his own death warrant, and Elisa's along with him.

CHAPTER 6

The waitress at Paul's Tavern—*We Serve Good Food! Best Breakfast In Town!*—greeted Chris with a smile the next morning.

"You're becoming a regular, honey," she said. "Coffee?"

"Yes, please."

"Room for cream?"

"No, thanks."

"You'd think I'd know that by now," she said, with a raspy laugh, and went off to get his coffee.

Chris opened up the newspaper he'd purchased from the Save-a-Lot, and looked at the front page. More trouble in Syria. More controversy about the state budget. More people outraged over deservedly obscure celebrities trying to gain notoriety in outrageous ways.

Funny how none of it mattered when you might be dead in a few hours. How could he know how far they'd infiltrated? Maybe one of them was in the back of the restaurant right now, slipping poison into his coffee.

As if on cue, the waitress reappeared, still smiling, carrying Chris's cup. She set it down in front of him.

"Know whatcha want, hon?" she said, pulling out a pad.

"Two eggs over easy, bacon, toast," Chris said.

"White or wheat?"

"Wheat."

"Comin' right up. Anything more to drink?"

"Small orange juice, please."

"You got it." She snapped her pad closed and went off toward the kitchen, leaving Chris staring at the coffee, his newspaper forgotten.

I can't be afraid of everything, can I?

The key was to pick up on the important things, notice what's different. Even if guessing wrong, or missing something, meant he was dead.

"Well, I'm not going to start suspecting my morning coffee," he said quietly, and picked it up and took a sip.

Consuming his coffee, and then his breakfast, while showing no signs of heart attack, stroke, or fatal lethargy, he smiled and paid up, thanking the waitress for not killing him by leaving a nice tip. Chris left the restaurant, pressing the electronic unlock button on his key ring as he approached his car.

There's another change, he thought. *Locking my car. I never locked my car before this. Maybe Hargis is right, I am learning.*

But the thought of Hargis wasn't comforting. As he drove home, he tried to recall everything the agent had said to him, trying to puzzle out if there was a way to tell from his words whether he could be trusted or not. These people were too smart to be obvious about things. They hadn't gotten this far, killing five people and barely raising a suspicion, by leaving footprints.

But that was the problem. If Hargis was honestly trying to protect him, then he'd say exactly the same things he would if he was trying to kill Chris.

So how could he know what to do when there was no way to tell truth from lies?

Maybe I should call the local FBI office, verify these guys are on the level.

He turned onto his street, looking for the telltale white sedan, but it was nowhere in sight. The only thing unusual was a New York State Electric and Gas truck parked across the street from his house, its familiar orange and white logo blazoned on the side. One man was standing in the bucket of the cherry-picker, and had the transformer box open. The other was feeding him cable from a large spool. Both wore yellow safety vests and hard hats.

Chris felt the panic rise in him, but immediately he laughed at himself. NYSEG workers.

He parked his car and shut off the engine, then walked down his driveway and across the road.

"Hi. What're you working on?" he asked the man paying out cable.

The man gave him a genial smile. "Routine maintenance," he said. "Replacing some old junctions and wire. There've been a lot of power outages in this area, and we're hoping to head off a few of them before the weather goes bad."

"Oh. So nothing I need to be concerned about?"

He laughed. "Nope."

"Have a good day, then," Chris said.

"You, too."

Chris walked back up the driveway, his thoughts still in an internal war.

He couldn't go around suspecting everything and everyone, but he also realized that lack of caution was how the others got killed. He had the advantage of having at least some idea of what was going on.

But there was a difference between "forewarned is forearmed" and shrieking paranoia. He knew that to stay alive, he had to be smart, be skeptical, and question what he saw, but not assume that everything was out to kill him.

Baxter greeted him with a thwack of his tail against the floor, but it was mid-morning, right in the middle of canine nap-time, so he didn't even get up. Even Jabberwock was asleep in his cage on the bookcase.

A whole day, and nothing to do but sit around and fret. Just like the previous day. And the day before.

I'm going to go batshit crazy if something doesn't change. I'm freaking out over some electrical service guys, for chrissake.

He sat down, turned his computer on, and checked his email. Nothing new from Elisa. Nothing, in fact, except an email from a Nigerian prince who promised him a million dollars if he'd reply with his bank account and social security number. Chris deleted it and shut off his computer. He leaned back, and gave a harsh sigh.

The idea from earlier came dancing back into his thoughts—verification. At least there was one thing he could settle. He could cross the NYSEG workers off the list of things to worry about.

Getting out his telephone directory, he looked up the number for New York State Electric and Gas, and dialed the number. After going through several menus of options, he finally got a real person on the other end of the line, a harassed-sounding woman who clearly was not in the mood for inane questions.

"I'm calling about some service being done on my road," Chris said.

"Address?" the woman said.

"515 North Glen Road, Guildford."

There was a pause, and then the woman said with an audible sigh, "I'm sorry, sir, there is no scheduled service being done on your road."

Chris's stomach clenched painfully. "I… what?"

"I said," the woman said, her voice becoming even more peevish, "that there is no service being done on your road."

"But I just talked to them. Two guys in a NYSEG truck. They were working on the transformer."

"Sir," the woman said, in a tone that made it sound like an insult, "I have access to the itinerary of all scheduled service and maintenance being done in the entire region. I can tell you for certain that there is no work scheduled anywhere along North Glen Road. If there were, I would know, sir."

"I…" Chris started, and then said, "thank you," and hung up.

He stood there staring into space, listening to the sound of his heart hammering in his chest, as his conscious mind tried its best to fly away.

They're… *Them.* The NYSEG guys are… *Them.*

Maybe the waitress at Paul's is, too. So far they haven't left footprints, but at what point will they give up being subtle and just go for the kill and be done with it?

Maybe everyone is in on it.

Something cold and wet nudged his hand. Baxter, sensing Chris's distress, had roused himself from slumber and was standing next to him, his face questioning, worried, his tail down.

Still feeling like he was dissociating, Chris went back to the front door, Baxter trailing him. He opened it, went down the steps onto the sidewalk, and past his car and out to the road.

The NYSEG truck was gone.

Chris said, "What the hell is going on here?"

That's when his house exploded behind him.

The concussion knocked Chris and Baxter both off their feet. Chris landed on his belly, which was how he narrowly missed being beheaded by a whirling chunk of his screen door. Debris rained all around him, and he reflexively put his hands over his face. Baxter gave a terrified whine and pressed into him, shuddering.

Then, with hardly any conscious awareness of what he was doing, he was back up and running for his car. He flung the door open, called once for Baxter—who needed no additional encouragement—and stuffed his hand in his pocket to find that he still had his car keys, cellphone, and wallet. He slammed the door behind him, turned on the ignition, and peeled out of the driveway as his house's natural gas line went up in a second, much larger, explosion.

It was fortunate no one was coming down the street, or Chris would have been t-boned. He screeched out onto Glen Road, gravel spitting from under his tires, and took the first left onto Martin Street. Forcing himself to slow down, he turned up Hyland Street and into a maze of suburban neighborhood lanes, which he drove in no particular pattern.

Gone. My house is gone. They blew up my house. And if I hadn't made that call to NYSEG, I'd be dead now.

His pulse accelerated, but his thoughts had an odd, detached calm, as if he were hearing a story about someone else. He wondered if they had waited around to see the explosion. Probably not. These people set their traps and assume they'll work. No way would they be around the scene of the crime. They were too careful for that, too cocky. But what about Hargis and Drolezki? Where the hell were *they?*

Chris passed the house of his friend, Janina Vannoy, the high school choral music teacher. He knew that Janina wasn't there. She had mentioned to Chris at the last faculty meeting of the year that as soon as school was out, she and her family were heading off for a three-week family vacation to Belize, where they were all going to take scuba diving classes.

And the last thing I said to her was, 'Wow. Your summer is sure going to be more exciting than mine.' Ha!

He drove his car around and behind a forsythia hedge, screening it from the road. He turned off his motor, and started to laugh—a panicked, desperate sound that would have looked to a passerby as if he were sobbing uncontrollably.

And honestly, it probably wasn't far from that.

The storm passed, and he realized he felt completely exhausted. Fighting sleep, he looked out toward the road, wondering if any neighbors had seen his car go up the driveway, and saw, driving slowly along the street, a white four-door sedan.

There were sirens in the distance now. Fire trucks, no doubt, coming to deal with the blazing remains of his house.

"Oh, God, I can't deal with this. I can't fucking deal with this," he said out loud.

If they find me here, they can kill me. That's all. They can just fucking kill me and be done with it.

And he closed his eyes.

• • • •

He awoke to rain striking the windshield of his car. The light was dim, and lightning flashed in the distance. He consulted his watch. It was only a little after two in the afternoon, but the sky was dark with rolling clouds.

He blinked groggily, and looked over at Baxter, who was sitting upright in the passenger seat, as if on guard duty.

"That's a good boy," he said, and Baxter looked over at him and wagged. "I bet you need to pee, but I don't imagine you'll want to go out in this, do you?"

Chris started his motor, and cautiously backed out of the Vannoys' driveway. He looked up and down their street. No cars visible. He pulled out, heading away from what was left of his house. In his rearview mirror he could see a reddish glow on the underside of the clouds, the unmistakable ruddy glare of fire. He barely gave it a glance. His car was headed north, out of Guildford and into the hill country beyond.

Even if Hargis and Drolezki were on his side, they couldn't protect him. Some fake electrical workers were able to get in and sabotage his house, right under their noses. Or maybe he'd been right, and the two FBI agents were in on it, too. Either way, Chris knew he had to get out of there. Anywhere was safer than Guildford.

He took a winding, circuitous route, north and west, checking frequently for any sign of pursuit. If there was anyone trailing him, they weren't being obvious about it.

Chris was surprised at how little he worried about the idea of someone following him. Whatever happened after this he wouldn't be able to predict, just like he hadn't been able to predict anything else connected to this insanity. Up till now, though, he'd been trying to pretend that he could parse it, make sense of it, anticipate the next move. No more of that.

It was like a deer pursued by hunters. The deer has no idea of why it's being hunted; all it knows is that its life depends on its next move. So no more intellectualizing, no more puzzling over why all this was happening. Instincts and reflexes. Just run.

Be the deer.

He came up to the junction with Interstate 90 in Geneva, went west, toward Buffalo. The same road that ran right through Seattle. One long, continuous piece of pavement running across the entire United States, connecting this place to where it all started.

By this time, the wind was howling, the rain was coming down in sheets. He pulled off into the Seneca Service Area to wait out the worst of the storm.

After about forty minutes, the rain tapered off to a drizzle, the storm passing away south and east. He let Baxter out to pee, and hit the road, again heading west into the lengthening shadows of dusk.

"Let's see how many miles we can put behind us before dark," he said to Baxter, who just sighed and went back to sleep.

He stopped for the night at a Super 8 in Erie, Pennsylvania. He didn't tell them about Baxter. Chris followed his father's dictum that it was always easier to beg for forgiveness than to ask permission. He waited until the coast seemed clear, and then snuck his dog down the hall and into his room, which fortunately was on the first floor.

Chris grabbed a hurried dinner in the hotel restaurant, brought leftovers back to his room for Baxter, and then went to the computer in the lobby. He signed into his email account, despite a nagging voice in the back of his head that told him every time he connected with anything electronic, he was leaving a footprint.

But I've got to let her know, he though, hitting the return key. There were no unread emails. He clicked on *New Message*, and wrote ereed@orionsbelt.com into the address line.

> *Elisa,*
>
> *I'm a little worried that you haven't written, but I hope everything's all right. I don't want to tell you where I am, for the same reason I didn't want you to tell me where you are. I'm on the run. I don't know if you were right about the FBI men, but whichever way, they weren't able to protect me. My house was blown to pieces this afternoon, and I only escaped by dumb luck. Two near misses are enough, so I'm gone from Guildford. I don't know where I'll go now. So far, "away" is as far as I've thought this through.*
>
> *I don't know how easy it will be to track me. I have my cell with me, but I'm not going to use it, or even turn it on, unless I have to. The number is 607-555-2904. ONLY call it if there's an emergency. I'll try to be back in touch soon.*
>
> *God, I hope you're okay. You have no idea how much I hope you're okay. Sorry if that seems forward, or weird, or whatever. I don't think I've ever felt as alone as I do now, and I can't bear thinking that maybe they've got you, too. So as soon as you get this, send me an email to let me know how you are. I'll be back on the road tomorrow, but I'll check in before I leave the hotel.*
>
> *Take care.*
>
> *Chris*

Chris clicked *Send*. There was no familiar whooshing sound, as his computer had done, only a little note that said, *Message Sent*. Chris's computer, along with everything else he owned, was now buried under a pile of charred rubble on North Glen Road in Guildford, New York.

Chris went back to his room. The clothes he wore, his car, his wallet, his cell, and his dog. That was all that was left of his life. He had, at times in his life, been what he'd considered poor, down to almost nothing in his bank account by the end of the pay period, eating instant noodles and peanut-butter-and-jelly sandwiches for dinner because he couldn't afford better.

He had never before been homeless.

He unlocked his hotel room, turned on the light, peered in. Nothing seemed amiss. Baxter was lying on the bed, and his tail thumped against the mattress in greeting. He closed the door behind him, shot the deadbolt and slipped the chain lock into place. Only then did he sit down on the end of the bed and slump over, his hands over his face.

Can they find me here? I probably shouldn't have given my actual name at the register.

He'd had to, though, because he'd given them his credit card. But he knew they could track him that way. Next time he'd make up a name. He'd use his credit card at an ATM to get a few days' worth of cash, and then pay for everything that way.

If they catch up with me here, I'm done for, but there's nothing I can do about that now. And whatever happens, I'm going to get some sleep. I wonder how bad it hurts if you are killed in your sleep?

Holy hell, I'm tired.

There is only so long that the human body can ride an adrenaline high. Chris felt a fatigue like he'd never experienced before, not even on his days of long, uphill back-country hikes. He realized suddenly that if he didn't stand up now, he was going to fall asleep where he sat.

He stood, and got undressed, leaving his clothes in a pile on the floor. He slid between the sheets, and rested one hand on Baxter's furry back. Then he gave a deep, hitching intake of breath, and was asleep within one minute.

CHAPTER 7

Chris awoke at 7:32 AM from a combination of a full bladder and Baxter snoring loudly in his face. He opened his eyes, squinting at the line of bright sunlight gleaming at him from between the opaque plastic window shades, then got up, and stumbled into the bathroom.

He stood under the shower, marveling at the fact that he was still alive. Either that meant that they didn't know where he was, or else they were letting him live for the time being, perhaps to see what he was going to do next.

He had a momentary jolt when he considered the direction he'd chosen to drive. They knew he'd tried

to contact Elisa, and perhaps also knew that he'd succeeded. Were they letting him live so that he would lead them to her, hoping to get them both at the same time? If so, it would be crazy to keep heading west. Running toward her would be the most obvious move he could make.

But the drive to find her, keep her from getting killed, was too strong, and he put it out of his mind.

He successfully sneaked Baxter out to take a hurried pee in the garden behind the hotel, and got him back to the room without being seen. Baxter gave him a hopeful look, but was rewarded only with some water poured into the ice bucket.

"Look, dude, I know you're hungry. At least I saved you some of my burger from last night. I promise, we'll pick up some dog food today. Yesterday I was mostly focused on how not to get us both killed."

Baxter wagged his tail, which he took as understanding.

There were two messages on his cell. A text from Matt van Valen, one of the high school history teachers, asking if Chris wanted to get together for a game of tennis. Evidently he hadn't heard about the explosion. There was also a voicemail from Hargis, exhorting him to call back immediately.

Chris deleted both without answering.

Back to the hotel restaurant for breakfast, and another newspaper that described trouble in Syria, controversy over the state budget, and foolishness about celebrities. The news never changed.

Humanity always keeps doing the same things over and over. We're programmed to act a particular way by our brain wiring. It's why we're so predictable.

If Chris had a chance of outwitting these guys and getting away, it would be because he'd done something that went against his programming, something that they honestly didn't think he'd do. So far, all he'd done was make it easy for them. And yet, he was still planning on heading west. There was no doubt in his mind about that.

He stopped in the lobby after breakfast, sat down at the computer, and signed into his email account. Several new emails, mostly from recognized addresses.

From his principal:

> *Chris,*
> *I heard about your house fire, and I wanted to offer to you to come stay at our place for as long as you need. Gail and I have a spare bedroom and would be happy to put you up. I'm so sorry this happened. If you need anything, let me know.*
>
> *Andy*

From the head of the science department:

Chris,

I hope you're okay. I'm off on vacation but heard about what happened from Dolores, who said that the news said that no one was hurt in the fire. But that sucks even so. I just wanted to say that I'll be back next week and if you need any help, I'm happy to do what I can.

Lynn

There were several other offers of help, sympathy, and questions from curious friends and coworkers. Obviously, the news stations had reported that he'd survived the fire. The emails were unanimous on that point.

Even before sifting through the ashes looking for bodies, the police would have seen that there was no car in the driveway and figured he was away when the house went up. After the fire was out, they'd have confirmed it by going through the debris. So that meant that everyone knew he was still alive, which was both good news and bad.

The next one was from an unknown email address, jch292@gmail.com.

Mr. Franzia, it is imperative that you return to Guildford as soon as possible. You're taking a tremendous chance by being on your own, where there's no way we can protect you. Contact me immediately.

J. Hargis
p.s. I am assuming that my business card was destroyed in the fire. My cellphone number is (703) 555-1003.

Chris gave a grim chuckle. *Protect me? You did fuckall to protect me from getting my house blown up. I think I'll take my chances.*

He deleted it without responding, just as he'd done with Hargis's voicemail message.

The next one was the one he was looking for—ereed@ orionsbelt.com.

Chris,

That is horrible! I'm so sorry I didn't write yesterday, but I thought you were safe, and so was I, and I didn't have anything new to tell you. I got busy with other things and didn't see your email until two hours after you sent it, by which time you were probably sound asleep.

Has it occurred to you that it sounds like they're getting a little desperate? Think about it. All of the others were killed quietly, simply, nothing flashy. Nothing that would attract notice. The fact that they destroyed your house – that's going to make the news, cause some attention. Either they've given up trying to be subtle about things, or maybe they have some reason for changing their tactics. I don't know if that's accurate, but I thought of that and thought I should mention it.

I'm still fine where I am. I am so worried about you,

though. I hope you're being careful. Please contact me when you can to let me know how things are, and that you're okay.

Take care.

Elisa

Chris clicked *Reply.*

Elisa,

I'm so relieved to hear from you. I'm okay for now, and am going to hit the road shortly. I don't want to stay in one place for long. I don't know how many traces I've left, nor how easy it is to track my whereabouts. I was so dog-tired last night that I didn't care, but today I'm going to be more careful. I'll be in touch as soon as I can.

Chris

Chris sent the email, then signed out. He stretched, then stood up, and headed back toward his room. There was nothing to pack up. Just grab Baxter and go.

He used the ATM in the lobby to withdraw the maximum amount of cash his access card would allow, which turned out to be five hundred dollars. He was able to get another five hundred as a cash advance on his VISA card. He looked at the stack of bills sitting in his hand in some amazement; he'd never held that much cash before.

One less set of footprints. Once he left the hotel, no more using plastic unless it was imperative.

As he was passing the front desk in the lobby, the clerk, a middle-aged African American woman with short-cropped salt-and-pepper hair and a brass nametag that said "Luanne," said, "Sir? Excuse me, sir?"

Chris turned. "Yes?"

"I'm sorry, but I thought… you're staying in 107, right?"

Simultaneously, two thoughts flashed through his head. The first was: *Shit, the hotel staff found Baxter.* The second was: *How the hell does she know who I am?*

But he said, trying to keep his voice steady, "Yes, that's me."

She smiled, and said, "I thought so. I remembered you from yesterday, when you arrived. And I wanted to let you know. There were two men here looking for you."

Chris's heart gave an uneven little gallop against his ribcage. "Really?" he said.

"Yes. They wanted to know your room number, but hotel policy is that we can't give those out unless we've received prior authorization. I offered to call your room for them, and they said to, but you weren't there."

"I was at breakfast," Chris said. It was becoming increasingly difficult for him to modulate his voice. His thoughts were screaming at him, *Run! Run! They've found you! Get out of here!*

"It occurred to me afterwards that you might have been," Luanne said. "Well, they said they'd be back in fifteen minutes. So I thought I'd let you know."

"Okay," Chris said. "Thanks." He frowned. "Was one of them kind of small, with dark hair, and the other this big blond guy that looks like a linebacker?"

Luanne shook her head. "Nope," she said. "They both looked like generic suits, to me." She laughed. "Sorry, that's not much help. But they had a kind of business-professional look. White guys, maybe mid-forties, both had brown hair. One of them wore glasses."

"Oh," Chris said. "Okay. Thanks."

"If they come back, do you want me to give them your room number?"

"No!" Chris said, a little more forcefully than he intended.

Luanne didn't seem surprised at his response. "No problem, sir. I'll call you if they come back, then?"

"Sure," Chris said. With any luck, he'd be long gone by then. He added, "Can I go ahead and check out now? I've got to pick up my stuff, but I can leave the card key in the room, and it'll save me another walk to the lobby."

"Of course," she said. She clicked on her computer keyboard, and called up his account. "Are you leaving this on your VISA card, Mr. Franzia?"

"Yes."

Another few clicks. "Then you're all set. Would you like a receipt?"

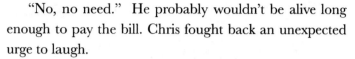

"No, no need." He probably wouldn't be alive long enough to pay the bill. Chris fought back an unexpected urge to laugh.

"Thank you for staying at the Super 8. Hope to see you again soon."

Not likely. He said instead, "Thanks."

He made it back to his room without running. He opened the door, called for Baxter, tossed the card key on the coffee table, and made it out into the parking lot without incident.

A minute later, he was pulling back out onto the road and following the signs that said, *To I-90 West.*

· · · ·

Chris crossed into the state of Ohio at a little before ten in the morning. He drove a steady seventy miles per hour with the sun shining into his rear window and Baxter snoozing on the passenger seat. Near Euclid he started catching glimpses of the flat expanse of Lake Erie. The traffic began to increase as he approached Cleveland.

Even staying on the interstate, Cleveland was a snarled mess of twisty roads, lane changes, and traffic jams, and it took him nearly an hour to clear the city and continue west. At least the proximity to the city made the selection of music on the radio better. He finally settled on 100.7, WMMS—*Cleveland's Rock Sta-*

tion—and passed the time listening to the Gin Blossoms, Linkin Park, and Green Day.

By the time he got past the last of the Cleveland sprawl it was nearing noon, and his stomach growled. As he crossed into Elyria Township, he saw a sign saying, *Last Exit Before Toll,* and decided he'd wait to stop until the first service plaza on the Ohio Turnpike.

Middle Ridge Service Plaza turned out to be a sprawling, dome-shaped building housing the usual assortment of fast food restaurants, a mini-mart, and the Ohio Heartland Gift Shop. He got some takeout Chinese food for himself, was able to pick up a bag of dog kibble and a pair of small plastic bowls for Baxter in the mini-mart, and bought two Ohio State University t-shirts for himself in the gift shop. He could keep wearing the same jeans day after day, but a clean shirt was more important. He made a mental note to pick up a couple of pairs of boxers and a package of socks next time he saw a K-Mart.

He sat at a picnic table in the sunshine, eating his General Tso's chicken, with Baxter sitting next to him contentedly munching kibble from one of the bowls. He watched the people going into and out of the service plaza, idly wondering if any of them were suddenly going to turn and kill him.

Weird how quickly you get used to an idea.

Any of these people could be one of *Them*. No way of knowing.

The desk clerk at the hotel said that the two men who were looking for him were 'generic.' After all, that'd be an advantage, wouldn't it? It's only in action-adventure movies that the bad guys look visibly evil. In real life, evil looks like everything else, until it acts.

As he retrieved Baxter's food and water dish and deposited the takeout containers in the trash can, the thought crossed his mind that maybe the people who were looking for him in the hotel could have been FBI, dispatched by Hargis and Drolezki to catch up with and protect him, or bring him back to Guildford.

There was no way to tell whether that was right until it was too late, though. It all came of having enemies and friends that looked exactly alike.

Back in the car, back on the Turnpike heading west toward Indiana and beyond. The terrain was mostly flat and getting flatter. Behind were the rolling hills of the western Alleghenies, ahead the pancake cornfields and straight-edge horizons of the Midwest. Exits for Sandusky, Fremont, and Elmore zipped by. Then there was the Rust Belt urban jungle of Toledo, its skyline graced by two huge glass-fronted skyscrapers and a dozen smaller, grime-stained office buildings. After crossing I-75, there was nothing but farms, silos, and billboards advertising evangelical churches and revival meetings.

Chris saw the sign saying, "Last Ohio Exit" at just before four in the afternoon. By then, the sun had swung around to the west and was shining into his eyes, and the glare had given him a headache. He was torn between pushing onward out of fear and finding a place to stop out of simple fatigue.

Where was he headed? West. Stupid choice, probably, but he knew it wouldn't turn him back. Whether it was because that was where he thought Elisa was, or because it was where the whole thing had started thirty years ago, it was impossible to know. But now, this moment, he needed somewhere to hole up for a while. Some little pissant town in Iowa where no one would ever think of looking for him. Continuing to drive was pointless.

After all, he didn't even know for sure if Elisa was still in Minnesota. She could be anywhere. Going to St. Cloud was a good way to get caught. Going west at all was crazy.

And yet he kept driving.

He saw the sign saying, *Pay Toll Ahead*, and slowed down, pulling into the "Cash" lane to pay his fare. Ahead of him were a pickup truck and a minivan packed with luggage and children.

He couldn't hide forever. It had to end at some point, most likely by his getting caught and killed. What other outcome could there be?

I'm one guy, one naïve high school teacher from Nowheresville, upstate New York, against people who are capable of creating unde-tectable poisons, sneaking into your house and tampering with beer in your fridge, executing a fatal hit-and-run, and impersonating electric workers to rig your house to explode, all without getting caught. How can I hope to get away from people that powerful?

The pickup pulled through, and Chris edged his car up.

A surge of determination rose in him. He might not have a chance, but he'd sure as hell evade them for as long as he could. Even if they caught him, he'd give them a good hard run.

He certainly wasn't going to lie down and give up just because he was alone.

The minivan pulled through, and Chris moved up to the tollbooth. The toll collector was a young man who already had a deep summer tan, whose shaggy brown hair was streaked with obviously dyed blond highlights. He looked like he couldn't be much beyond a teenager. A college student, possibly, with a summer job working for the Turnpike Commission.

Chris handed him the ticket through the open window. The boy took it, and said, "That'll be ten dollars, sir."

Chris handed him a ten dollar bill.

The boy said, "Would you like a receipt?"

Chris said no.

"You might want to consider not getting on the Indiana Turnpike," the boy said.

Chris stared at him for a moment. "What?"

"I said," the boy replied, in a conversational tone, "you might want to consider not getting on the Turnpike. You are going to Indiana, aren't you?"

"Yes," Chris said. "Why?"

The boy shrugged. "Whenever you go through one of these toll booths, there's a camera that takes a photograph of your license plate. It automatically records where your car is. So, where you are."

Chris looked at him, his eyes wide, and said, "Oh."

"Just a thought," the boy said. "There are lots of ways to cross Indiana besides the Turnpike. Might be a little slower, but I wouldn't let that influence the decision."

"No," Chris said, swallowing.

The boy grinned at him, showing a row of perfectly even white teeth. "Have a nice day, sir."

"You, too."

Chris drove forward, feeling the sweat standing out on his skin, trying to breathe steadily and return his heart rate to normal. He got a ticket at the Eastpoint Toll Barrier at the state line, but ten miles later got off on Exit 144 toward Angola, Indiana.

The sun headed toward the horizon in front of him.

Who was that kid? And why would he tell me that?

He wasn't one of *Them,* apparently. Or maybe he was, and was trying to divert Chris onto a different path, one where he'd be easier to find, in small towns, on small roads, in unpopulated areas, instead of the teeming bustle of the interstate.

But he'd been telling himself to go on instinct, and his gut told him to trust the kid. If he was one of *Them,* why any warnings at all? Why tell him that his license plate was being photographed, and that they could keep track of his whereabouts that way?

My friends and my enemies look exactly the same. So I have to tell them apart a different way. Think about what they say, how they act. I'm smart enough to figure this out. And I'd better be.

My life depends on it.

CHAPTER 8

I t wasn't until 9:30 at night, right outside of Elkhart, Indiana, that Chris found a motel, the Belmont Inn, that would let him stay without requiring that he submit identification.

He signed the register as "Chris Lake," which seemed like a generic enough name not to be memorable, but didn't have the invented quality of "John Smith." Nothing would look as suspicious as hesitating over your own name. It was easy to remember, as well. Lake was his grandmother's maiden name.

He signed the register, made up an address, and a phone number of random digits. The clerk, a greasy-haired young woman with too much eye-liner, took his registration form and glanced at it briefly. He held his breath, expecting to be asked at least for a driver's license, but she just said, "Sixty dollars."

He handed over the cash, and the clerk slid a key across to him without once meeting his eyes.

"Room 9," she said.

"Thanks," Chris said, but she was already reading her newspaper again, and didn't respond. There was a sign that said *Continental Breakfast, 6 AM – 9 AM* on the wall, but no restaurant in sight. He decided not to ask about it. No sense attracting attention.

And the fact that she wouldn't look at me means that she'd be unlikely to be able to identify me, if someone comes asking about me.

Could she be one of Them? *It doesn't seem likely. Whoever* They *are, I doubt they would show up in the person of a slovenly twenty-something woman who needs to take a shower.*

Of course, there was the boy in the tollbooth. Even if he wasn't one of Them, he knew what was going on. He was just as unlikely.

So rule one, don't trust appearances.

Chris went down to his room and unlocked the door. There was a faint odor of stale cigarette smoke, but it wasn't too bad. Flipping on the light revealed worn carpet that had once been beige but now was patterned with a variety of stains and snags. At least the bed looked reasonably clean, despite a glossy spatter of some unknown substance dried onto the wall next to it. The bathroom had a rust-stained shower and sink, but soap, shampoo, and clean towels were provided.

Chris went back out and peered down the hall. There was a back entrance, perfect for sneaking in a dog. Given the untidy state of the room, he doubted dog hair would be high on the list of concerns of the housekeeping staff even if he got caught.

Baxter was safely retrieved from his car, the door shut and bolted, and Chris turned the television on and lay back on the bed. He flipped channels until he found a rerun of *The X-Files*. He smiled. It had been his favorite television series from the time it started, and he owned the whole series on DVD.

Used to. He sighed, his smile vanishing. *It burned up with the rest of my house.*

The episode was a continuation of the Alien Conspiracy story, and he'd caught it in the middle. Mulder was sneaking around in the Russian countryside with his erstwhile arch-enemy Alex Krycek. This one, Chris remembered, ended badly, with Mulder bound to a rusted bed frame with chickenwire and infected with the evil, mind-controlling Black Oil.

Chris used to be obsessed with the show, especially the episodes about aliens and government conspiracies.

Now that he was living it, though, it wasn't nearly so appealing.

He turned the television off.

Thinking about his previous life brought his mind back to the fateful field biology class. His life had intersected with six other people—five of whom were now dead. None of them could have predicted such an outcome at the time. The only one who'd had any inkling, apparently, was Gavin. That email to Glen was the only unifying theme, the only thing that gave any hint that there was more going on than a string of accidental deaths.

Why couldn't he have given more information? But the answer came right away. He'd been afraid that his emails were being monitored. Which they probably were. But something, anything that gave a clue about what he was up against would be preferable to this blank, terrifying suspicion of everyone and everything unknown.

Gavin, of course, had always loved mysteries. He was a little on the odd side even back then. Fascinated with the fringe areas of knowledge, with topics that most of the rest of them considered nonsense. Chris recalled a conversation they'd had over coffee after class, shortly before their first expedition into the Cascades. Deirdre Ross and Glen Cederstrom had been there.

· · · ·

"I'm going to have to spend some extra time before the next test in the bone room," Glen said. "I'm not looking forward to having to learn all of those scientific names."

"Pity they didn't have a Bigfoot skull in the bones collection," Chris said. "What's the scientific name of a Bigfoot, anyhow?"

Gavin leaned forward, his round face flushed with excitement. "Well, organisms aren't assigned scientific names until they're catalogued. Bigfoot hasn't been. But it will probably turn out to be some sort of Australopithecine."

Deirdre rolled her eyes. "Really, Gavin?"

"I was joking," Chris said.

"No, but really," Gavin said, undaunted as always. "How could there be all of those reports, and not one of them is true? Not one single report, not one photograph, not one video recording? All fakes?"

"Easier to believe that than there being some kind of hairy wild man out there in the mountains," Deirdre said. "Funny that they've never found any bones. Chris hit it exactly. There's no Bigfoot skull in the bone room. That's because it doesn't exist."

"I don't know, Deirdre," Gavin said. "You're not a little worried, going up into the Cascades next week? It hasn't crossed your mind, not once?"

Deirdre took a sip of her coffee. "Not until now."

"What about you, Glen?"

Glen Cederstrom shrugged and smiled. "I don't know. There are lots of things that people thought didn't exist, and now we know they do. How about that fish? You know, the coelacanth. Known only from *fossil records until fifty or so years ago, and then someone catches one. It could be that Bigfoot is like that."*

"But people have seen Bigfoot," Gavin said.

"People who have been drinking," Deirdre said with a curt little laugh.

"Not all of them," Gavin persisted.

"Why do we have to decide?" Glen said. "I'm okay with not knowing. Everything doesn't have to be settled. The jury can stay out until we have evidence one way or the other."

"How can you have evidence against?" Deirdre said. "There's nothing that would disprove Bigfoot's existence. That'd mean you're content to remain in ignorance forever."

Glen gave her a slow smile. "Yeah," he said. "Pretty much."

"Well, I'm not," Gavin said. "At some point, you have to make a decision. I've looked at the evidence, and I think if you're fair, you can't argue against it. Bigfoot exists."

"By the same logic, so do aliens, ghosts, and the Loch Ness Monster," Deirdre said.

"Yes," Gavin said. "They do."

"Seriously? You believe all that bullshit?"

"It stands to reason."

"Reason is exactly what it doesn't stand to," Deirdre said, her voice becoming sharp with derision. "You can't just believe something because lots of people say it's so. Science doesn't proceed by majority vote."

"No, but that's it," Gavin said. "The problem is that there are cover-ups. The actual scientists don't want you to know about what's really out there. You've heard of Roswell, haven't you?"

"City in New Mexico," Deirdre said.

"Yes! The site of one of the best-documented alien spacecraft crashes. The military covered it up. There's a film out there that shows a dissection of the body of one of the crew. I watched it. That thing was not human."

"But Gavin," Glen said, "why would scientists want to cover it up? If aliens were real, or any of the other things you claim, don't you think scientists would be eager to investigate it? Why would there be cover-ups? The results of an autopsy on an extraterrestrial, if that could be proven? It would make a scientist's career. You think Einstein is famous? He'd be a minor character next to the first scientist who could prove the existence of an alien intelligence."

"But that's exactly it!" Gavin said, his voice rising with excitement. "The establishment doesn't want this to happen! It would overturn our place in the universe. They're trying to keep us manageable, and that means controlling the flow of information. You think we know even ten percent of what the government does? Why is it so hard for you to believe that some of this stuff might be real, and that there are people, powerful people, who want to keep us in the dark about it?"

Deirdre laughed; it was not, Chris recalled, a particularly nice laugh. "Oh, c'mon. Glen is right. Humans are lousy at keeping secrets. That's why conspiracies never last long. Look at Watergate. Those clowns couldn't even wiretap a hotel room and keep it a secret; how could anyone keep evidence of aliens and Bigfoot and all a secret? Someone would blab."

"And then They take care of the informant," Gavin said darkly.

"They?" Deirdre said, raising an ironic eyebrow.

"Yeah," Gavin said. "Them. You never know who they are. They could be anyone. They could be you or me or Chris or Glen or the lady you bought your coffee from. You'd never know it."

Deirdre looked at Gavin for a moment, and then slowly shook her head. "Well, if They made my coffee, They need to learn how to make a decent brew, because this stuff is swill. Or, I dunno. Maybe it's poisoned, or something. Mind-altering chemicals."

"Yes," Gavin said, not cracking a smile. "Yes, it could be."

Deirdre laughed. "You seriously need to stop watching bad thriller movies," she said.

And that had ended the conversation.

• • • •

Chris stretched, cupped his hands behind his head. Gavin had given up after that. He knew when he was beaten, perhaps, or simply drifted off onto another weird mental pathway. He always seemed to be into new things. It was yoga for a while, Chris recalled, and then Tarot cards and crystals and herbal supplements and numerology and Native American mysticism. He never stayed with one thing for long, but there was always a stack of books tucked into his backpack that had nothing to do with any of his classes. But Gavin was a genuinely kind individual, and had the earnest enthusiasm of a cocker spaniel. On the whole, though, most of his friends tolerated his flights of fancy. If anything, most people seemed to think the two most judgmental members of his circle of friends, Deirdre Ross and Lewis Corelli, were too harsh on him, and occasionally, simply unkind.

But Gavin had been right, at least about that. "They" were real. It remained to be seen if he was right about anything else—Bigfoot and Nessie and aliens and the rest of it. But *They* were very real. And evil.

He looked at the beat-up digital clock on the nightstand. 11:04. He stood up and called Baxter, who gave a heavy sigh and jumped down from the bed. Chris peered out into the empty hall. He went out to let Baxter pee in the grass next to the door, and stood for a moment watching the traffic go past on the highway. Lights glittered in the distance.

Any of those lights could be *Them*. Gavin was right. *They* could be anyone. The girl who checked Chris in to the hotel. Someone in one of the four other cars in the parking lot. Maybe *They* were catching up with him, and would be pulling up soon, Generic White Men in Dark Suits, and one of them would pull out a gun with a silencer, shoot him in the head, and drive away.

He gave a little laugh. *Well, if* They're *here, then* They *have had about a hundred opportunities and haven't taken them.*

"C'mon, Baxter, let's go," he said aloud. "Shouldn't tempt fate."

The hallway was still empty, and he made it back to his room unobserved. He shut, bolted, and chain-locked the door, got undressed, and climbed into bed. The last thing he thought, before he fell asleep, was what Deirdre had thought, right before she drowned. Whether she recognized she was the victim of her own disbelief, or if she died never knowing she'd been wrong.

· · · ·

Chris woke up the next morning at a little before seven, ravenously hungry. He yawned and stretched, and felt Baxter's tail thumping against the mattress.

"Survived another night, dude," he said. "That's the way to start the day."

He didn't bother checking out. No reason to. He'd paid for his room fair and square and had given a false name and address in any case. All the clerk would tell him was "Thank you," if that. Just before leaving his room, he checked his cell and deleted another voicemail from Hargis. Then he tossed the room key on the nightstand and headed back to the car. They were on the road by 7:30.

· · · ·

Highway 20 paralleled the St. Joseph River for a few miles before they veered apart, the road dipping off southward as the river, glittering in the gray morning light, angled sharply toward the lowlands of southern

Michigan. The traffic picked up as he got closer to Gary, and for no particular reason other than wanting to stay out of the urban mess that was Chicago and its environs, he took Highway 31 south for an hour, through a flat expanse of corn and wheat fields that seemed to have no boundaries but melded seamlessly from one into another with only the occasional house or silo to break the monotony.

He was starving by the time he stopped at the Café Tourelle in Peru, Indiana for breakfast. He parked in the shade, let Baxter out, and leashed him to a sapling in a grassy area using a nylon lead he'd picked up earlier at a hardware store. He put the water bowl down near him, filled it with some water, and went into the restaurant, stomach growling.

The café had computers with free internet access, and Chris sat eating a ham-and-cheese omelet while checking his email. There was another email from jch292@gmail.com:

Mr. Franzia:
I need you to respond to this email immediately. It is urgent.

J. Hargis

"You just won't take no for an answer, will you?" Chris shook his head and gave a grim chuckle. "Not too bloody likely, my friend," he said as he deleted it.

The next one was from Elisa, with a timestamp of the previous day at a little after four in the afternoon. He opened it, feeling his pulse quicken. Every time he saw Elisa's name, it reassured him that they could win this game.

We've eluded them this far. We can keep eluding them.

The email read:

> *Chris,*
>
> *I wanted to send you this so you know I'm still okay. I haven't seen anything amiss around here, but I'm keeping my eye out. I'm in a place where I'd know if there was anything out of the ordinary, so you shouldn't worry.*
>
> *I hope you're okay. Just let me know if everything's all right. I feel like we need to be each other's lifelines, even if no one else can know what's going on, we both do. I check my email several times a day. I know you probably won't have much opportunity to write, but a quick note when you have the opportunity would let me know that you're still okay.*
>
> *I was looking at a map of the United States yesterday, and wondering where you were. I know you can't tell me, but I kept looking at different towns and different states, and imagining that you were out there, on the road, maybe in the South or the Midwest or maybe even back in the Northwest. Not knowing simultaneously makes me feel reassured that you're safe and makes me feel lonely. I hope you can find a way to get somewhere where you don't have to run any more.*
>
> *I miss you. That may sound strange to say, since we*

haven't had any contact for thirty years. Maybe it's losing all of the others that makes me feel this way. And maybe, somehow, we can meet when this is all over. It sounds like a ridiculous hope, but I'm clinging to it anyhow.

Elisa

Chris smiled as he read this. He could hear it, in his mind, in Elisa's voice. It was a gentle voice, low and sweet. A beautiful voice, he remembered. He hit *Reply*, and wrote:

Elisa:
I got your email, and I'm fine. I've had a couple of scary near misses. One in a hotel, where the clerk in the lobby told me that two guys had been asking about me, and one completely inexplicable one at a tollbooth, where the ticket-taker somehow knew what was going on. I don't want to give you more than that because who knows who else might be reading this, but it shook me up enough that I'm being a lot more careful now.

But so far, so good. I don't know where I'm heading, and couldn't tell you even if I did, but I'm still alive and unharmed and trying to keep one step ahead. I promise I'll get back in touch as soon as I can.

Don't worry about me.
Chris
p.s. I miss you, too. A lot.

He hit *Send* before he had time to talk himself into deleting the p.s.

He finished his breakfast, paid his bill to a fresh-faced girl who would have been a contender for that year's Miss Perky Midwesterner contest, and went back outside into the sunshine. An elderly woman with a shopping bag was bent over, petting Baxter. Baxter's tail was going like mad.

"Your dog?" she said, looking up with a smile.

"Yes," Chris said. "His name is Baxter."

"He's a darling," the woman said. "I simply love dogs. I have two of my own, but I never can pass a sweet doggie like this without saying hi."

"Oh, Baxter loves people," Chris said. "He's about the friendliest guy on earth. He's been that way since he was a puppy. Not a mean bone in his body."

"No, I can see that," the woman said, laughing. "I wish I had a doggie biscuit for him, but I don't."

"No problem. He appreciates the petting as much as food, honestly."

She looked into Baxter's brown eyes. "You be a good boy, Baxter," she said, scratching him under his chin. "Take care of your daddy."

Chris laughed and said, "He will."

The elderly woman put her hand gently on Chris's shoulder and said, "God bless both of you. Have a nice day."

"You, too."

She walked off down the sidewalk, taking little, mincing steps, the shopping bag hanging from her hand.

Chris unhooked Baxter's leash from the sapling, and then unsnapped it from his collar, and let him into the car. Baxter jumped into the passenger seat and put his paws on the dashboard, his tail still wagging furiously.

It was only after Chris started the engine that the thought came to him, seemingly out of nowhere. . . *She's one of* Them.

Chris's rational mind spurred him to laugh out loud. Her? She looked like his grandma. A stiff wind would blow her over.

Well, the boy in the tollbooth didn't look suspicious, either. Not until he told Chris to get off the freeway.

He looked into his rearview mirror. The old lady was still visible, walking away from him, now almost two blocks away.

All she is is an old lady who likes dogs. You can't suspect everyone.

But the relief was short-lived. That was the old way of thinking and had nearly gotten him killed. He had to suspect everyone, even if they looked harmless.

Maybe especially if they look harmless.

Chris reached over and ran his hands over his dog's fur. Nothing amiss, so far as he could tell. Baxter, pleased with the attention, gave him a wet kiss on the cheek.

Chris unsnapped Baxter's collar, and held it up.

It was five minutes before he saw it. He'd been about

to give up and put the collar back on, and write his feelings off to paranoia. It was a tiny, rectangular black metal chip, wedged into the blue nylon fabric of Baxter's collar. At first, it looked to him like a fleck of dirt or rock, but he used his fingernail and thumbnail to lever it out, and then it sat in his palm. A little dark, flat object, obviously man-made, with a minuscule hook on the back.

He stared at it in silence, his heart thrumming in his chest.

Chris considered dropping it onto the pavement, but after a moment, he tossed it into the open window of a battered pickup truck parked nearby. The truck had Indiana plates and a bumper sticker that said, *This Truck is Protected By Smith & Wesson.* After a moment's thought, he tossed Baxter's collar in, too.

At least the owner of the truck looked likely to be able to take care of himself should the Men in Black show up.

Then Chris was out onto the road, driving down the highway, looking in his rearview mirror every thirty seconds for signs of pursuit, the wind of his speed drying the sweat standing out on his skin.

It wasn't until he hit Logansport, an hour later, that his heart rate returned to normal.

CHAPTER 9

As Chris was crossing into Illinois, at a little before eleven in the morning, he began to wonder how he was being tracked.

In the hotel two nights ago, he'd been careless, signing in under his actual name, and using his bank card to get cash the next morning. It was no mystery how the two nameless men in generic dark suits had located him. In fact, it was lucky they hadn't gotten there sooner, found what room he was in, killed him as he slept. After that, he'd been on the Turnpike the whole way across Ohio. If the boy in the tollbooth was right, they would have known the instant he crossed the state line, and knowing the speed the traffic was going, and that he hadn't exited, it wouldn't have been difficult to keep track of where he was the entire way across the state.

But now? He was no longer using toll roads. He hadn't used his credit or bank access cards since Erie, Pennsylvania. He had no GPS, and even the all-powerful They couldn't have tracked him to the café by his email and shown up within minutes. So how had the little old lady found him in a parking lot in Peru, Indiana?

Then Chris realized he was making an assumption. He didn't know that the microchip in Baxter's collar had been put there by her. It could have been there days or weeks earlier. Chris had only checked because he'd been suspicious. The fact that he'd found it right after talking to her was not proof that she was the one who put it there.

Maybe she was what she appeared to be. An old lady who liked dogs.

Still, the encounter had set off Chris's intuition. In his memory, she had the feeling of an optical illusion. She seemed real, seemed to be authentic, but he was certain she wasn't. She was part of the conspiracy, like the boy in the tollbooth, like the Men in Black in Erie, Pennsylvania. Like the NYSEG workers who blew up his house.

So how did she find him?

It would be easy to put a tracer on his car. Stick something inside the wheel well or underneath the bumper, and no one would be able to find it. But he couldn't get rid of his car.

He could, however, get rid of anything else that *They* could use to track him. Such as his cellphone.

Chris knew that cellphones sent and received signals from satellites, although he didn't know much about it beyond that. He was beginning to regret his general anti-technology bent, in fact. In any case, there had to be something in a cellphone that tracked where the user was. Chris had seen posts on Facebook that read, *posted from mobile phone in Philadelphia, PA.*

If the phone kept track of where he was, why couldn't someone use that to monitor his whereabouts?

He reached in his pocket and pulled out his cell, looked at it as it sat in his open palm. It was one of the old-fashioned flip phones. He'd intended to upgrade to an iPhone and never gotten around to it. Chris knew that iPhones were equipped with a GPS. Were old cellphones?

Maybe. And "maybe" was enough. He had to shake *Them* loose from his trail, vanish from the map. Any way they could track him was one too many.

Just west of Watseka, Illinois, Chris rolled down his window, and with a swing of his wrist, sent his cellphone flying into a cornfield.

No calling the police now if he was in trouble, not that there was any guarantee whose side the police would be on. Nor could he contact Elisa if there was an emergency. But Chris knew he had to get ahead of *Them*. If he could lose *Them* once, completely, then maybe after that he could stay safe if he kept moving.

He stopped for lunch at a McDonald's east of Peoria. His food was handed to him by a bored-looking girl who recited his order in a nasal monotone, a regular cheeseburger with the works, a kid's hamburger with no ketchup or pickles for Baxter, large fries, a bottle of water. He thanked her, and then paused, waiting, he realized afterwards, for her to say something cryptic, to reveal herself as one of *Them*.

She didn't. As Chris drove away, he started to laugh, quietly at first, and finally in paroxysms so helpless that he had to pull over.

"Oh, God," he said, as the storm finally passed, and reached up to wipe his streaming eyes. "I'm cracking up, I really and truly am."

He reached into the bag to pull out Baxter's burger, unwrapped it and set it on the seat. It was gone in under a minute. Chris ate his more slowly as he drove. The heat was already oppressive, and he considered turning on the AC, but instead opted to open the windows and take off his shirt. The wind felt good on his bare skin. Baxter put his paws on the windowsill, face out in the slipstream, tongue flapping.

Chris could have enjoyed this, he realized. Under other circumstances, it would have been fun. No connections, nowhere to be, free to go when he wanted to and stop when he wanted to. Just him and his dog, like that song from the 1970s, *Me and You and a Dog Named Boo*, about not being beholden to The Man, having no restrictions, having no responsibilities.

They've tried more than once to end me. And I'm still alive. Damned if I'm going to waste that.

• • • •

He crossed the Mississippi River into Missouri at a little after four in the afternoon. The Bayview Bridge, its steel girders and fanlike array of cables looking almost white in the westering sun, leaped across the expanse of flowing water, of impressive breadth even this far north. Hadn't Mark Twain grown up somewhere near here? Chris couldn't recall the name of the town. But this was definitely Tom Sawyer and Huck Finn country, and even now, with metropolitan St. Louis to the south and Kansas City straight ahead, there was an old-fashioned feeling to the place, as if the entire Midwest still had one foot in the nineteenth century.

Missouri went by in a string of small towns that all looked alike, with quaint names and even quainter slogans, along a stretch of highway that could have been drawn with a ruler. Shelbina, "Queen City of the Prairie." Macon, "City of Maples." Brookfield, "Home of the Great Pershing Balloon Derby." Chillicothe, "Home of Sliced Bread." In between were miles of flat farmland. He drove at a steady sixty-five miles per hour, moving with the flow, only slowing when the speed limit changed as he passed the "Welcome To" sign for the next village along the way. The traffic picked up as he approached the city of St. Joseph, on the western edge of the state. The weather had been beautiful all day—sunny, hot, humid, white puffy cumulus clouds—but by six o'clock the sun was descending into a line of ominous thunderheads forming on the horizon, and he began to think that he had covered enough ground for one day.

He passed up a Hampton Inn, a Ramada, and a Holiday Inn, knowing that he would have to give identification there. He wandered aimlessly for a while, wondering if he would have to cross into Kansas before finding something suitable. He finally pulled off Highway 36 into the parking lot of a place that looked like a possibility, a disreputable-looking low building with a sign that said, *State Line Motel, Vacancy* in garish neon. His was the only car in the lot. Apparently no one else that evening was desperate enough to opt for lodging this questionable.

He turned his engine off, pulled his shirt back on and buttoned it, and got out. Huge, widely-spaced raindrops spattered the pavement, carried on a wind that ruffled his hair in angry gusts. The sky had turned a nasty color, greenish-gray, like algae-coated slate. The clouds were roiling, their undersides twisting and bubbling into bizarre shapes.

A homeless man sat slumped in the entry to the motel. Despite the heat, he was wearing an oil-stained red plaid flannel shirt, tattered jeans, and a dark stocking cap. A paper bag with the neck of a bottle sticking out sat next to him on the stoop. He looked up at Chris as he came in under the awning, and said, his voice slurred, "Help for a guy down on his luck?"

Chris looked at him, wanting to say, "I'm very down on my luck at the moment, too, bub," but instead he took out his wallet and dropped a five-dollar bill into the man's grimy hand. "God bless," the man said, and then added, "weather's gettin' bad, sir. Tornadoes. Seen my share of 'em. Hope never to see one again. But this is the way it looks when they come. Can't outrun 'em."

"I guess you can't," Chris said, not knowing what else to say.

"Certain things you can outrun. Certain other things as you can't. Tornadoes is one o' them you can't. Best to know which is which."

"Yes," Chris thought, and his mind went spinning. What does that mean? Is he one of *Them?* Was that a warning? Or a threat?

"You can't outrun God," the man said. "I found that out, sir. Yes I did."

Chris took a deep breath, let it out slowly. No. He's only an old wino. An ordinary person, not one of *Them.*

"That's... good," Chris said.

"Yes, sir, it is. Gonna meet God soon, I am. Leave this place behind."

The wind was roaring now, and the sound of the rain behind him on the pavement sounded like bacon sizzling in a pan.

"I have to go," Chris said.

"You go, then, and God bless you," the man said, waving one hand vaguely in his direction.

"Same to you."

Chris pulled open the door and entered a dingy lobby. This was a step down even from the Belmont Inn. The check-in desk was topped with stained and torn contact paper, and the only places to sit were two dented folding chairs. A grimy oil painting of a landscape, hanging crooked on the faded wallpaper, was the only concession to décor.

Behind the desk was an old man, his face grizzled with two days' growth of beard.

"I'd like to rent a room for the night," Chris said.

"Yeah," the man said, and pushed a clipboard across at him. "Nightly rates are forty dollars. Fill this out."

Chris filled the paper out with his pseudonym and fake address, and pushed it back toward the man along with two twenties. The man looked it over, and said, "You're in room four. Out the door, left down the sidewalk, third on the left." There was a tremendous thunderclap, and the man said, "Helluva storm. They say we got a tornado warning, all o' Buchanan County and out across the river into Kansas. Best get inside while you can."

That seemed like good advice, and Chris went back out through the front door. The homeless man was still sitting with his back to the wall, but seemed to have fallen asleep despite the noise of the storm.

Maybe he's not asleep, maybe he's dead, Chris thought. Maybe he finally went back to God, like he said he would.

He stood, looking out into the downpour for a few moments, and finally decided to go for it. The rain was showing no sign of slackening, and he didn't want to stand there in the entryway with only a sleeping (perhaps dead) wino for company. Besides, he figured that he could dry off as soon as he got to his room.

Hunching his shoulders and squinting his eyes against the storm, he walked out into the parking lot. Cold rainwater soaked him to the skin almost immediately, poured down his neck, plastering his shirt to his back.

He went up to his car and opened the door, and called for Baxter. The dog looked terrified. He was a complete wuss about thunderstorms, which fortunately had been infrequent back in upstate New York. He was sitting in the passenger seat, shivering, and looked at Chris with wide eyes that seemed to say, "You're not really going to make me go out in that, are you?"

"I'm not going to stand here in the rain all night waiting for you," Chris said. "Man up, dude."

He reached in and picked the dog up. Baxter weighed a little under fifty pounds, and it was a struggle to lift him over the driver's seat and out onto the rain-soaked pavement.

There was another lightning flash and thunderclap, and Baxter whined and huddled against Chris's leg.

"Just come on, and we'll get inside where it's nice and dry," He shut the car door. And that's when he saw that his front driver's side tire had been slashed. It was completely flat, a gaping hole sliced in the side.

Dear God! It's the car. They were tracking me by tracing my car.

He looked frantically around the parking lot, searching for who could have done this, but there was no one there. The parking lot was empty. The lights from the traffic on Highway 36 flashed by, tires hissing on wet pavement.

With the suddenness of a snake, a hand grabbed Chris's upper arm in a viselike grip. Chris twisted around, lost his balance, and almost fell. Baxter growled, his hackles rising, and backed up against the car. It was the homeless drunk, who had roused himself and now stood very close, rain pouring down his lined face like tears, his fingers still clamped on Chris's bicep.

The drunk's eyes were wide, showing bloodshot whites. His pupils were huge in the dim light. He pulled Chris to him, until their faces almost touched, and said, in a hoarse whisper, "Run."

Chris yanked his arm free, gasping for breath, and his butt pressed up against the closed car door. He felt frozen in place, as if his body had been turned into stone, as if he were a statue left out in the rain in this desolate parking lot. Then there was a loud crack from somewhere near the motel, and one of his car's windows shattered in a cascade of shards.

"Run!" the drunk said, his creaking voice rising to a shout. "*Run!*"

There was another sharp report and the man lurched forwards, almost into Chris's arms. Chris's chest and face were spattered with blood.

The drunk spun around, arms flailing, and landed with a splat on his back on the wet pavement. His eyes had rolled back to show nothing but whites, and there was a spreading dark stain on the grubby red plaid of his shirt.

The paralysis broke like a dam bursting. Chris turned and sprinted toward the highway. There was another gunshot. Afterwards, he was certain that he'd felt the wind of the bullet's passing ruffling his hair. Baxter, whining with fear, was right at his heels. Heedless, he ran across the eastbound lanes, the grassy median, and launched himself into the westbound lanes.

The reflexes of the driver who almost hit him were amazing. Compression brakes roared and groaned. Even so, the truck's front wheel barely missed Baxter's tail as the two of them cleared the lane and stumbled onto the shoulder of the highway. Both panting, Chris crouching down into the high grass, hoping desperately that the distance and dim light would defeat whoever it was that was trying to shoot him. But the eighteen-wheeler continued to slow, and to pull onto the shoulder, finally coming to a complete stop about fifty feet further along the road.

Chris stood and ran toward it, the soles of his sneakers making splatting noises on the wet asphalt. By the time he reached the front end of the truck, the driver had already slid over and opened the door, and was shouting, "What the hell was you thinking, running in front of me like that? You coulda got yourself killed!"

But then he looked at Chris's face, and his own expression changed from anger to concern.

"Buddy, you okay?" he said.

"Help," was all that Chris could get out. "Help me."

"Climb on in." He reached out a sinewy arm, hand open toward him. Chris took it, and once he was seated reached down and grabbed Baxter by the front legs and hauled him bodily into the cab. A minute later, they were pulling back out into traffic, and Chris saw a sign that said *MISSOURI RIVER*, followed by one moments afterward that said *Welcome to Kansas!*

· · · ·

"I'm Thomas T. Champion, from California, P-A," the truck driver said, gesturing with one hand. "Gotta add the P-A part, 'cause people always think it's California state. That's a place I never been, not yet, at least. I been all through the Midwest, and far west as Montana, but that's about it."

Thomas T. Champion turned out to be loquacious and friendly, once he was convinced that Chris wasn't on the run from the law.

"Police ain't after you, are they?" he asked, as the truck rolled on through the rainy Kansas night. "'Cause I don't mind helping a guy who needs help, but I don't want to get mixed up in nothin' illegal."

Chris assured him that he hadn't broken any law.

"Kinda figured not," Thomas T. Champion said. "Dumb of me, but I looked at that dog of yours, and I knew somehow that you weren't no jailbird. I guess there's nothin' stoppin' a criminal from gettin' a friendly old dog like that, though, right?"

"Guess not."

"What was you runnin' from, though? I swear to Jesus, you almost got turned into road pizza out there."

Chris thought for a moment, and then decided that there was nothing for it but the truth. He was too tired to make up a plausible lie in any case.

"There's some people who are trying to kill me," Chris said. "The FBI tried to warn me about it. I have no idea why. I think it might be something that happened in my past, that for some reason I've forgotten about."

Champion's grin flashed out in the dark. "Really? Like in that movie, what the hell was it? The one with Matt Damon."

"*The Bourne Identity.*"

"Yeah! That's the one! So you think you might be some kind of international spy or somethin', and you got, whatchacall, amnesia?"

"No, nothing like that. I really don't know what's going on, or why they want me dead, but I'm pretty sure it's not that."

"Hey, that Bourne guy didn't know, either," Champion said. "It could be."

"Yeah, I guess it could."

"Where you from, Mr. International Spy?"

"I grew up in Corvallis, Oregon, but I've lived in upstate New York for about twenty-five years. Little town named Guildford. South of Syracuse."

"Huh. What brought you out there?"

"A job. I'm a high school science teacher."

"Mild-mannered high school teacher by day, top-secret international spy by night," Champion said, laughing at his own joke. "Betcher popular with the kids on account of that."

"Oh, yeah, they'd like that," Chris said.

"So how'd you end up in St. Joe?"

"I was stopping there for the night. Traveling west.

Trying to stay one step ahead of the guys who are after me and keep from getting killed. But I think they had some kind of tracking device on my car. If you hadn't picked me up, I'd probably be dead by now."

Champion's smile faded. "So, you're really serious? All that stuff is true, you being hunted and all?"

"Yes. All true." Chris looked out of the window again. "I think a guy who tried to help me got killed because of it, too. Shot in the back."

"No shit?" Champion said, in a hushed voice.

"No shit."

"How're you not freakin' out?"

Chris shook his head. "I don't know. It hasn't sunk in yet. People are dying because of me, and I still don't know why."

"Jesus," Champion said. "Well, that's a helluva thing. And you got nothing else with you? Just you and your dog?"

"By now, yes. Seems like I've been gradually stripping myself of everything. The last thing I ditched was the car. Somebody slashed the tires, most likely to keep me stuck there, so I couldn't get away. Probably for the best, since they had it bugged. That has to be how they found me." Chris paused, looked out into the night. "Now I really do have nothing but the clothes I'm wearing, and what's left of the money in my wallet."

"It's like them Native American spirit quests."

"What is?"

"You never heard of that?" Champion said, taking one hand off the steering wheel to point forward, toward the west. "Out there, some o' them Native American tribes, I forget which ones—maybe the Cheyenne, but I could be wrong about that. When the boys of the tribe would reach a certain age, they'd send 'em out into the wilderness, bare-ass naked. Can you imagine? Out in the middle o' nowhere, not even a pair of skivvies to cover your privates. And they had to survive for a few days like that. Not only survive, they had to have a vision while they was out there. It was like, go out there, and come back and tell us what you saw, and what you learned, and if it's good enough that'll mean you're a man. Some of 'em never come back, of course. They starved or died of thirst or fell off a cliff or got snakebit, or whatnot. Some of 'em had to be rescued, and those ones was always kinda second-class citizens after that. But there was the ones as came back into camp on their own two bare feet, and had a story to tell. And those were the men. Those were the warriors."

Chris looked out into the darkness, listening to the rhythmic thwack of the windshield wipers. Rain was still falling, but more gently now, and there were occasional lightning flashes in the distance.

A spirit quest. Is that what this is? Gradually getting rid of everything that connects me to the world? Going out naked into the wilderness, just me and my dog, to see if we can survive, and maybe come back with a story?

"So," Champion said, his smile returning, "you think you'll have a vision?"

Chris looked at him for a long time without speaking, and finally leaned back in the seat, stretching his legs. "You know," he said quietly, "If I can survive long enough, I think maybe I will."

They took Highway 75 north and crossed into Nebraska at just before nine at night. Thomas T. Champion was still going strong. Chris, on the other hand, was at that stage of fatigue that bordered delirium.

"It's a lucky coincidence I was comin' through St. Joe on 36 at all," Champion was saying. "Got a report there was an accident blockin' up Interstate 29 just shy of the Iowa border, probably on account of the bad weather. Thought I'd avoid that mess, cross into Kansas and then cut north and hit I-80 that way. I got to be in Salt Lake with this lot of furniture in three days. No real need to rush, but I hate gettin' stuck waitin' for them to clear a wreck."

Chris had his eyes closed. Baxter was already snoozing at his feet. "Lucky for me you did," he said, a little indistinctly.

"That's the truth," Champion said. "And I'd like to get some more miles between us and those guys as was after you. Once we hit I-80, there's a rest stop, this side of Lincoln. We'll pack it in for the night."

"Sounds good," Chris mumbled.

Champion said, with a smile in his voice, "Okay, I'll stop my jawin' now and let you sleep. Guess even spies gotta get some shut-eye."

Chris didn't respond, and the roar of the engine, the swish of cars passing in the night, and the low sound of country music on the radio all faded seamlessly into sleep.

• • • •

He awoke thirsty, hungry, and needing to pee as the first rays of sunshine tinted the interior of the truck cab with crimson. He came to full wakefulness with the abrupt realization that Baxter was gone.

He sat up, his neck cracking as he straightened, heart hammering in his chest. He called once, quietly. Maybe Baxter had gone back into the truck's sleeping area with Thomas T. Champion. At least that's what he assumed was in the back of the cab. He'd been too tired to inquire the previous evening, and had never been inside an eigh-teen-wheeler before this.

No response.

He got up, maneuvered his way between the seats and through a sliding door left partially ajar, into a narrow room with a bed, mini-fridge, television, and an open lap-top, with the screen glowing. The bed had a rumpled blan-ket and pillow, half fallen onto the floor, and the whole place smelled faintly of body odor and beer.

No one there.

He returned to the front of the cab, fighting down a sense of panic, opened the door, and climbed out.

"G'mornin', sunshine," came a cheerful voice from behind him. Chris turned, and saw Champion walking toward him from the direction of the rest stop building, Baxter trotting at his heels. "Your old dog seemed like he needed to go out and water the trees, so I took him with me. Hope you don't mind. He took to me right away. I've always had a way with dogs. Helped that I had some day-old roast beef for his breakfast, o' course. Don't expect either of you was thinking much of dinner last night, but he was lookin' at me with those 'feed me' eyes, you know?"

Baxter came up to him, tail wagging, and Chris scratched him behind the ears.

"Anyhow, you can go visit the men's room and wash up a little. We'll find a place with some pay showers today, there's a couple of 'em along the way. One thing about this life is you get used to grabbing a shower when you can find one. Expect you're hungry. We'll stop and pick somethin' up when we get to Lincoln."

"That sounds good," Chris said, and then addressed his dog. "Baxter, you go with Mr. Champion, now." Baxter trotted over to Champion as if they'd been best friends for years, his tail still doing the slow wag that indicated calm good cheer.

As Chris walked to the men's room, he reflected that his dog's reaction, more than anything else, had convinced him that Champion was okay. Baxter was generally a pretty good judge of character. But then, the more paranoid side of his brain chided him for being simple-minded.

Some dogs will trust anyone with a doggie biscuit, and Baxter is one of them. Don't fall for the "dogs have a sixth sense about people" bullshit. Stay on guard.

Chris didn't know if Champion was all right, yet, but there was nothing wrong with remaining cautious.

He went into the restroom, which was otherwise empty, and after a much-needed visit to the urinal, went to the sink to wash his face. He was looking pretty scruffy, with three days' dark beard, peppered with gray. He'd always been clean-shaven, but he rubbed his rough chin, and thought, *The hobo look kind of suits me. And after all, that's what I am at the moment. May as well look the part.*

He washed his face, made a cursory attempt to getting his hair to lie flat, but gave that up when it became apparent that without a shower, he wasn't going to get any cooperation. He went back out into the sunshine, and looked out over the rolling Nebraska hills, with alternating patches of brown and green showing where the center-pivot irrigators were doing their job of watering perfectly circular fields of wheat, corn, and oats.

They were back on the road ten minutes later, and the miles slid by in a constant stream of conversation, underscored by the low, intermittent crackle of the CB radio. Perhaps because he spent so much time alone, Thomas T. Champion turned out to be an eager conversationalist. Chris was happy to have someone to talk to and take his mind off the omnipresent worry about whether he was going to be killed.

"Sorry I'm yakkin' at you so much," Champion said, after a forty-five minute long monologue about his twentieth high school reunion, which he'd attended the previous year. "You give me a thermos o' coffee, a bag o' potato chips, someone to talk to, and put me behind the wheel of a truck, I can go all day long."

"It's okay," Chris said. "It's nice to have a pleasant conversation. I haven't had one of those in the last two weeks, since all of this nonsense started."

"Yeah, you know, I was thinkin' about all that last night, right as I was tryin' to get to sleep," Champion said. "You really got no idea why these guys are after you?"

"Not really, no."

"Helluva thing," he said. "How did the FBI find out they were after you, so they could warn you? I mean, if you want to talk about it. You don't have to get into all of the gory details with me. I'm just curious."

"No, it's no problem," Chris said. "Some people I knew in college had already gotten killed. Me and one other were the last two left."

"Seriously? That's like somethin' out o' one o' them, you know, Agatha Christie novels. People gettin' picked off, one by one. And you and some other guy are the only ones left? What was it, people who were in a frat together or something?"

"No, people in the same biology class. And it's a girl. She's the only other one who's still alive." Chris hesitated, afraid to reveal too much. But there was something about the truck driver's manner that engendered trust.

And as if reading Chris's thoughts, Champion said, "Now, you got no reason to tell me anything more. After all, I'm still a stranger. "

"Well, you saved my life last night, and you didn't kill me in my sleep."

Champion burst out laughing. "Yeah, I guess that's true enough," he said. "And for the record, I got no intention of killin' you. I'm not one of the Bad Guys."

"I think I believe you," Chris said.

"Well, after what you been through, that's the best I could hope for."

"And actually, I was thinking… I'd like to try to get in touch with the other survivor. We've been emailing each other every so often, just to…" He trailed off.

Champion's face became serious. "Just to say that you're still alive. That they haven't got you, yet."

"Yes."

"That's gotta be scary. The two of you, waitin' to see which one gets got first, hopin' all the time that you'll both escape in the end."

"That's it exactly. And she'll probably be worried. I haven't written since yesterday morning."

"Aren't you afraid of… you know, them being able to trace your emails? You said they had something tracking your car."

"I don't know. I got rid of my cellphone yesterday because of that. Is it possible to tell where an email originated?"

"I dunno," Champion said. "But it wouldn't surprise me."

"Do you have an internet connection?"

"Yeah," he said, his hesitancy sounding clearly in his voice. "I use it to keep in touch with my brother and his family. I got a satellite modem last year. I'm connected anywhere there's cell service."

"Could I use it to check my email?"

Champion looked dubious. "Look, Chris, I'm not gonna tell you you can't, but seems to me you got away by the skin o' your teeth last night. You might want to find a way to leave no tracks for a while."

Chris knew the driver was right, but he suddenly felt a desperation to see if Elisa had written to him. The sensation bordered on physical pain. Despite being in the company of an apparently friendly person who seemed to have no problem giving Chris a ride for as long as he wanted, Chris suddenly became aware that he was, more than he ever had been, entirely alone. Out on the roads of this spinning globe, cast adrift like a shipwrecked sailor, and Elisa was the only one who truly understood, who shared that isolation. Thomas T. Champion could, when his load of furniture was delivered to Salt Lake City, go back to his home and his friends and his life.

What did he have? His dog, his clothes, and the remaining $732 from his thousand. In other words, not much.

And he was willing to run a risk to contact the one other person in the world whose fate resembled his own.

"I'll read my email, I won't respond," he said to Champion, at the same time knowing that it was a lie.

"Okay," Champion said. "Your decision, my friend, and I understand it's gotta be hard not knowin' how she is. But I gotta say that in your place, I'd be scared to take a piss for fear they'd track me down by the flush."

"I think I haven't stopped being scared since I first found out about those people I knew in college dying," Chris said. "But being alone is worse than being scared, I think."

Champion nodded. "I get it. Laptop's in the back, in the cabinet next to the bed. If we got cell service out here, it should work just fine. Gets a little spotty further west, but I think around here there shouldn't be a problem."

"Thanks," Chris said. Standing, he made his way into the living quarters. The laptop was right where Champion said it would be, and he pulled it out, lifted the cover, and turned it on, sitting on the edge of the bed with the computer balanced in his lap.

Opening up a web browser, he signed into his Gmail. He had several new emails—two, he saw, from Elisa.

"Yes," he said under his breath, feeling relief wash over him. One of them had been posted only ten minutes earlier. Ignoring the other emails, and skipped right to the older of Elisa's messages.

> *Chris,*
>
> *I'm so glad you're still okay. I am too. I really don't know how they'd find me here, unless they could somehow trace where my emails are coming from. I've done some research, and it seems like the most that could tell them is that they're coming from my laptop, not where my laptop actually is. So I think I'm safe. Please don't worry about me.*
>
> *But your mention of scary near misses has me afraid for you. How are they finding you? I don't imagine you're being*

careless, not after what's already happened. Please take every precaution you can. I'll be waiting for your reply.

Elisa

The second message, posted that morning, was much longer:

Chris,

I'm really concerned that I haven't heard from you, and I am hoping that it's only that you haven't had a way to get to an internet connection. But you know me; when I care about someone, I worry.

To pass the time, since I haven't been able to do much else that's productive, I decided to do a little online research. I thought that I might be able to figure out what we had in common—the seven of us—besides having been in Field Biology together, thirty years ago. I don't know why I thought I'd find anything, because after all, the FBI men who contacted you didn't seem to know what was going on, right?

Well, if they gave you that impression, I think they must have been lying, or at least not telling you the whole truth. I spent the better part of yesterday evening online, and I came up with something that seems to be another significant link between us all. And if I could find it with a little bit of online digging, I can't imagine that they don't know.

Did you know that all of us are involved, in some way,

in astronomical stuff? I found right away that you were the
president of an Amateur Astronomers' Club. I do paintings
of deities connected with the sky and stars. It's been a pas-
sion ever since college. I have read everything I can find on
it. I don't recall ever thinking about the subject when I was
a kid, or even an undergraduate. But after graduate school,
it became as near to an obsession as I have. Maybe you've
looked at my gallery website and seen some of my paintings.
I am in love with the mythological creatures of the skies.

Well, we're not the only ones. Each of the seven of us
has a different twist on it, but it's true of all of us. Gavin
was all over UFO websites. I found him on Reddit. He's
got over a thousand posts on subreddits like "Conspiracy"
and "UFOs" and "Ancient Aliens." Not much of a surprise, maybe——remember how he always was into that stuff?
Maybe he was the only one who already had a seed of the
interest before, prior to whatever it was that happened in
class. But, Chris, it's all of us!

Mary was a fiend about Star Trek. She was one of those
conventioneer types, can you believe it? I found a photograph
of her online, at a costume ball, dressed up like Lieutenant
Uhura!

Lewis took award-winning astronomical photographs.
Deirdre had volunteered to be on the team of consulting phy-
sicians for the astronauts on the International Space Station.
She even had research proposals out there for experiments to
be run in space. And you probably know that Glen taught

at a community college, but do you know what he taught? Despite a master's degree in biology?

Astronomy. He must have gone back and gotten a second advanced degree, after we knew him.

This has to be significant. I don't know how, but it has to. What's the likelihood of seven people as different as the seven of us, and all of us have some kind of passionate interest in space?

It's like whatever happened, up there in the Cascades, gave us some kind of post-hypnotic suggestion. Maybe there was an alien ship in that cave, or something. I know that sounds ridiculous.

Write when you can. I hope you're okay. I'll be waiting for your response.

Elisa

Chris reread the message twice. He sat, uncertain, finger poised above the touch pad to click on *Reply*. Both Elisa and Thomas T. Champion had brought up the possibility that he could be tracked by his emails, but then Elisa had added that she didn't think it was possible unless *They* knew the location of the computer where the emails had originated. Chris remembered reading something a while back about ISP addresses and the police using them to nail people involved in child pornography rings. He didn't remember much about it, if they identified each computer uniquely, could tell specifically where that computer was located, or did something else entirely.

It didn't seem likely that they could figure out where a computer was located from an email. If they could do that, they'd have caught Elisa by now. Chris rationalized that if they were monitoring Elisa's emails, and she got one from his Gmail account, sent from Champion's computer, they wouldn't know that the computer was on a truck in the middle of Nebraska.

Elisa,

First, I'm still alive, but I no longer have a car or a cellphone. I had another near miss last night. Someone took a shot at me outside a motel. I got away, but they shot an old guy who tried to help me. I had to leave my car behind. I probably shouldn't say more than that in case someone's reading this. But so far, I'm still okay.

Second, what you found is really bizarre. Like you said, too much of a coincidence to be a coincidence. But what the hell could it mean? Like you, it makes me wonder what we saw in that cave.

It's funny you mentioned alien ships. And you're right, it seems laughable, now that I wrote it. Like you, I've been fascinated with the stars, but just since I was in graduate school. I wasn't really into it in high school, or as an undergraduate. I went into biology because it was my favorite science, I never was much good at physics (nor very interested in it, frankly). But ever since I got my master's degree, I've had this thing for space research, and especially, alien life. You know all of those exoplanets that have been recently discovered? Elisa, when I read about that—it's like, my heart is pounding with excitement. I dream about alien worlds. I remember once thinking—it was after our Field Biology class, but not sure exactly when—that I wished I hadn't been almost done with a master's in biology, because if I had it all to do over I would have majored in astronomy, my issues with understanding physics be damned.

You said this sounded like a post-hypnotic suggestion. I think it's more insidious than that, you know? Because if you're right, if that is the link, five of us have died because of it. What it reminds me of is a kill switch. Do you know about those?

It's a gene sequence that's implanted in some genetically modified organisms. It can be for a lot of reasons, but the outcome is the same for all of them. It's a bit of DNA that is inserted into the host's DNA, and it sits there, dormant, sometimes for years. Then, when it activates, it causes havoc. The most innocent of them cause the individual to be unable to reproduce. Those have been used in crops when they don't want people to do seed saving. The seeds form, and look normal, but they're dead, they don't sprout, so if you want to replant the same crop next year, you have to buy new seed from the company.

But some of them are wilder than that, and a little scary. There are DNA sequences that have been inserted into mosquitoes that cause them to aggressively seek out mates, but the mating produces tons of babies who all die when the kill switch activates, before they reach adulthood. I heard about another one that has been used with microbes. When they come into contact with a specific substance, they self-destruct.

Maybe this sounds fanciful, I dunno. And I don't think that it's literally our DNA that is affected. But maybe we had something implanted in us, perhaps at that cave. It activated in all of us, and created our fascination with aliens.

And now, thirty years later, the bad guys are trying to eliminate everyone who was infected.

Chris

He glanced out of the narrow window in the sleeping quarters, looking at the drab, tan Nebraska hills sliding by. By launching that email, had he given some central monitoring device his exact location?

Didn't matter. He had to let her know he was all right.

But the thing about astronomy, that was bizarre. She must be right, though. It had to be the link. And she was surely right that Hargis and Drolezki know about it. If Elisa, working on her own from a laptop in some small town somewhere, could find this out, certainly the FBI could. They had pretended they thought the commonality between the seven was the Field Biology class;

but now it was clear that there was a second, and more curious, connection.

Five minutes later, the Gmail screen auto-refreshed, and there was a new email from ereed@orionsbelt.com.

> *Chris,*
>
> *A "kill switch." What a terrifying concept. But I think that feels right, you know? I think we somehow need to find out what was in that cave. It was somewhere near Lake Ingalls, I remember that, but the Cascades are full of trails, so that doesn't narrow it down much. I think I could probably find the spot if I were there. You know how memory is. You don't think you remember something, but then when you're pressed, it turns out that you do.*
>
> *I'm really relieved you're okay, and I hope you're not endangering yourself by emailing me. Wherever you are, I hope you're being careful, and that you've really gotten away this time, to somewhere they can't find you.*
>
> *I wish I could see you. I know that's probably impossible, but this would be more bearable if we were together. I can't imagine how we could arrange to meet, though, since there's no way either of us can say where we are without the bad guys finding out.*
>
> *But I can still wish, right?*
>
> *Elisa*

Chris hit *Reply*.

> *I wonder if there's a way we could give each other infor-*
> *mation so that only you and I could understand? Like some*
> *kind of a code?*

Her response came right away.

> *Maybe. Let me think about it. I'm not sure what kind*
> *of a code we could use that the bad guys couldn't crack, but*
> *maybe there's something.*
> *Then you and I could meet up, hop the next spaceship to*
> *Alpha Centauri, and live happily ever after out in the stars,*
> *right?*

Chris smiled, and wrote:

> *I think I'd like that.*

He turned off the computer and stowed it back in the cabinet. When he returned to the front of the truck's cab, Champion looked over at him, a wry smile on his face.

"You wrote to her, didn't ya?"

Chris looked out of the window, blushing a little. "Yes."

"I knew you would. You had that look on your face when you went back there, and you came out just now looking like a guy who's got just what he wanted."

"I had to let her know I was all right."

"I get it. And I hope you keep bein' all right, you know? You and your lady friend both."

Chris didn't answer for a while. Finally, he said, in a quiet voice, "Me, too."

CHAPTER 11

They stopped for lunch at a rest area east of Brady, Nebraska. Champion had a well-stocked fridge, with cold cuts, a loaf of bread, half a head of lettuce, and even some mustard and a small jar of mayonnaise. They made themselves sandwiches and then left the truck for a picnic bench in the shade of the building that housed the restrooms and snack machines. Baxter sat next to them, munching contentedly on dog chow they'd picked up at a convenience store in Kearney.

The weather was sunny and hot, with an incessant wind that dried the slices of bread before they could fin-ish their sandwiches. The terrain was still flat, but the wheat and cornfields had been largely left behind for wide, bleached grasslands given over to herds of cattle. As they drove that morning, the slow, shallow, meandering course of the Platte River could sometimes be glimpsed to the north of the highway, marked by a low line of green showing the only place where lush vegetation had enough water to survive the blazing heat. Elsewhere, the predominant color was brown.

"Least it's not humid out here," Champion said, taking a pull on a bottle of water. "Where I come from, it gets this hot, you'd be wringing wet in five minutes from the humidity."

"That's like upstate New York," Chris said. "It's not often that hot, but when it is, it's like a sauna."

Champion looked thoughtful. "You think you'll be able to go back home, at some point?"

Chris didn't answer for a moment. He looked out over the level expanse of prairie behind the rest stop building, the wind fluttering hair that was by now in need of a trim. "I don't know," he finally said. "I honestly hadn't thought about that. When you feel like you're in imminent danger of dying in the next five minutes, what might happen five years from now doesn't seem all that important, you know?"

"I guess that makes sense."

"I don't even have a house to go back to. They blew up my house, did I tell you about that?"

Champion's eyes opened wide. "Seriously? Like, blew it up, with dynamite, or something?"

"Something like that, I suppose. It's lucky Baxter and I were outside at the time. There were some electrical workers out there, and I thought it was odd, so I called the electric company. A pissed-off-sounding woman told me there wasn't supposed to be any work done in my neighborhood that day, so I went back outside to ask them what the story was. They were gone, but as soon as I got to the end of the driveway, my house exploded. If we'd been inside, we'd both be dead."

"No shit," Champion said, in an awed voice. "You got more than your fair share of luck, sounds like."

"In one way, I suppose. Lucky, though, would be having none of this happen in the first place."

"I guess that's fair enough," the truck driver said. He took another drink of water. "But hell, Chris, you can't keep runnin' forever, right? And you gotta have people who care about you, family and friends. They got to be frantic by now, with all this shit happenin', and then you disappearin' and all. You got any kind of plan, here?"

"Nothing beyond 'stay alive' and 'keep moving.' What I'll do if this all ends, somehow, I don't know." He looked down. "And frankly, I don't see how this can end except with me dead, you know? It's me and my dog against these guys who can track my movements, rig up explosives and poisons and God knows what else. Who apparently have a network of people all across the country that are part of the conspiracy. How can I hope to hold out more than a few days, really?"

Champion looked thoughtful. "Well, you got your luck. That's somethin'."

"I guess."

"It's not like everyone is against you, either. I'm not. Most o' the people you run into aren't, either, I'd bet. Most of 'em are ordinary Americans doin' their ordinary American stuff, who know nothin' about this. But I can see how you could get to thinkin' that everyone's part of it. Oh, I get that. It's like when a dog lives with people that beat it, you know? Poor dog, all it knows is people bein' mean and cruel, so pretty soon the dog decides that everyone is mean and cruel and'll bite the hand of the guy who's tryin' to rescue it."

"Can't blame the dog," Chris said. "He can't tell the difference between enemies and friends. Neither can I."

"I think you're sellin' yourself short, there," Champion said. "You trusted me, and that was right."

"That was luck. I think I'd have jumped in anyone's car at that moment."

"But that's it. When you rely on your luck, you survive. You gotta trust your instincts. I think you might just get out o' this alive if you do that."

Chris smiled a little. "Earlier, I was thinking along those lines. I felt like a deer being tracked by a hunter. The deer that survive are the ones whose instincts are the best. They don't think, they don't use logic, they act. And some of them survive." His smile vanished. "Of course, some of them don't."

"C'mon. You got a chance, here. Trust your gut." Champion looked around him. "And so far, it's been quiet, right? We haven't had any trouble today. Maybe we lost 'em."

"Could be," Chris said, and finished the last bite of his sandwich. But he doubted it. They weren't done with him yet. After all of the trouble they'd gone to, there was no way they were going to let him get away easily.

· · · ·

Chris checked his email after they got back on the road, and found to his delight that he had another email from Elisa.

> *Hi Chris,*
>
> *I've been thinking about what you suggested, to see if there was a way we could communicate so that no one would understand but us. And I think I have something. Maybe it's silly, but I think it could work, depending on how good your memory is. It has to be something only you and I would know, right? Well, I came up with an idea. And if it works, maybe we can use it.*
>
> *Remember when we were studying for all of those quizzes in Field Biology, where we had to learn all the*

scientific names of the animals we might run across? I know we all hated them. They seemed pointless, memorizing lists of names that we could easily look up if we needed to. But we did it anyway, and we had all these mnemonics for remembering the names. And then, there were all the trips we took, and animals we saw, and stories attached to them. I'm hoping you remember enough of what we did together to make this work.

Let's give it a try. If you can figure this one out, maybe that will be a way that we can tell each other where we are, and maybe meet?

Okay, so here goes.

We were on an offshore trip, right near the beginning of class, out in Puget Sound. We hadn't started doing any banding yet, or taken our first trip up into the Cascades. It was kind of an orientation, getting to know some of the species in western Washington. And we kept seeing these little birds, lots of them. None of us had ever heard of them before. And Mary thought they were hilarious. Every time we saw one, she'd laugh, in that stage-laugh way of hers, but finally, we were all pointing them out, because they were funny. If you take the name of the genus of these birds — you may need to look it up, I did — and number the letters, and write out letters 12, 7, 1, 16, 2, 9, and 15, in that order, you'll get a message.

I hope this works.

Elisa

Chris smiled to himself. Brilliant idea; only the seven of them would have any idea how to decode the message, although if they were going to send more serious information, they'd have to be more careful about the clues. How many kinds of "funny little birds" could there be in Puget Sound? But Chris remembered the trip, and the incident, well. Mary had made a big deal about it, at first commenting that they looked like flying penguins. She really seemed to find them hilarious, however forced her laughter had sounded at first.

They were called murrelets. Chris looked up the Wikipedia entry for them, and the first line was, "Murrelets are a group of small marine alcids comprising three genera – Brachyramphus, Synthliboramphus, and Endomychura, living in continental shelf regions in the cooler parts of the Northern Hemisphere."

Chris counted the letters of the three names given. The one Elisa had referenced had at least 16 letters, so it could only be the middle one, Synthliboramphus. He fished around for a bit in Champion's cabinet, and found a pen and a three-day-old newspaper, and wrote down,

S1 y2 n3 t4 h5 l6 i7 b8 o9 r10 a11 m12 p13 h14 u15 s16

He then copied her message, 12, 7, 1, 16, 2, 9, 15, and moments later had written out, *MISS YOU*.

Chris burst out laughing, and wrote back:

Got it, Elisa. And that's brilliant.
And I do, too. Just so you know.

Her response came back quickly.

You have no idea how much better that makes me feel, that there really is some way for you to know where I am. Maybe we could get together, after all. Like I've said, I think I'm safe here, but I do feel very alone. Cast adrift, you know? I'm sure you understand. You don't even have a house to return to. I have one, but can't go back.

I'm not sure which is worse.

But either way, it'd be easier if we were together.

I'll see if I can give some thought to a way to tell you how to find me. The last one didn't take me long, but that was dumb luck, I think. I don't know how the professional cryptographers do it.

Elisa

Chris read her email twice, and then clicked *Reply*.

Elisa,
Be careful, okay? Only pick things that just the seven of us knew about. The last one—well, someone with a Puget Sound marine bird list could have figured it out pretty quickly, I think. It's got to be something that only we would know.

Now that the others are all gone, there's no way that the bad guys could get the key to deciphering the code.

This may be the only advantage we've got, at the moment. We don't want to get careless and blow it.

Chris

She responded moments later with:

You're exactly right. And no worries. I will be shrewd. I will be sneaky. They will regret ever taking on the likes of us.

Chris laughed again, and replied:

We'll show 'em a thing or two. Take care. I'll be in touch.

Chris shut the laptop, stowed it back in its spot, and returned to the cab. The scenery hadn't changed. The expanse of arid grassland seemed never-ending. But he sensed, through a combination of intuition and actual knowledge, that they were approaching the end of the flat midsection of the country. Ahead lay the Rocky Mountains, piled in ever higher peaks, through the states of Utah, Colorado, and Wyoming, and up into Montana and Idaho.

And after that, more grassland, with the dry fields of

eastern Washington and Oregon, and then the volcanic cones, glaciers, and fir forests of the Cascades. Where all of this started. And to where, he thought grimly, he was being drawn, like a moth to a candle.

• • • •

It was a little past two in the afternoon, and they were approaching the town of Ogallala. Chris was dozing in the passenger seat, Baxter at his feet dreaming of chasing rabbits, to judge by the twitching of his paws and his occasional low woofs. But Chris roused when Champion moved suddenly, leaning forward and turning up the volume on his CB radio.

A voice, crackling with static, said, "*… all I can say is it's a fuckin' inconvenience. Over.*"

Champion lifted the microphone from its hook, depressed the key on the side, and said, "Breaker 1-9, can you repeat that?"

The same voice came back, "*Goddamn roadblock on 80 westbound. They're stoppin' everybody. I'm stuck in the line waitin' to clear. I'm runnin' behind schedule already, so this is pissin' me right off. Over.*"

"Copy that, thanks," Champion said, and gave a quick glance over to Chris. Chris felt a light sweat break out on his forehead.

"You got any idea what they're lookin' for?" Champion said, into the microphone. "Over."

"Just heard from up ahead. Searchin' for some kind o' fugitive. Said he's armed and dangerous. Probably some guy escaped from the state pen in Lincoln and hijacked a car to get away. With all the ways he could go from there, though, don't know why the fuck they're stoppin' up the interstate. He could be damn near anywhere. If that's what's actually goin' on. Hell, I dunno. Fuckin' nuisance, is what it is. Over."

"It is that," Champion said. "State cops, then? Over."

"Naw," came the voice. *"Don't look like it. Feds, I'd guess. I'm still a ways back, but they're in unmarked cars. Got the whole fuckin' highway blocked, lettin' people through one at a time. It's gonna be a long wait. Over."*

"'bout what mile marker? Over."

"Around 120. Maybe 122. Passed Ogallala about ten minutes ago, I'd say. Over."

"Might be time to pull over and take a nap. Over."

"I dunno. Don't expect these guys are gonna give up any time soon. Roadblock like this, they mean business. You're gonna have to deal with it unless you're packin' it in for the night. Over."

"Guess you're right. Thanks for the info, buddy. Over."

"No prob. Out."

Champion rehung the microphone from its hook, and looked over at Chris.

"Whaddya think?" Champion said.

"You know what I think," Chris said.

"It's them again, isn't it?"

"Of course. I should have taken your advice about the

emails. That's how they know where I am. It has to be. There's nothing else left for them to track me by, unless they somehow put a computer chip under my skin while I was asleep."

Champion's forehead creased with worry. "I guess it's pretty likely you're right about that. I understand why you did it, though. I was all alone in the world, except for one friend, I'd take any kind of risk to get a hold of her. But hell, Chris, this sucks, you know?"

Chris laughed grimly. "Yeah, you could say that."

"What do you want me to do?"

"I don't know," he said. "What can you do? I'm out here in the middle of nowhere in Nebraska. There's nothing but fields and ranches and a whole lot of nothing between me and some guys who intend to kill me. Unless I'm prepared to strike out across the hills and hope like hell I can get somewhere safe, I don't think I've got a lot of options here."

In the distance, Chris saw a green sign on the right hand side of the highway that said, "2 miles. Exit 126, Ogallala, Rt. 61, Rt. 26."

"That's your last way out," Champion said. "Right there. We take that exit, you got a chance. We keep going, they get you." He looked over at Chris. "You're not ready to give up, are you?"

Chris looked out of the window at the dry hillsides rolling by, with the smooth, glittering waters of the Platte

River still following them, hugging the highway to the north. He thought about Elisa, waiting for him. There could be a way for them to connect, to face this menace together instead of alone, and an almost painful pang of longing grabbed his heart and held on.

"No," he said quietly. "I'm not ready to give up. Take the exit. Take the exit, drop me off, and then keep going. I'll walk into town. After that, I'll figure something out."

"Now, that's not what I meant," Champion said, his voice rising in panic. "I got no problem with taking a detour, here. I got a GPS. We can go right the hell around that damn roadblock, get back on 80 somewhere west of it, no problem."

Chris shook his head. "No. It's too risky. I was wrong about them. I don't understand computers that well, but I think I know how they did this. It's the only thing that makes sense."

"How?" Champion said.

"It's got to be that they pinpointed your computer. They're monitoring my emails, and they identified your computer from them somehow. They know where they originated. Somehow, they connected your truck with that computer. I don't know how they'd do that, but there has to be a way. Maybe you've used it for something official, something that allowed them to log your computer's identification in their databases. All it would take is once. And you're a trucker. You have to stop at weigh stations, you go through toll booths, everything like that. They know exactly where you are." He paused. "That has to be how Elisa has escaped so far. Even if they know that she's using her laptop to send emails, they haven't figured out where it is, yet. But once they have both pieces of information, you're pinned forever, like a butterfly to a mounting board." He laughed again. "I always thought the information age was cool, you know? And I thought the conspiracy theorists were paranoid idiots. What earthly reason could they have for monitoring our whereabouts? But I was wrong. When they have a reason, it's easy. All of the mechanisms, the infrastructure, are already there. We can be pinpointed in minutes, unless we swear off electronic communication entirely."

"Damn it, this is so crappy," Champion said, sounding genuinely distressed.

"Yes. It is. But I don't need to drag you down with me. When you get to the roadblock, if they ask you—which they will—don't deny that you gave me a ride. They'll know that much already, and if you lie, you'll be in worse trouble. You're much better off playing innocent, that you gave me a ride out of Lincoln, that I was hitchhiking. That's the first time I used your computer, so they wouldn't know that wasn't true. I haven't touched the computer for over an hour, so tell them that I told you to drop me off in Sutherland. That was the last town we passed, right?"

"Yeah."

"Tell 'em that I told you I was meeting up with friends in Sutherland. If they fall for it, maybe they'll think Elisa is there. Or maybe they'll try and see if I have relatives there. Either way, it might get them off my ass for a while." He sighed. "And I guess I can't email Elisa any more."

The sign for the exit appeared on the right, the off ramp curving up from the highway onto a hill that supported the Highway 61 overpass. Champion put his turn signal on, and the truck moved smoothly off the interstate and onto the ramp.

"You sure about this, Chris?" he said, as he braked to a halt at the top of the hill, where there was a stop sign and a right-turn arrow pointing the way to Ogallala.

Chris nodded. "I'm sure. I can risk my own life. But I'm not risking anyone else's, not if I can help it. I've already cost two people their lives. If you got caught with me, you really think they'd let you go?"

"No," Champion said. "I guess not."

Chris opened the door, and with a little urging he got Baxter to jump down onto the gravel on the road's shoulder. Champion tossed him a full water bottle, which Chris caught in mid-air.

"You take care, buddy," he said. "Guess we'll probably never see each other again. But man, I hope like hell you get away. I really do."

"So do I," Chris said. "And thanks. Thanks for everything you did for me."

"I wish I could do more."

Chris shut the door of the truck. Champion raised one hand in a solemn wave. Then with a groan, the big engine propelled the truck past the turnoff for Highway 61, and down the on ramp back toward I-80.

Chris watched the eighteen-wheeler roll back onto the interstate, and stood, with the sun in his face and the wind pushing on him in hot gusts, like the breath of some distant dragon, until Champion's rig was lost to view. Then he turned right, toward the bridge across the Platte and the town of Ogallala, Nebraska.

He had never felt so completely alone in his life.

CHAPTER 12

Chris walked across the broad bridge over the South Platte River, Baxter trotting contentedly by his heels.

He has no idea what's happened, Chris thought. *Fortunately. For a dog, this kind of thing might be a big adventure. As long as he has food and a place to sleep and gets a pat on the head occasionally, he's none the wiser. I wonder what will happen to him if They get me? Will someone take him in? I sure hope so.*

But this seemed too elegiac a train of thought for him to follow very far, so he pushed it aside.

Ogallala is a small town, with the flat topography allowing a grid of streets running parallel and perpendicular to the river front. First Street seemed like a major road; there were many passing cars and curious looks as he walked down the wide sidewalk past a realtor's office, the Keith County Senior Center, and a small grocery store. Further along seemed to be mainly occupied by auto dealerships, so he turned right up a side street, and soon found himself wandering through block after block of neatly kept houses, past large shade trees that provided the highest concentration of the color green he'd seen since entering the state of Nebraska.

He passed an elderly gentleman out mowing his lawn with a push mower, and responded to the one-handed wave in kind. A slight frown crossed the old man's face as his eyes followed Chris down the sidewalk. His mind played with various reasons for the man's reaction. Was it because Chris was a stranger? Or because he looked shabby? Or because his dog wasn't on a leash?

Or was it because the elderly man was one of *Them?*

But that seemed ridiculous. He turned, unable to stop himself from checking. The old man was giving the scruffy stranger and his dog no further attention, and had returned to mowing his lawn in perfectly lined-up parallel stripes.

Rely on your intuition to tell your friends from your enemies from the people who have no connection to you at all. And this guy is one of the latter.

He continued walking for about a quarter-mile, and

the tidy suburbs were beginning to straggle off into larger lots with less well-kept houses. He saw old cars, some with gaping spots of rust, and unkempt tangles of children's toys, farm equipment, and oddments like spools of chicken wire and empty steel barrels lying on their sides. The whole place had an air of desolation.

One of the last buildings before the pavement turned to a dirt road was a small, square white building with a steeple. A sign in front said, *Ogallala Full Bible Church of God*. Without knowing exactly why, he turned up the walkway, past rows of marigolds flowering orange and crimson in the blazing sunshine, and then up to the door.

Chris had never been religious. He'd only been in a church a few times in his life, for friends' weddings and for the funerals of his father's parents—both of his paternal grandparents were the children of Italian immigrants, and devoutly Catholic. His mother's side of the family had mostly been freewheeling agnostics. His father, once freed from the lockstep attendance at Mass he'd been forced into as a child, had jumped straight into atheism without a backward glance.

As a result, religion was something that had hardly been on his radar at all. He'd run, a couple of times, into the devoutly religious as a result of his teaching of evolution, and had reacted to their objections mostly in puzzlement. Other than that, he hadn't given much thought to it.

So it was a mystery to him why he went up that walkway in a town he'd never been in before, to a church he'd never heard of before, and opened the door.

Inside the building was cool and dim and silent, and had that distinctive smell of old books that Chris always associated with libraries. Baxter followed him, his claws clicking on the hardwood floor, and the door swung shut behind them with a clunk. Row after row of dark wooden pews were lined up facing a raised altar on which sat a table, two chairs, and a lectern. A rather battered-looking spinet stood in the corner. Other than a large, unadorned cross, there was not much in the way of decoration on the walls. It was about as far from the ornate cathedral where his Grandpa and Grandma Franzia's funeral masses had been said as he could imagine.

Chris sat down in one of the pews, wondering what he should do next.

A door opened at the back corner of the church, behind the lectern, and artificial light shone out from what seemed to be a small office. A tall, heavyset man, balding and walking with a steel cane, came out, and met Chris's eyes with an unsmiling, but not unfriendly, gaze.

"Can I help you?" he said.

"I'm… I'm not sure," Chris said. He looked down at Baxter, who had sat down next to him, and was panting. "I'm sorry, but my dog was with me and I didn't want to leave him outside."

"Oh, I've never heard Our Lord had problems with

dogs, so I don't either," he said, and smiled, revealing a pair of front teeth with a large gap. "Got two of them myself. For hunting, mostly, but that doesn't mean I don't spoil them in the meantime. He looks like a good boy. What's his name?"

"Baxter."

"Well, that's a good name for a dog," he said, leaning over and scratching Baxter's ears. "Any case, though, what can I do for you today?"

Intuition. Luck. Maybe he wouldn't have come in here if it weren't safe. "Can I ask you a question?" he finally asked.

The man shrugged. "Certainly."

"Do you know who I am?"

One shaggy eyebrow rose a little. "Far as I know, I've never seen you before in my life. Is there a reason I should?"

Chris looked into his eyes. "No. But can I just say that if you're planning on killing me, I wish you'd cut to the chase and get it over with."

The man stared at him in complete incomprehension, and finally sat down, first leaning on his cane and finally dropping ponderously into the pew across the aisle from where Chris sat.

"Son," he said, "you're making no sense at all. Either there's a story behind this, or you're plain crazy, and at the moment the jury's still out on which it is. Why would you walk in and ask a man if he wants to kill you?"

"I don't know who I can trust," Chris said. "What I've been through… I don't know if you'll understand."

"Well, I don't know either, till you tell me about it. But I do know that now you're in the consecrated house of God. And I am a minister of the Gospel. You have nothing to fear here. But you want help, you need to level with me. What's all this about?"

"I need someplace safe to be," Chris said. "I've been running for days. There are people who are trying to kill me."

The man's broad forehead creased, and both eyebrows shot upwards. "That's the second time you mentioned someone killing you. Why's someone trying to kill you?"

Suddenly Chris felt both mentally and physically exhausted. He leaned forward, and put his forehead into his hand. "I don't know. I honestly don't know."

There was silence in the dim, musty sanctuary for some time. Finally, Chris raised his eyes. In his imagination, he wondered, in the moment before he looked up, what he would see. The heavyset man now holding a gun, its barrel a black, empty eye aimed at his head. The man flanked by grim-looking individuals in black suits. Or that the man would have mysteriously vanished, leaving Chris alone in this dingy little church.

But all he saw was the man still sitting there, in exactly the same position as before, his large, calloused hands laced across the handle of his cane. Their eyes met.

"I'm Reverend Joseph Harper," the man said. "Most folks call me Reverend Joe. Whatever evil's been following you, it cannot enter herein." His eyes never wavered from Chris's. "You have nothing to fear here," he repeated.

Chris sat with Reverend Joe alone in the church. No one else was nearby, at least no one Chris saw.

What possible reason could They *have to spare me now? Given that* They've *been trying for almost three weeks to get rid of me? So either he knows, and is on my side, like the boy in the tollbooth. Or he's telling the truth, and doesn't know anything.*

If he was one of *Them*, Chris knew, he would already be dead.

"My name is Chris Lake," Chris said. "I'm from Syracuse, New York. In the past month, I've survived at least three murder attempts. I'm telling you the honest truth that I have no idea who it is that is trying to kill me, nor why. Right now I seem to have shaken them off, but I don't know for how long that'll be. I don't want to put you at any risk, but a place to hide out for a few days would be wonderful. I can pay, at least something, even if it's to crash on your sofa, or sleep in the church, or wherever."

Reverend Joe stared at Chris in silence for another few moments. Chris had never believed in souls, but the preacher seemed to be trying to see into Chris's. Finally, Reverend Joe said, "The Lord Jesus commands us to care for the downtrodden. It's a commandment that a good many of his followers like to forget. In Matthew, chapter twenty-five, Our Lord says, 'Then shall the King say unto them on his right hand, "Come, ye blessed of my Father, inherit the kingdom prepared for you from the foundation of the world; for I was hungry, and ye gave me meat; I was thirsty, and ye gave me drink; I was a stranger, and ye took me in; naked, and ye clothed me; I was sick, and ye visited me; I was in prison, and ye came unto me."' How can I do other than what the Lord commands?"

Chris looked at him, a sudden sensation of detachment washing over him. A dizzying succession of bizarre feelings slipped past. This elderly man, in his flannel work shirt and khaki pants, was a link in a chain extending back in time, back through Cotton Mather and Martin Luther, and earlier, Thomas Aquinas and the Venerable Bede and St. Augustine and other, less-remembered names from long-ago college history classes. Despite his long life of disbelief, Chris felt that Reverend Joe really was drawing down some kind of celestial power to shield Chris from harm. He sensed that this moment, right here and now, was some kind of pivot point on which his very life might depend. A deep shudder ran through his body. Baxter whined, and looked up at his master, uncomprehending worry in his brown eyes, and he leaned heavily against Chris's leg.

The moment passed. Chris said, "I don't know how to thank you."

Reverend Joe said, "The Lord has given me to understand that you are telling the truth. That is all the thanks I need." He stood up, assisted by his cane, and said, "Come with me. My wife and I have a spare bedroom, now our son's grown and gone. No reason you can't stay in it for a while."

· · · ·

Chris rode in an aging Ford pickup to Reverend Joe's house. The windows were open, and with the wind, the heat no longer felt oppressive. Baxter sat next to him on the seat, head out in the slipstream, tongue flapping. A Christian music station was playing low on the radio.

The Reverend and his wife, Dolores, a rawboned woman with steel gray curls and dark eyes set in an angular, high-cheekboned face, lived in a neat ranch-style house on the north end of the town. It had rows of glowing marigolds along the walk and underneath the windows, leaving Chris no doubt as to who looked after the landscaping at the church. An embroidered sampler with the legend "God is Lord" hung in the entryway. The interior of the house was spotless, but had few knick-knacks and other adornments. A framed photograph of a smiling man of about forty leaned on the mantelpiece above a wood stove, with a blond woman and a boy and girl in their early teens. The man's oval face and dark eyes left no doubt that Chris was looking at the Harpers' son, whose bedroom he'd be occupying.

Dolores Harper didn't question her husband's statement that Chris was a poor man who needed help, "as the Lord hath commanded us." However, she was also eminently practical. She offered Chris a shower and a change of clothes, and to launder Chris's own garments, which were, by now, very much in need of it. Baxter was given a saucer of water and a bowl of kibble, and took care of both in short order. He then acquainted himself with the Harpers' two spaniels, Zeke and Jimbo. After a moment's suspicious circling, tails started to wag. The canine pleasantries exchanged, all three dogs lay down on the long throw rug in the living room.

Chris took this as a sign that he could excuse himself and take advantage of Mrs. Harper's offer of a hot shower. He stood under the spray as long as he felt was reasonable. There was something ineffably comforting about feeling the warm water running down his skin. Finally, he got out, toweled off, and dressed in the clothes—rather too large for him—that Mrs. Harper had given him to wear until his were laundered, and then he went back out into the living room.

He was immediately struck with the smell of frying food, and his stomach gave a loud rumble. His time with Champion had been pleasant enough, but his meals had been lacking both in quantity and quality. Whatever Mrs. Harper was cooking smelled better than anything he'd had to eat in the previous month.

It turned out to be fried chicken. With biscuits, green beans, and a big glass of cold milk. Grace was said before eating, another novelty for Chris, who simply bowed his head until Reverend Joe was finished praying. Then all three dug in, for the most part in silence. Dinnertime conversation was, apparently, not something the Harpers indulged in. The whole affair was about as different from the noisy meals he remembered growing up as anything he could imagine.

After the last of the chicken was eaten, hands were wiped and napkins crumpled up and added to the plates full of bones and biscuit crumbs, Reverend Joe leaned back in his chair, patted his ample belly, and said, "That was a mighty nice meal, Dolores."

"It was wonderful," Chris said. "Thank you for your hospitality."

Dolores nodded toward Chris. "I'm happy you enjoyed," she said. Then she looked at her husband. "Chase Ballengee called while you were out."

Reverend Joe smiled and frowned at the same time. "Chase? Haven't heard from him in an age. What'd he want?"

"Just to see if we had any odd jobs he could do. I told him the first thing was for him to attend Sunday services for a change, and stop spending his money on beer. He just laughed."

"I expect we could find something for him to do, if it

came down to it. I could use help with the lawn mowing, both here and at the church, now that my knees're so bad. You can only do so much yourself, you know. We're neither of us getting any younger. And for all of Chase's bad habits, he's a good worker."

"He is," Dolores said. "He means well enough, I suppose."

Conversation lagged. *What do I do?* Chris thought, after about five minutes had passed. *Just excuse myself, at some point? Do they spend their evenings sitting at the dinner table, silently staring at the dirty dishes?*

Reverend Joe spoke again, interrupting his thoughts, and this time directing a question to Chris.

"You have family you need to get a hold of? Let them know you're okay?"

"I don't know if I can," Chris said. "I think that the people who are after me can somehow track my emails and phone calls."

Reverend Joe absorbed this in silence. Mrs. Harper didn't react. Chris suspected her husband had told her about Chris's plight while he was in the shower. Or perhaps she didn't question Reverend Joe's decisions. Didn't the Bible say something about wives being obedient to husbands?

"You married, Chris? Any kids?" Reverend Joe asked.

"No. Neither."

"Still, you must have family and friends, right?"

"Yes. But I'm afraid to contact them. I don't want to put them in danger."

Reverend Joe nodded. "Lord Jesus bless you, son. That's a hard road to travel, being alone like that."

"I wouldn't have made it this far without people like yourselves who are willing to help me," Chris said. "In fact, I'd be long dead."

"You must be tired," Mrs. Harper said.

"I'm exhausted," Chris admitted.

"I keep the bed made up for guests," she said. "I'll throw your clothes in the washing machine, and hang them to dry tomorrow, if the weather's good. Till then, you'll have to make do with those castoffs of the Reverend's. Better than nothing, although they wouldn't fit unless you put on a few pounds."

"They're fine, Mrs. Harper. But if you don't mind, I think I'll head to bed. It's been a while since I slept in a comfortable one. Thanks again for dinner. It was amazing."

He stood, and went out into the living room and then down the hall to the room that had been pointed out to him earlier as their son's old room. He opened the door, and flipped on the light switch. A digital clock glowed red, its display reading 8:14, but he felt like it was after midnight, and that he could sleep for days. The room was as sparely decorated as the rest of the house, with only a bed, a dresser, a chair and small writing desk, a night stand, and a small set of bookshelves containing a Bible, a book called Daily Inspirational Readings from the New Testament, and a hardcover with a glossy, brightly-colored spine called *Jesus Guides My Life*.

Chris considered the Harpers as he prepared himself for bed. His first encounter with serious Christians had left him with the impression that they were, other than the frequent mentions of God and Jesus, pretty ordinary folks, and a significant distance from the shrieking maniacs from the Westboro Baptist Church that made it onto the nightly news every so often. Even so, he felt no particular inclination toward the devotional reading available from the books on the bookshelf, so he shut the lights out, undressed, and climbed into bed. Baxter was already snoozing at the foot of the bed. He hadn't asked the Harpers if it was okay for his dog to stay with him, but he figured that he could always apologize afterwards if he'd breached protocol.

The bed was supremely comfortable, and he relaxed into it, feeling his joints creaking as the stress of the previous days drained from him. Moments later, he was deeply asleep.

• • • •

Chris woke out of a sound sleep, some uncertain amount of time later, when the light switch turned on.

He sat up, blinking and dazed, the blanket slipping from his bare chest.

"I think you may owe us an explanation, son," came Reverend Joe's voice.

Chris frowned, and squinted. Reverend Joe was standing in the doorway, a piece of paper in one hand, and a hunting rifle held at his side. "I brought my gun with me for my own protection, because Mrs. Harper insisted. But I'm open to talking, and I need to hear what you have to say."

"What…" Chris began. "About what?"

"About this." He held out the sheet of paper to Chris. "You need to give me some answers. This… it doesn't cast you in the best of lights."

Chris slid a hand out from under the blanket, feeling like he was in the middle of some sort of dream, where everyday objects and words no longer make sense. He took the sheet of paper, turned it over.

Two things jumped out at him immediately, even given his sleep-addled condition. The first was the word, bolded and capitalized: ***WANTED.***

The second was a smiling photograph of himself. It was, he realized, his last school nametag photo.

"Mrs. Harper told me this morning that I should check out your story," Reverend Joe said, his voice heavy with what sounded like disappointment. "She's more suspicious than I am, sometimes. So while I was drinking my coffee, I got on the computer and did a search for 'Chris

Lake, fugitive.' I wasn't expecting anything to come up, and honestly, I don't believe she was, either. I think she was as caught up short as I was when something did. Now she's telling me I should call the sheriff, and you need to tell me why I shouldn't."

Chris looked back down, and continued to read the fine print underneath the photograph.

WANTED

Christopher David Franzia, age 52, of Guildford, Schuyler County, New York. 6'1", black hair, brown eyes, slim build. May be traveling under the name "Chris Lake." Should be considered armed and dangerous. Do NOT approach if seen, but contact the authorities at the number listed below.

Last known to be in Sutherland, Nebraska. May be traveling west. Law enforcement agencies in western Nebraska, Colorado, and Wyoming should be on the alert for this dangerous fugitive.

Wanted in connection to a series of murders in Oregon and Washington state.

Reward available for any information leading to Christopher Franzia's arrest.

Contact 1-800-555-9003 with leads, or email gpd292@ctis.gov.

CHAPTER 13

I didn't kill anyone," Chris said. He looked into Reverend Joe's eyes as steadily as he could, given the situation. Sitting in bed, wearing only a blanket, and having a man standing there with a gun and a wanted poster with your picture on it didn't really foster self-confidence.

Reverend Joe frowned, shook his head.

"I want to believe that, son, I truly do, but that's not enough. You need to explain why that poster says you did."

"I told you that there were people who were trying to kill me," Chris said. "They're the same ones who committed the murders they're referring to in this wanted poster.

Five friends of mine in college have been hunted down one by one and murdered. I, and one other person, are all that's left. Neither of us has any real idea why we're being targeted. But now, the ones who are after me have changed their tactics, it looks like. Before this, they were trying to kill me themselves, by whatever it took. Since that hasn't worked, it seems like they're hoping to get someone else to do it for them, for the reward."

"That's quite a story," Reverend Joe said. "But most people, hearing your tale, would say that's exactly what someone'd say, in your situation. How would you answer that?"

Man, I am getting sick of this.

"I don't know," he said, and gave a harsh sigh. "I don't really have any evidence. The people who are chasing me haven't been leaving a lot of footprints. But as for you, I thought you said God told you I was telling the truth, yesterday."

"So He did," Reverend Joe said. "So He did. And God never speaks anything but the truth."

"Then why are you even questioning me?"

"Our finite minds don't always hear His words correctly."

"Well, that's convenient," Chris said, a little peevishly. "So, I guess that throws you back on your own brain to figure it out."

"Now, there's no need to get angry, son," Reverend Joe said. "But put yourself in my place. If you took in a man, and saw a wanted poster with his face on it, wouldn't you ask a few questions? Especially if it said he was armed and dangerous." He frowned. "You aren't armed, are you?"

"Look," Chris said, and pulled the blanket back. "It's a little hard to carry a weapon when you're not wearing any clothes. Unless I have a hand grenade stuck up my butt, I'm pretty much defenseless."

Reverend Joe stared at him for a moment, and then broke out in a belly laugh. "Heck, son, you got me there."

"If you want to make sure, the clothes you lent me are in a pile next to the bed. You can feel the pockets. The only things in them are my wallet and keys, the latter of which won't do me a lot of good, given that the people who are trying to kill me blew up my house, and I had to abandon my car in some town in Missouri to keep from getting my head shot off."

"All right," Reverend Joe said, holding one hand up. "Settle down. I believe you. Either you're telling the truth, or you're the best liar I've ever met." He went over to the jeans and flannel shirt that Chris had dropped on the floor when he'd undressed for bed, and gave them a cursory check. He tossed boxers and the jeans to Chris, who caught them in midair.

"Get yourself dressed, son, and come on out into the dining room. Join us for breakfast, and tell us what you can of the story. You've got me convinced, now you need to convince Mrs. Harper. I should warn you, though. She's a harder sell than I am."

• • • •

Twenty minutes later, Chris sat, working his way through several links of sausage, leftover biscuits from the previous evening's dinner, and orange juice. Despite her feeding him well, Mrs. Harper stared at him the whole time through narrowed eyes, like a hunter waiting for her prey to make the first move.

Reverend Joe's laptop was open on the table in front of Chris, and he saw on the screen the image that Joe had printed out. He shuddered involuntarily at once more seeing his smiling face underneath the word **WANTED**.

"What is 'ctis.gov?'" Chris asked.

"I'm not sure," Reverend Joe said. "I can't keep up with all those government agencies and their initials."

Chris typed in *www.ctis.gov* and pulled up a site that said, *Central Terminal Information Services*. The Official Seal of the United States figured prominently on the page, but other than that, there wasn't much information about what it actually did. The website had some vague verbiage about "Acting as a clearinghouse for data involving issues of national security," and "Seeking to ensure justice and the safety of American citizens both at home and overseas." Clicking through the associated links didn't provide much in the way of additional information, although on a page titled *Current Cases Under Investigation*, Chris did find an entry for Elisa Ann Reed (also known as Elisa Ann

Howard) whose last known residence was St. Cloud, Minnesota. She was, like Chris, said to be involved in a string of murders in the Northwest, and was described as armed and considered dangerous, but her current whereabouts were listed as "unknown." Her photo was an old one, and looked like it had been culled from a newspaper.

"Elisa is the only other one of us who is still alive," Chris said, pointing at her blurry image on the screen.

"So you say," Mrs. Harper said.

"Yes," Chris said, his voice tight. "So I do say. Because it's the truth." He opened up a Google search page, and typed in "Central Terminal Information Services," and got a series of hits, all of which brought him back to the ctis.gov pages.

"You'd think if this was a real agency," he said, "there would be more online about them."

"It's a dot-gov site," Reverend Joe said. "You can't get one of those unless you're legitimate."

"There are probably ways around that. Even if it's official-looking, it might not be for real."

"That's true. But it still could be a government agency."

"Government doesn't mean it's good," Chris said.

Reverend Joe snorted. "Especially these days. I can't stand Obama and his liberal lackeys. Leading the whole country down the road to perdition."

Chris looked up. He wasn't going to waste time discussing politics. "Look, I know I don't have any hard evi-

dence to convince you with. Just think about it, though. What's the likelihood that I'm some kind of most-wanted criminal? Here I am, fleeing across the country, with nothing but my dog." He gestured down at Baxter, who was sitting next to him, leaning against his leg. "No car, no gun, nothing. Just me and a dog. Does that seem plausible to you?"

Baxter, seeming to sense that he was being talked about, began to wag his tail. Chris gave him a bite of sausage.

"Seems like you got the Reverend convinced," Mrs. Harper said. "I'm a little more cautious, I guess. I mean, Joe, think about it. Besides the up-front danger of harboring someone who might intend us harm, there's the fact that we could get in a lot of trouble if we make a mistake. If he actually is a criminal on the run, and they find out we sheltered him? Knew about the wanted poster and didn't tell anyone? We'd be charged as, what are they called…"

"Accessories," Reverend Joe said. "Accomplices."

"Right," Mrs. Harper said. "We're law-abiding citizens, Mr. Lake. Or is it Mr. Franzia?"

"It's Franzia," Chris said, trying to keep an angry tone from his voice and only partly succeeding. "I was going by Lake because they could track me otherwise. But seems like they found out, anyway, probably in Missouri, where I lost my car. I'm guessing they checked the motel register there."

"I don't know," Mrs. Harper said, her lips tightening into a grim line. "Joe, I know you want to help this fellow, but I'm worried. Why shouldn't we call the number on the wanted poster, and let the authorities sort it out?"

"If you do that, I'll be dead before nightfall," Chris said. "I'll put it that bluntly. You may as well get Reverend Joe to take his hunting rifle and put a bullet in my head. It'll amount to the same thing."

For the first time, an uncertain expression came into her eyes. She looked at her husband and didn't say anything further.

"Look, son, it's just if there was some proof," Reverend Joe said.

"I don't have any. There's only one other thing I can show you as evidence, and it's pretty thin." Chris signed into his Gmail account. "This may be the dumbest thing I've ever done," he said in a quiet voice as he typed. "They were tracking me by my emails before. But maybe if you only read the emails between Elisa and me, it'll be all right. I suspect that they found me when I sent an email. Maybe it'll be okay if you just read them." There was a new, unread message from Elisa, but there was no telling what the content was, so he ignored that one. He decided that if he could convince the Harpers he was innocent, he could go back and read it later. And if he couldn't, it was better that they get as little information about her as possible.

He clicked on the last message he had sent to Elisa,

and scrolled down to the bottom, where the previous messages back-and-forth were arrayed. He turned the laptop around so that they could both see the screen. "There. If that doesn't convince you, then you'll have to call the number on the poster."

The next few minutes were spent with first Reverend Joe, and then Mrs. Harper, slowly reading through the emails from bottom to top, Mrs. Harper peering at them nearsightedly through reading glasses.

"Well," she said, finally, "that's something."

"Do you believe me?"

Reverend Joe leaned back in his chair. "You have to admit, Dolores, it'd be hard to see how he could make all that up."

"They had a warrant out for her arrest, too," Mrs. Harper pointed out.

"Now, look," Chris started, but Mrs. Harper put up one hand.

"Now, don't mistake me. I have to say, of all the things I've seen, that bunch of emails is the most convincing. Hard to see how you'd have had the foresight to fake that. But even if you're telling the truth about it all, I'm not a bit sure what to do about you."

"The Lord commands us to look after those in need," Reverend Joe said.

"That he does, Joe," Mrs. Harper said. "But you got a lot of people here in this town that need looking after, too.

They depend on you. This fellow here, he may need help. Begging his pardon for accusing him of being a criminal, and all, although I will say I think I had sufficient justification for doing so. It's still to be figured how much risk we can take on his behalf. Joe, you're the leader of this community of Christ, here. You have to put that into your calculations, if you take my meaning."

"I do," Reverend Joe said. "But I have to point out that it's mighty easy, in these kinds of circumstances, to be afraid or selfish or lazy, and to attribute your decisions made from that kind of sin to God's will."

"Whatever you decide to do," Chris said, "it's nice to be believed."

"I can see how it would be," Mrs. Harper said, and then turned to her husband. "But you see, don't you, that if we accept that he is telling the truth, and I must admit I can't see any other explanation, that these people who are chasing him, they're murderers, evil men right from the pit of hell. They won't be stopped by you or by me."

"That is the risk you take for doing God's will," Reverend Joe said, an authoritative tone entering his voice. "If we cannot stand up to the enemies of God in times of danger, what good was our faith in the first place?"

There was a knock on the front door, and Baxter gave a single woof. The Harpers' dogs, out in the back yard, barked with considerably more force. Chris felt his heart give a painful jump in his ribcage.

Chris panicked. *Shit! They've found me. Can they have homed in on the Harpers' computer that fast?*

Mrs. Harper recognized the danger before her husband did. She gave a tug on Chris's arm, and said, "You go back into the bedroom, now. Take your dog. I'll give a yell if it's safe." Her dark eyes glittered dangerously, and she leaned toward him and said, very quietly, "There's a hunting knife in the top drawer of the dresser in there. You use it if you need to."

Reverend Joe's eyebrows flew upwards when he suddenly realized what his wife was implying. Chris stood, snapped his fingers for Baxter, trotted back down the hall to the bedroom, and shut the door behind him.

There was the sound of the front door opening, and closing, and then muffled conversation of which he could not make out any words.

How long can someone live in fear?

Probably a long time, but what does it do to your psyche? People in a war zone are in a perpetual state of fear. So are the survivors of concentration camps and prisoner-of-war camps. So, to a lesser extent, are people in prisons. Some people come out of those situations damaged for life; others survive and can go on to live relatively normal lives.

It dawned on Chris that if he survived this, he might have post-traumatic stress syndrome, and spend the rest of his life jumping every time the doorbell rang or someone called his name.

At least Mrs. Harper believed him. That woman was capable of changing her mind in a flash. A half hour ago, she was ready to let her husband shoot him. Now, she was arming him and telling him to defend himself if he had to.

Must be nice to see the world so black-and-white.

Despite her directions, Chris didn't go to the dresser. The thought of finding the knife, taking it out of its sheath, evoked a superstitious fear that if he did so, a confrontation was inevitable. He crouched by the door, listening. The conversation going on in the living room was quiet. There was no indication that there was anything alarming about the Harpers' visitor.

Ten minutes passed, and finally there was the sound of a door opening, then closing. A short time later, there was the coughing rasp of an old engine catching. Then a soft voice said, "Chris, you can come out."

Chris opened the door. Reverend Joe was standing there, a sheepish half-smile on his face. "It was nothing. Just Chase Ballengee. He's the one who called yesterday about odd jobs. I set him to mowing the lawn. Best to give that boy's hands some work to do." He turned and walked back down the hall, and Chris followed. "I tell you, though, son, after your story, and especially how Mrs. Harper reacted, I halfway thought we'd open the door and find a couple of guys from the Mafia or whatnot. When I saw it was Chase, I about laughed right in his face. Of course, he wouldn't have known why, he'd probably have thought I'd lost my mind."

"It's how I've been living for three weeks," Chris said. "I suspect everyone I meet."

"You trusted me," Reverend Joe said.

"Yes, and I'm not sure why. No offense, but you see what I mean."

"Of course, I take your meaning," Reverend Joe said. "And I have to say, that by itself counted a lot. Something about your manner makes it hard to imagine you're a mass murderer, like those people claim. Mrs. Harper's to be excused for not believing you for longer. She didn't see you, sitting in the church like that. And maybe, she didn't hear God's voice, the way I did."

Chris looked at him curiously. *On a fundamental level, I really don't understand these people. It is a completely different way of figuring out the universe than the one I've always bought into. But even so, I'll accept their help as long as they're willing to give it.*

A shadow passed across the living room window, along with a crescendo of the noise from the lawn mower engine. Chris got a glimpse of a narrow, olive-complexioned face, and curious brown eyes that glanced into the room and met Chris's in a quizzical glance that lasted only a fraction of a second. Then the noise receded.

$$\bullet \quad \bullet \quad \bullet \quad \bullet$$

Mrs. Harper, once she was convinced that Chris was telling the truth and that it was her duty before God to protect him, approached the situation with down-to-earth pragmatism. Over lunch—grilled cheese sandwiches—she talked to Chris about what he intended to do next. Reverend Joe was in his study, working on his sermon for the next day's services. Mrs. Harper brought her husband his sandwich and a glass of milk, and then set out lunch for herself and Chris in the dining room.

"What are your plans?" she asked him.

"Well, up to now, I haven't really had any, other than trying not to get killed," Chris said.

"Why'd you head west?" she asked.

"I'm not sure. At first, it was random. I was running, anywhere, trying to get somewhere safe. No reason."

"There's a reason for everything," Mrs. Harper said, with such certainty in her voice that Chris found himself half believing it despite his rationalism.

"Out there, out west, is where it started, you said," she said to him. "God is leading you back. You think you could have survived everything you have without the Lord Jesus placing his hands over you?"

"I don't know," Chris said.

Mrs. Harper nodded. "It's hard work, faith," she said. "I know that all too well. But even if the Lord leads, you got to move your own feet. Are you going to continue on west?"

"I suppose. But I'm not sure how I'll get any further along. I was lucky enough to get picked up by a trucker, before, and he took me from Missouri all the way here. I'm not likely to have something like that happen again."

"If it's meant to be, it'll happen," Mrs. Harper said.

"I wonder if I could use Reverend Joe's laptop again," Chris said. "There was an email from my friend, Elisa, that I'd like to read. I can't respond to it, there's too great a chance that they could find me that way. But I don't see how there's a danger simply from reading it. If it's okay."

"No harm I can see," Mrs. Harper said. The laptop had been left on the table after breakfast. She unfolded it and slid it toward him

He signed back into his email account, and clicked on the message from Elisa. As he did so, the front door opened, and the man Chris had seen mowing the lawn came in. He was about twenty-five years old, small, slender, and dark, with straight black hair that was in need of a haircut.

"Just wonderin' if I could use your bathroom, Mrs. Harper," he said.

"Of course, Chase. You know where it is."

"Thank you."

"Say, Chase," she said, "you must be hungry. Would you like me to put a sandwich on for you?"

"That's awful kind of you," he said, and gave her a shy smile. "I'd very much appreciate it, Mrs. Harper."

Chase vanished down the hallway, and Mrs. Harper stood, picked up the plates, put them in the sink, and set to work making another grilled cheese sandwich.

Chris read:

> *Chris,*
>
> *No news here. Everything is quiet, and I am fine. I hope you're still safe. I worry pretty much constantly, but I know you can't write to me over and over just saying, "Everything's okay," so I have to be patient and trust that all will be well.*
>
> *I do want to let you know where I am, though. Now that we have a way to communicate that no one else can figure out, it should be safe. I don't know why that's important to me; it feels like I'm more connected to you if you know where I am. Since I'm safe—for now—maybe if you can get here, you can be safe, too.*
>
> *So, here goes. I'm staying with a friend who's the bird specialist for a wildlife refuge—kind of ironic, isn't it? She has a big house and plenty of room. She'd invited me to visit before all of this crazy stuff started. Fortunately for me.*
>
> *So, once you know the town I'm in, it shouldn't be hard to find me. So here's the clue:*
>
> *Remember when we were having to memorize the scientific names of animals, and there was one that you found really funny? I still remember, sitting there in the coffee shop, laughing, because you said that it sounded like the name of an ancient Greek stripper. It kept coming up, and we thought it was hilarious. And it worked—I still remember when we got our quizzes back, and none of us missed that one! Deirdre said, "Well, chalk one up for the stripper!"*

*So take that name, and if you write out the letters num-
bered 1, 12, 14, 15, 5, and 10, you'll get the first part of
the town I'm in. It's not the complete name, but it's the best I
can do, and you'll be able to figure it out from there.*

*I hope I'll see you soon. Let me know if you figured out the
message, and if you might be able to get here. Until then, be safe.*

Love,

Elisa

Chris stifled a surprised smile at her signing off "Love,"
and picked up a pen that was sitting on the table, and began to write on his hand.

He remembered the incident well. The animal in
question was the Night Snake, Hypsiglena torquata. For
some reason, the scientific name had struck him as slinky
and sexy, and the hilarious image of an exotic dancer in
ancient Greece had forever been attached to it.

He hurriedly numbered the letters, and counted off,
his heart pounding with an inexplicable excitement.

H-O-Q-U-I-A.

"My God," he said, under his breath. "She's in Hoquiam!"

Chris looked up. Mrs. Harper had stopped in the act
of handing a plate with a sandwich to Chase Ballengee.
Both of them turned and were looked at him with expres-
sions that could have meant almost anything.

CHAPTER 14

The moment hung, suspended, between the three of them. Everything seemed to have stopped. There was no sound but the whistling of the wind outside the house. Chris realized he was holding his breath only when it became painful, and let the air out in a rush.

And all at once, it was over. Mrs. Harper said, "Sandwich got toasted a little dark on one side, Chase, hope you don't mind."

Chase said, with a grin, "'Course not, Mrs. Harper, it's fine. Nice of you to feed me lunch." Then he turned to Chris and said, in a conversational tone, "Is that Hoquiam, Washington? I got a buddy lives right nearby there."

Chris opened his mouth, and then closed it again. "Yeah," he finally said, and his voice sounded thin and hoarse in his own ears. "It's that—I just—got an email that mentioned it."

Chase sat down at the dinner table, and took a bite of his sandwich. "You probably know the fellow, too, Mrs. Harper," he said, in a tone that seemed to indicate that he was completely unconcerned with Chris or his email, and was still pursuing his own train of thought. "Van Spaulding."

Mrs. Harper nodded. "Van," she said. "Of course I remember him. He went up that way, what was it, five years ago?"

"Somethin' like that." He turned back to Chris. "Van worked for the BIA, out o' Winnebago."

"BIA?" Chris said.

"Bureau of Indian Affairs. I used to see him every few weeks or so. My grandpa always had him up for dinner whenever he was in this part o' the state. My pa's pa was full-blood Arapaho. I'm half, 'cause my ma's ma was Cheyenne. Van's the one who got my sister the scholarship to the University of Nebraska. But he got a little fed up with all the drivin'. They were sendin' him all over the state, seems like. He took a job for the BIA out in western Washington. Lives in Aberdeen. That's right next to Hoquiam, isn't it?"

"I think so," Chris said.

"We still get Christmas cards from him every year," Chase said. "He got married out there, already has a couple o' kids."

"That's nice," Mrs. Harper said, "but I'm sure Mr. Lake here doesn't need to hear all about folks he's never met."

"Well, he said 'Hoquiam,' and it got me to thinkin'," Chase said.

"Be that as it may," Mrs. Harper said.

"Sorry," Chase said, meekly, and returned to eating his sandwich.

Chris looked back down at the email, trying to fight down a rising sense of panic. Had he just, in a careless slip of the tongue, given Elisa's location away?

No, he rationalized, Mrs. Harper was ready to arm me against whoever was at the door. Nothing she has said has given me any reason to think she's not who she claims to be. And Chase? The Harpers have known him for years. He can't be part of the conspiracy. If the Harpers were okay, so was this Chase dude.

And indeed, once Mrs. Harper got him to stop talking about his friend from the Bureau of Indian Affairs, he turned to chattering about other things—the weather, his sister, his grandparents, local politics. It came out that Chase and Mrs. Harper were second cousins, and that Mrs. Harper's grandfather and Chase's grandmother were siblings who had lived their entire lives on a reservation down in Concho, Oklahoma. Finally, his sandwich was finished, he thanked Mrs. Harper profusely, and went back outside to finish mowing the lawn.

There was silence for a while, largely because Chris's mind was only occupied with one thing. He now knew where Elisa was, and he felt a sudden, overwhelming need to be with her, not to be alone in this terrible situation. Everything else—the Harpers, Chase Ballengee, the memories of his former life—faded into obscurity compared with the desperate desire to be with the only other person in the world facing this terror.

Mrs. Harper was standing at the sink, her back to Chris, washing the dishes. When she spoke suddenly, Chris jumped.

"Whatever it was you said, earlier, in front of Chase and me. It must have been important."

Chris cleared his throat, and finally said, quietly, "Yes."

"I thought so. You looked like you'd bitten into a thistle."

"I felt that way."

"You needn't fear speaking plainly in front of us," she said, still without turning. "It's safe here. We have no desire to harm you."

"Even Chase?"

Mrs. Harper laughed softly. It was the first time he had heard her laugh. "No," she said. "I've known Chase since he was a baby. He's a good man. A good man who's had a hard life so far. But no, you needn't fear Chase."

Chris didn't answer.

After a moment, Mrs. Harper turned, pulled a tea towel from a hook by the sink, and dried her hands. "You know," she said, "I think I see now that you were as scared of us as we were of you."

"I've been scared of everyone, since this started."

Mrs. Harper rehung the towel, came over, sat down at the dinner table across from him and looked at him appraisingly. "It's all too easy to think that everyone sees what you see. We all do it. I didn't trust you at first, because of that wanted poster, and the fact that you're a stranger. But it never occurred to me that you looked at us the same way. Not until now."

Chris nodded slowly. "I never have been paranoid," he said. "I always trusted people really easily."

"Better to, I'd say. Better than the opposite."

"Trusting people now could get me killed. I still don't know how to tell who is trustworthy and who isn't."

"Only God can see what's in a man's heart. The rest of us... well, we have to pray for guidance, and then do the best we can."

"What am I going to do?" Chris said. "I can't stay here forever. It's only been a day, and I'm already feeling that way. I need to keep moving west. I think that time is running out."

"Yes," Mrs. Harper said. After a moment's pause, she said, "These men who are after you. Do you know who they serve? I'm not talking about God and the Devil. I'm talking about here on Earth."

Chris shook his head.

"When you fight evil, the first thing you need is to know its name. Knowing an enemy's name keeps him in his proper proportion, you might say."

"How do I find out his name?"

Mrs. Harper looked at Chris for a moment without responding. He wondered if she was going to ask him to pray to Jesus again. But she finally reached out, and patted the back of his hand with her work-hardened one, and said, "When you need to know, you will."

· · · ·

Chris asked if there was anything he could do to help around the house, and the afternoon passed in menial chores that he suspected were more to give him something to occupy himself with than from any particular need. Late that afternoon, as Mrs. Harper prepared the evening meal of pork chops, broccoli, and cornbread, Chris checked his email again, and found another message from Elisa. It was a long one, this time.

> *Chris,*
> *I'm getting a little fretful that I haven't heard from you,*
> *but am consoling myself with the thought that it's probably*

that you haven't had access to a computer. I don't know if you got my last message. I hope so. And I hope that means you'll be able to find your way here.

In any case, I've continued trying to do some research, and I found something interesting.

Do you remember how I told you that I kept running into Gavin's posts on conspiracy websites, especially ones having to do with aliens? Well, I began going back through them, and I found that a couple of years ago, he started posting under a different name. Something spooked him, it seems. The link between the posts he made under his real name, and the ones under a pseudonym, was given away by someone else. Someone who posted under the name "Iktomi7979." Someone who appears to have known Gavin, and known about the entire episode. The seven of us, and what we supposedly saw.

It was on a thread on Reddit where people were making fun of alien abduction stories and that sort of thing. Here's what Iktomi7979 posted:

"It's fine for all of you to sneer and scoff. Keep doing it till they catch up with you, and yeah, I'm talking about the big THEY. I have a friend who's afraid to post under his real name now because THEY are after him. He and some friends had an experience when they were in college, and now he's afraid that THEY are trying to clean up the loose ends by getting rid of them. There are seven people who saw SOMETHING, and sooner or later, THEY will erase

them. All of them. Check out the posts from Reddit user "7MenInWhite7" and his blog, Shadows in the Cave."

I had already found Gavin's blog and his Reddit posts under "GMcCormick555," but the "7MenInWhite7" username was new. He apparently adopted it in 2011, when he thought it wasn't safe to post under his own name any more. And Chris—what he's posted, if it's real, is horrifying.

There's too much there to quote directly. Go to Reddit, if you can, and search that username. But the gist is that up in the Cascades, there's a government facility of some kind, entirely underground, that was engaged in some kind of surreptitious research into alien technology and biology. Scary stuff. Extending human life span through genetic engineering, mind manipulation, new types of weapons, faster-than-light propulsion.

He was cautious about giving too much detail. You could tell he was scared, but at the same time wanted the information to get out there. And the place he was talking about sounds, from the little bit of description he gave, like the area around Teanaway Pass and Lake Ingalls.

It sounds crazy, I know. But I think this has to be the connection. Now, the question is: if whoever is after all of us has killed five of us to keep us from giving away what we know, does that mean that all of Gavin's stuff about aliens and bioengineering and futuristic technology is true? Or is there another reason? Maybe we did see something in the *cave, and Gavin's memory filtered it through what he already thought was true. Remember, he was already into all that stuff, beforehand. So maybe part of it is true, and that's why they're after us.*

But if so, which part? How can we tell?

I should send this and get off the computer. I've already been at this most of the morning. In any case, I thought this was important.

Keep in touch if you can. Stay safe.

Love,

Elisa

Could that be it? Was there something there, in that cave, that none of them completely remembered? That Gavin, more than the others, was able to access, perhaps because he'd already been primed by his interest in the paranormal? It seemed far-fetched, but Chris had no better theory of his own. And somehow, there was another person, the mysterious Iktomi7979, who knew about the incident, and what it implied. Who that Iktomi7979 could be was uncertain. There was no one else in their circle of friends who had been close to all seven of them. Perhaps it was someone Gavin knew. Someone he'd become acquainted with during one of his flights of fancy in the world of conspiracy theories. But how, then, did he know about the six other members of the class? All of it had to tie back, somehow, to that trip into the Cascades. And it was beginning to seem inevitable. He was going back there, back to the rocky pass and the little glacial lake, back to where it had all begun thirty-odd years ago.

Perhaps if he could find Elisa, he could make sense of all of this. The two of them together might have a chance. But just him alone?

Not likely.

To Chris's rational mind, the idea that merely adding another person would make a difference in his likelihood of surviving seemed ridiculous. Especially given that the person in question was a fifty-something artist from St. Cloud, Minnesota. But on an instinctive level, it felt more than important, it felt necessary.

He *had* to meet up with Elisa. He had no doubt about it. If he wasn't able to do that, it would be tantamount to giving up and calling the number on the wanted poster himself.

Then a more sinister idea came to him.

Maybe his obsession with heading west was just another kill switch. Chris felt a shudder twang its way up his spine. Maybe whatever happened in that cave, it had somehow programmed him to return there if things started going awry. What if the people who were chasing him had introduced into him some sort of homing beacon thirty years earlier, and even now were using it to lure him in? Or worse, that it was impelling him to find Elisa, allowing Them to catch both of them together?

But there seemed no good answer to that. Whatever the reason, he knew that he would continue to travel west, as long as he was able to do so.

• • • •

Dinner was consumed in silence. Pork chops, fried until browned and bubbling with juice, were consumed, and then the best broccoli Chris had ever had, with butter and a little bit of garlic salt. The drippings of all of it mopped up with fresh-baked cornbread.

Sated, Chris leaned back in his chair, and Reverend Joe wiped his mouth and then his hands on his napkin, and said, "So, son, Mrs. Harper and I have been talking about what your next move should be."

Chris raised his eyebrows. As far as he'd seen, Mrs. Harper spent most of her time in housework, and the Reverend had been in his study for most of the day. When they'd had time to consult about their impromptu visitor's fate was hard to determine.

"We both agree that you can't stay here. But don't mistake me, it's not because you're any kind of a bother, or because we're concerned about our own safety. My sense is that you've given the people who are after you the slip."

"You really think so?" Chris tried to keep the doubt out of his voice, but he sounded dubious even in his own ears.

"I do," the Reverend said firmly. "If the men who are pursuing you knew you were here, they would have fallen upon this place like a pack of wolves. What, after all, could we do to protect you? It's been over a day, now, and there's been no sign of them. I believe that the only explanation for that is that they do not know where you are."

"But," Chris said, and let the word hang.

Reverend Joe laughed a little. "Yes," he said. "But. You can't stay here, as I said before. The Lord has given me to understand that you are to continue your journey, west. I don't know how to say this other than straight out. It is only by throwing yourself into the midst of lions that you will come forth unscathed."

Suddenly, Chris had a sense that they had connected. His rationalism and the Reverend's religion, though light years apart, had swung around to within the range of a handshake, only for a moment, and Chris knew for certain that the Reverend was right. Just as he had known earlier, without logic or reason, that he had to meet up with Elisa, he knew that it had to be soon.

"Yes," he said. "I think so, too. I said to Mrs. Harper earlier that I need to head west again."

Reverend Joe nodded solemnly. "I called Chase Ballengee. I told him that I would pay him to give you transportation, for as long as you needed it. I told him that it was risky. I didn't tell him everything, because Chase is a talker and sometimes doesn't know who he should talk to.

I told him that he should call his friend, Van Spaulding, and tell him that he's coming out for a visit. It's a reason that most everyone would think was natural, on account of Van's being a friend of the family."

"But why would Chase do something like that?" Chris said. "Even knowing the risk?"

"It's a fair question," Reverend Joe said, and frowned for a moment, as if trying to choose his words carefully. "I think the best way to explain it is to say that Chase has been waiting for something like this. Something bigger than he is, something bigger than drinking beer with his buddies down at the bar and grill. Something bigger than just earning enough to pay his rent and keep his car's gas tank filled. Chase needs this as much as you do." He regarded Chris with a level gaze, and added, "It's how redemption works, sometimes."

"I—" Chris said, and then stopped, swallowed. "I can pay him. You don't need…"

Reverend Joe held up one hand, and Chris stopped. "I'm doing this as much for Chase as for you. Chase hasn't had an easy time of it. It's hard, being an Indian. Harder still being a half-breed like Chase is, and his family from two different tribes. He doesn't belong anywhere. He's not white enough to pass for white, and not Indian enough to really be one of them, either. His parents split when he was three and his sister was one, and his father raised them both, till he was killed in a car wreck, driving drunk, when

Chase was only eleven years old. Then they moved in with their grandfather down in Oklahoma. Chase stayed down there until he was old enough to leave, then came back here and settled in to living hand-to-mouth, as he still does. His sister was luckier. Smarter, too. When the BIA helped her to get that scholarship, she took off and never looked back. And it's seemed to me that ever since then, Chase has been waiting. Waiting for something to happen, waiting for something that needed doing that only he could do."

"The Lord sent you," Mrs. Harper said to Chris, who regarded her with wide eyes and did not answer.

"So I talked to Chase about it. I told him the danger, that there were men after you, evil men who'd kill you, and kill him, too, without thought or conscience. He knows the danger. He said yes."

Without warning, Chris felt himself near tears. He wasn't a crier. The last time he'd cried had been at his father's funeral, ten years earlier. But before he could stop himself, his eyes had brimmed over. He only managed to say again, "I can... I can pay him," and then looked down, overcome, unable to speak, and wiped his eyes with the back of his hand.

Reverend Joe's words, when he spoke, seemed to be coming from a distance. "All of the world, everything in it, is God's charity," he said, and Chris felt as if he were floating, hearing a message echoing from the walls of a cathedral. "There is nothing here that is not a gift. It is only up to us to accept the gift, or reject it."

Then Chris looked up, and the world appeared suddenly to shrink back into the Harpers' clean, spare dining room. Reverend Joe and Mrs. Harper were sitting across from him, looking at him gravely over the plates and bowls and silverware and pork chop bones.

"If you decide to take our offer, you leave with him tomorrow at dawn."

•   •   •   •

The sun had not yet angled its first rays over the horizon when Chris, with Baxter at his heels, walked out of the Harpers' house into their front driveway. Chase Ballengee was already standing there, grinning and wearing a University of Nebraska baseball cap, leaning against a rusty blue Chevy sedan of uncertain age.

"Mornin', Mr. Lake," Chase said, and gave a little wave of his hand. "Nice we're startin' in the cool of the mornin'. It's gonna be a hot one today, I think."

"It's Chris, please," Chris said. "And thanks. It's nice of you to do this."

"Oh, hell, it's no problem," Chase said. "I'd do anything for the Reverend and Mrs. Harper. They're like parents to me. And it'll be nice to go out and visit Van Spaulding. I haven't seen him in an age. I'll get to meet his wife and kids."

"How long do you think it'll take us to get there?"

"I was lookin' at a map last night. I figure we'll take Highway 26 up toward Scottsbluff and into Wyoming, and then pick up Interstate 25. That'll take us all the way into Montana, and then it's I-90 the rest of the way to Washington State." He shrugged. "Don't guess we'll get much further than the Montana border by tonight, and that's probably pushin' it. But we'll get as far as we can get. I'm guessin' that day after tomorrow, probably late afternoon, we should see the Pacific Ocean."

"Have you ever been there before?"

"Nope." Chase looked off toward the west, his back to the horizon where the sun was staining a thin line of clouds rose-pink. "Always been a dream o' mine, to see the ocean. I called Van last night, he said he had a boat and'd take me out on it, right the hell out into the Pacific." He turned back to Chris, his smile gleaming in the dim light. "Always gets me to thinkin', you know? When I see pictures of it. You're standin' on the beach, lookin' west, and there's nothin' between you and Japan and China and Russia. Nothin' but a big ol' bunch o' salt water. How can you look at that, and not feel like, man, I am so small."

"I don't know," Chris said.

"I'm not sure I'd want to live there. Hard to imagine how you'd want to be reminded of that, day in, day out. How little you are, how huge the world is. I do want to visit it, though. See it, stick my feet in it, just so I can say I did."

"It's cold," Chris said, with a smile.

"Don't matter. Still gotta do it."

"I suppose so."

The front door of the Harpers' house opened, and Mrs. Harper walked out, followed by Reverend Joe, leaning heavily on his steel cane. Mrs. Harper was carrying a plastic shopping bag, weighed down and bulging.

"Can we get you some breakfast, Chase?" she said. "There's more bacon and eggs, it'd be easy to fix you a plate before you go."

"No, thank you, Mrs. Harper. I had some coffee and a donut before I left, that'll keep me fine for a while."

She nodded, and handed him the bag. "Here's some sandwiches for your lunch. You've got some miles to cover before you get anywhere there'll be a place to find food, so I wanted to see you off provisioned."

"Thank you kindly, Mrs. Harper."

"Before you leave," Reverend Joe said, "I will ask for God's blessing on your journey."

Chase's smile vanished, and he removed his cap, and bowed his head. Mrs. Harper closed her eyes. Chris, a little uncomfortably, looked down at his feet.

"Dear God our Father," Reverend Joe said, "I ask your blessing on these two men as they undertake this journey. Place your hand over them, and see them safely to journey's end. Lead them by the hand to where you intend, and may all work out as you have in your great wisdom planned. And until they arrive home, keep their steps sure-footed on the high road, with their eyes facing forward and their hearts and wills always guided by the Divine. We ask this in the name of your son, Jesus Christ. Amen."

Chase and Mrs. Harper said, quietly, "Amen."

Chris just cleared his throat, and looked up.

"There is a reason to all of this," Reverend Joe said, looking Chris directly in the eyes. "Do not doubt it. Be of courage. There are greater forces than you or I know at work here, and I think you will face many trials before this is over."

"I know," Chris said.

"Then go, and be steadfast. And you, Chase, take care and come back soon. You will be in our prayers."

"Thank you, Reverend."

Chase got into the driver's seat, and Chris opened the back door of the Chevy for Baxter, who jumped in, totally unconcerned. Chris got into the passenger side and closed the door. The interior smelled like corn chips and cheap beer, but it had been cleaned recently. Most likely the previous evening.

Chase started up the engine, which coughed and shuddered before catching. He revved the motor and put the car in gear. The wheels crunched on gravel as he pulled out toward the road.

Chris turned in his seat, and saw, standing like statues bronzed with the first rays of sunlight, the figures of the

Reverend and his wife. Mrs. Harper raised one hand in farewell.

Then the old Chevy turned down the road toward the center of town, and the Harpers were lost to sight.

CHAPTER 15

By the time Chris had gone thirty miles in Chase Ballengee's car, he had noticed something decidedly odd about his traveling companion's conversational style.

Chase was friendly, open, and chatty. It wasn't fifteen minutes into their drive together that Chris found out that Chase had a girlfriend named Claire who was "sweet as anything" and also "awesome in bed." Chase's sister, in her last year at the University of Nebraska, was living with a graduate student named Rich Gaither, and she was afraid to tell their grandmother of their living arrangements. Chase was currently unemployed, but had been at times a letter carrier for the US Postal Service, a checkout clerk at the Ogallala Safeway, and a groundskeeper at the Ogallala Quality Inn. None of these jobs had lasted more than six months. "Got bored," was the comment append-ed to each.

But Chase didn't talk only about himself. He was curi-ous, too, about Chris. What was New York like? Chase expressed surprise to find out that Guildford was a rural farming community. "I always thought New York State was all city," was Chase's comment, along with a genial laugh at having been proven wrong.

"You got a girlfriend?" Chase asked, one hand resting easy on the wheel, his face in a broad smile.

"Not at the moment," Chris said.

"Well, why the hell not? Guys got needs, you know what I mean?" He thwacked Chris's arm with his free hand. "Of course you know what I mean."

"Never did meet the right woman," Chris said. "I guess I've gotten used to being single."

"That's too bad. You should keep looking, though. Never know when you'll find someone, and then, bam! You're in over your head. In a good way, of course." He frowned. "So, what is teaching like?"

Chris smiled at Chase's ability to switch gears with lightning speed. "It's a good job. I still like it, even after doing it for all of these years."

"How d'you put up with all of those teenagers?"

"I like their energy. Even if it's overwhelming at times. It keeps me from getting old, fat, and lazy."

Chase guffawed. "I suppose," he said. "But even so, I'd want to smack some of 'em. I couldn't barely put up with myself at that age."

That was when Chris noticed something peculiar about Chase's chatter. All through the conversation, as it flitted from one topic to the next, Chase never asked about the one thing that was most on Chris's mind. Why was he fleeing across the country? Who was chasing him, and why were there people who wanted to kill him?

They approached the rugged, windswept terrain south of where Highway 26 crossed the North Platte River, where bare limestone bluffs suddenly reared up from the rolling farm country behind them, like an omen of the Rocky Mountain foothills still invisible in the distance. There were few cars on the road, and Chase steered with one hand, his left elbow resting easily on the open window frame of the door, his free hand moving only to gesture as he spoke. Chris looked ahead, as the road looped forward over the hills. The sun was still low in the sky, but the temperature was already climbing.

Despite the warmth, a chill shuddered its way up Chris's backbone. Something was wrong. There was something abnormal about Chase, his easy acquiescence to driving him to Washington, his seeming lack of car-

ing about why he needed to do it. Thomas T. Champion
had asked Chris about his predicament. He hadn't pushed
when Chris didn't want to talk, but he'd shown ordinary
curiosity about this middle-aged schoolteacher, suddenly
flung out into the unknown, fleeing as if the hounds of hell
were at his heels.

Chase, though, hadn't asked a single question about
it. For all his interest in Chris's home town, his career, his
love life, Chase seemed to have no interest in the oddest
thing of all.

Which would make sense if Chase already knew what
was going on. If he was one of *Them*.

Seemingly unaware of Chris's dark thoughts, Chase
prattled on about his loyalty to the University of Nebraska
baseball and football teams. Chris suppressed an urge to
shout, "Shut up!" at this seemingly cheerful and voluble
young man, to demand that he pull the car over and let
him out, leave him by the side of the road.

He must be one of *Them*, Chris thought. Why else
would he not be at least a little curious? Why wouldn't he
ask questions?

I fucking sure would ask questions, if it was me.

But then a calmer voice carried the thought further.
What if the Reverend told him not to ask? That'd explain
it. Maybe Reverend Joe said to him, "Look, do this for me.
This guy is in trouble, and needs help." Chase said he'd
do anything for the Harpers. Maybe that's all there is to

it. Chase had been commanded by the Reverend not to mention Chris's plight. Maybe he had even been coached, in terms of, "you know, poor guy, he doesn't need you pestering him about it. Keep the conversation on other subjects."

Nothing sinister there. Nothing to worry about. Still, Chris thought he'd give it a test, and when there was a lull in Chase's chatter, Chris said, "I gotta wonder, though. After all of this is over, will I ever be able to return back to my home? Will it be safe to…?"

But Chase interrupted him, pointing excitedly up through the windshield, craning his neck. "Look! A Prairie Falcon! I love them. You ever thought what it'd be like to be a bird? Able to fly, and all? That's gotta be so much fun!"

Chris looked at him for a moment, and then said, "Yeah."

"Man, I'd love to have wings. Big ol' feathery wings, comin' right up from my shoulders. That'd be the coolest thing ever." He looked over at Chris and grinned. "Give you a hell of a time findin' shirts to fit, though, wouldn't it? And flyin' around with no shirt in the middle of winter'd get a little cold. Freeze your freakin' nipples off." He laughed at his own joke.

"I suppose so."

Then it was back to the topic of women (which seemed to be Chase's personal favorite), beer, and the various antics of his friends and family members, as they crossed the

North Platte, and angled west toward the Wyoming border.

Chris tried to test his hypothesis two more times. East of the little village of Torrington, Wyoming, he said, "I hope that we've shaken off the guys who…" but was immediately cut off by Chase.

"You know, this road takes the same path as the Oregon Trail? Keep goin' on it, and it'll take you all the way through Hell's Half Acre and over the mountains, and then down to the Pacific in Oregon. We're not goin' that way, o' course, but it's funny to think that there's a highway runnin' all the way from Ogallala to Oregon, and that it's the same path the western settlers took a hundred and fifty years ago."

Chris nodded, and the conversation spun off into talk about the Mormons and the Emigrant Trail and the Forty-Niners and the Donner Party.

It wasn't until after they'd passed the town of Lingle, Wyoming, population 476, that he had another chance. About five miles out of Lingle, Chase braked to a stop on the side of the road. Chris looked at him questioningly.

"Need to take a piss," Chase said.

Chase trotted around to the passenger side of the car, unzipped, and peed into the grass, unconcerned with the occasional car that zoomed past. After a moment, Chris gave a mental shrug, got out, let Baxter out of the back seat, and the two of them followed suit.

More comfortable, all three returned to the car, but

instead of starting the engine, Chase twisted around in the seat and picked up the grocery sack that Mrs. Harper had given him. "I'm hungry. You?"

"Definitely."

He opened the bag, and pulled out neatly-packaged ham sandwiches, each with lettuce (somewhat wilted by now, but still nice) and a big slice of tomato. There were water bottles for each of them. Suddenly Chase laughed, and said, "Man, she thinks of everything," and tossed Chris a ziplock bag full of dog kibble.

Once everyone was eating, Chris with the door open and one foot on the ground, he looked over at Chase and said, "It sure was nice having home-cooked meals. I hadn't had a meal like that since I had to leave my…"

"Traffic's picking up," Chase said, interrupting and gesturing with one hand at an eighteen-wheeler zooming by. "Guess we're not far from I-25. Bound to be more cars, I suppose. O' course, once we get on the interstate, we'll be able to make better time. See how fast this old baby can go, yeah?" He smiled at Chris, and then took another bite of his sandwich.

"Yeah," Chris said.

• • • •

They passed Fort Laramie—*Home of 250 Good People, and 6 Soreheads*—and Guernsey—*A Community of Good*

Neighbors—as the land gradually wrinkled into arid hills, studded with ponderosa pine and Rocky Mountain juniper. A little after one, they saw the sign that said, *I-25, Cheyenne/Casper, 1 mile,* and Chase gave an excited whoop and punched the accelerator nearly to the floor.

"That means we're really on our way," he said. "Long as we're on 26, it feels like we barely left home, you know? 26 runs right through town. But when we get on the interstate, then we're off and away. Out in the big ol' world, where no one can find us."

Chris looked over at Chase sharply, but Chase still had a genial smile on his face, and didn't seem to notice Chris's questioning frown. He swept upward on the turn signal lever as the on ramp to I-25 angled off to the right, and then merged onto the freeway, north toward Casper, and ultimately, the Montana border.

Chris asked if Chase needed a break from driving, and received a cheerful, "No, I love bein' behind the wheel. You relax and enjoy the ride!" Reassured, Chris dozed for a good bit of the afternoon. Casper went by in a fast-evaporating spike in the traffic, and soon they were heading north into craggy, ever-rising hill country. Chase seemed to have exhausted his topics for conversation, although he did alert Chris when they crossed the South Fork of the Powder River.

"Now that's crossin' into the Wild West," Chase said, gesturing at the steel span connecting the two sides of the gorge. Chris looked out his window at the rail zipping past, to the water glittering in its meandering course below. "There's nothin' but hard-edged cowboys out in this country, even today. Hasn't changed much in a hundred years, 'cept for the highway cuttin' through. Hard to imagine how they lived out here, back in the day, with no central heatin' and no grocery stores, and whatnot. It gets cold enough back home, but here they get blizzards, howlin' down from the mountains. Kill a man, if he's foolish enough to go outside. Then, in summer, it's hot as the hubs o' hell and dry as a bone, 'cept right next to the river, and the soil is too rocky to till. And still there's folks livin' here, folks have lived here for thousands of years. The cowboys, and before them, the Northern Cheyenne and Shoshone. They survived, somehow. I don't know how."

"You learn to survive, I guess. The ones that didn't, didn't leave any descendants."

"You're right about that. Or moved on to a place where they didn't have to work so hard to survive. No wonder some of the people passin' through didn't make it. It was hard ol' times, back then. Hard ol' times."

Chris looked at the arid, rock-strewn wilderness sliding past them, and tried to imagine surviving there in summer, much less in winter, when the temperatures could drop to fifty degrees below zero.

Chris was fighting to survive, too. He didn't know which was worse, to fight against the elements, or to fight against humans. The elements, at least, play fair. They may be unpredictable, they may not care about your survival. They might strike you down as casually as a person swatting a fly. But that was nothing compared to the worst that humans could do. The elements don't deceive, don't lead you into trust only to destroy it. Only humans do that.

•   •   •   •

The sun was dropping toward the western horizon as they approached Sheridan, Wyoming. Fifty miles earlier, they had hit the point where I-25 ended at I-90, the highway on which Chris had started his headlong flight west, and the one that would carry them all the way to Washington State. They merged smoothly onto I-90 West, heading toward Sheridan, the Montana border, and points beyond.

"Sheridan's gonna be our best bet for dinner," Chase said, and pointed to signs for restaurants zipping by on the right, hard to read in the failing light.

"Hey, how about that?" Chris said, as they passed a sign that said *High Point Café, Exit 23, 5930 Rt. 336 West— Breakfast/Lunch/Dinner—free computer use/WiFi hotspot.* "I'd like to check my email."

"Sure," Chase said, and when Exit 23 loomed up on the right, he took it. "How we gonna find the place, though? I don't have a map, and I'd prefer not to wander around too long lookin' for it."

"No problem," Chris said. "Just if it's convenient. Let's see if it's close to the exit. Otherwise we can stop anywhere."

As it turned out, the café had a tall sign and was near the freeway. It was busy, but there were several open computers along a row of windows at the front. Chris ordered a BLT and a large iced tea, Chase a reuben and a Pepsi, and after getting the username and password to access the café's WiFi network, they went to sit down.

"I'm just as glad to be away from them things," Chase said, gesturing at the monitor. "Can't stand computers, myself. I barely tolerate telephones, to be honest. I got my first cellphone last year, 'cause my girlfriend insisted."

Chris smiled. "I want to see if someone's contacted me," he said. He looked up at Chase, one eyebrow raised. "A lady friend."

Chase looked at him, his mouth hanging open a little, for several seconds, before leaning back and guffawing. "I knew it! I knew it! Nice lookin' fellow like you, and no woman? I shoulda known you were pullin' my leg. Well, go ahead, you check your email and whatnot. I don't mind."

Chris, still smiling, signed into his Gmail account, but a quick scan showed no new emails from ereed@orions-belt.com. He frowned a little, but realized that he'd been fairly intermittent in his contacts, too.

Chris shivered. He was fleeing across the country. She, on the other hand, was stuck in a friend's house, with nothing better to do. Every time he'd checked, there'd been a new email from her, and now, nothing.

Something was wrong.

The sandwiches and drinks were delivered by a smiling young waitress who looked like she was only about fifteen. Chase immediately took a big bite of his, and looked out the window at the cars whizzing by.

Chris ate his sandwich more slowly, as he looked back down his list of new emails. No, nothing from Elisa. There was another one from his principal, with the subject line, "Hope all's okay…" He didn't open it. Others were from the astronomy listserv he belonged to, or were obvious junk mail.

Then he noticed a message that he'd overlooked the first time, assuming it was spam. It had the subject line, "Open this. Important." The email address it was sent from was a Yahoo account, the username a random string of numbers and letters.

Chris clicked on it, and saw the following message:

Mr. Franzia:

We know where you are. You are putting others' lives at risk by your foolish attempts to evade us.

We have Ms. Elisa Reed in our custody. She is, as of right now, unharmed. If you would like her to remain that way, you should proceed to the Ranchester Turnaround, fifteen miles south of the Montana border on Interstate 90 westbound.

We will be waiting for you. We will give you until 9 p.m. this evening, Sunday, July 14, to meet us here.

It will be unfortunate if you do not check your email, or worse, choose to ignore it, because at 9:01 it will be our unfortunate duty to execute Ms. Reed. In the time between then and when we finally catch up with you and finish you off as well, her blood will be on your hands.

The decision is yours to make.

There was no signoff.

Chris set the remains of his sandwich back in his plate, his hand moving in slow motion. He swiveled around to face Chase, who had just popped the last bite of his reuben into his mouth.

"You," Chris said, his mouth dry. "You told them where Elisa was."

Chase looked at Chris, his perpetual smile fading a little. "Told them? Told who?"

"The people who are chasing me. You told them where she was. You overheard what I said yesterday, about Hoquiam, and you told them. It has to be you. You were the only one other than Mrs. Harper who knew."

"Chris…" Chase began, trying to smile again, and failing.

"You've been working for them all along, haven't you? It's why you agreed to take me. It's why you change the subject every time I mention anything about why I'm on the road."

"No," Chase said. "That's not true. The Reverend, he told me not to try to talk to you about your troubles. He says I talk too much, which is true, I guess, and he said that you had a weighty secret. That's what he called it. 'But it won't be lessened by you bothering him about it,' he told me. 'It's his burden to carry, his alone, and you see to it you remember that.'"

Chris's eyes were narrowed to slits, as he regarded Chase, who was squirming in his seat. "No. The only other one was Mrs. Harper. And you can't be asking me to believe that she is on the side of the people who are trying to kill me."

"No!" Chase said. "Mrs. Harper is a woman of God, she would never…"

"Then tell me!" shouted Chris, his anger bursting like a grenade. He grabbed Chase by the sleeve, and pulled him close, close enough to see the sweat standing out on his forehead. "You fucking bastard! Tell me why you did it! Tell me why you sold us out!"

"I didn't! I swear to Jesus Christ I didn't! I didn't say nothin' to no one with any ill intent, I promised the Reverend I'd protect you! He said you were in some kind o' bad danger, and that I was to do whatever I had to to see you safe where you were goin', and I swear by the Lord's name I did just that! I never talked about it to no one 'cept people like the Harpers who only want what's right and good!"

Chris let Chase's sleeve go, and slumped in his chair. Restaurant patrons, turning with concerned faces to see if a fight was about to break out, returned to their dinners and their laptops and their conversations. Chris put a hand over his face.

"How can you really expect me to believe that?" he said. "No one else knew. The message was in a code that only Elisa and I could break. The only other ones who could have deciphered it are dead, dead like Elisa and I will soon be. If it wasn't you, then who was it?"

"I don't know," Chase said, his voice quaking.

"Look," Chris said, looking up suddenly. Chase started, his eyes widening, as if he expected Chris to grab him again. "There's no more reason to lie. I'm here, out in the middle of a state where I know no one. Someone I care deeply about is in the hands of the people who are trying to kill us both, and I have no choice but to meet them and probably get killed myself in the process. I can't run any more, not if the result will be Elisa's death. There is no more reason for you to lie. Even if it's just to tell me I'm right, and that you're on their side, and that I'm going to be dead in an hour. Level with me. Just tell me the fucking truth, okay? That's all I ask."

And Chase looked him straight in the eye, and said, his voice still quavering a little, "Mr. Lake, I swear, with the Lord Jesus Christ Almighty as my witness. I never let the evil men know about where you were going, nor where

your girlfriend was, either. I only used my cellphone a cou-
pla times since we left, to call Reverend Joe, and let him
know we were okay, and to call my friend back in Ogallala
to tell him the same thing. If I sold you out, how would I
have done it? And when?"

Chris stood up, and shut off the computer, leaving
the rest of his dinner untouched on the plate. He threw a
twenty-dollar bill on the counter, and walked out.

A friend back in Ogallala. Who was the friend, Chris
wondered? It didn't matter now. The game was up.

Chris thought about people getting their last meal before being executed, and wondered how someone could
get down a t-bone steak and baked potato and dessert, all
along knowing that the electric chair was waiting for them
a few hours later.

Half a BLT was all Chris would carry to his grave.

He walked out of the café, Chase trotting after him.

"Where are you going?" Chase called out. "You gonna
run?"

Chris made a dismissive noise. "No. I'm not going to run.
I told you that. And you're coming with me. We're going to
the Ranchester Turnaround. It's only another ten miles further along I-90. And then we'll see if you're lying or not."

"I'm not," Chase said, as they climbed back into the
car, a stubborn note entering his voice. Baxter gave a hopeful wag to ask if there were leftovers, but Chris reached
back and gave him a skritch on the ears.

"Sorry, Bax, old buddy," he said. "In twenty minutes or so, we may have way bigger problems than no table scraps."

. . . .

The drive to Ranchester proceeded in silence, although Chris felt like his heart was pounding so hard that it must be audible to Chase. He was strung out to some extremity of emotion, scared, angry, desperate, resigned, furious at having been betrayed, grief-stricken that Elisa had been caught. There was even a slight tincture of hope there, that somehow, some way he would escape again, that he could free Elisa, that it would still all end okay.

Was Chase lying? The miles slipped past in the fading light. What reason would he have to keep up the subterfuge once he was found out, once it was obvious Chris wasn't going to try to run, that they had him cornered, and that he was going to the rendezvous to turn himself in?

He looked over at Chase, whose narrow, aquiline profile showed no more of the cheerful camaraderie he'd expressed during the first part of the journey. He looked terrified, to be truthful, his lips pinched into a thin line, his eyes wide as he stared straight ahead on the highway. He looked as if he were as scared as Chris was, perhaps more so.

Questions flooded Chris's mind. If it wasn't Chase, then how did they find out? Did they pinpoint Elisa's computer? Or was it some other way? How could they trace her computer now, if all the emails she'd sent before weren't enough? If it wasn't Chase, or one of the Harpers, then it had to be that someone was able to crack the code.

But *how?*

Chris saw a sign that said, *Exit 16, Decker Road, Decker MT, Next Right. Ranchester Turnaround, One Mile.* His heart gave a painful leap in his chest. He was going to need some serious therapy if he made it through this alive. He fought off a strange urge to laugh.

"There it is," he said, pointing.

Chase put on his turn signal and braked to slow down for the turnaround. It was nothing more than a looped bit of pavement with a picnic bench, a garbage can, and an open shelter with one light bulb glowing in the darkness. Chris could see a car parked there, its lights off. There was no way to tell make or model, or even its color. Everything around them was fading to slate gray.

Chase pulled in, stopped, shut off the engine, and then looked over at Chris.

"Whaddya want me to do?" he said, his voice thin. "The Reverend said I had to protect you."

"It doesn't matter," Chris said. "I know what I have to do. All the protection in the world probably wouldn't do me any good now. Save yourself. Get in the car, and drive. Take care of my dog, okay? That's all I ask."

Chris got out, and shut the door, leaving Baxter safely inside Chase's car. Much to his surprise, Chase got out, too, and followed, walking slowly about ten feet behind him.

Two figures came out of the shadows.

Chase gave an inarticulate squeak of terror, and got out only two words. "You? No…"

He turned, and sprinted back toward the car. Chris turned toward him, but one of the two figures elbowed him out of the way, knocking him sprawling onto the dry, dusty ground. A hand came up, then the other, and there was a gunshot.

Chase Ballengee flung both arms upwards, like a man shouting hallelujah at a revival, and fell headlong onto the pavement only five feet from his car. He didn't move again.

Chris scrambled into a crouching position, gasping for breath, as the second figure came running up to the first. At that moment, an eighteen-wheeler roared by on the freeway behind them, and the headlights briefly caught the two men who were standing over Chris full in the face.

Hargis and Drolezki.

CHAPTER 16

hris choked out, "What are you doing? He was helping me!" But neither man was looking at him.

They were facing each other. Drolezki, still holding the gun with which he had shot Chase Ballengee, was regarding his partner with eyes that had gone hard, glittering like pieces of quartz in the feeble glow of the light on the corner of the picnic shelter. Hargis looked at his partner with an uncomprehending frown, a dazed expression like that of a man just awakened from a sound sleep.

"Mark, what the hell? We were supposed to…"

"I know," Drolezki said, interrupting. "But you're

assuming that we're following orders from the same people."

And he shot Hargis in the middle of his chest.

Hargis staggered backward and collapsed to his knees, still looking up at Drolezki with the same perplexed frown. He opened his mouth, but no words came out. Then he pitched forward onto the dusty ground.

Drolezki, his formerly genial, teenage-boy face now ruthless and cold, turned towards Chris. Chris stared down the gun's barrel, the black hole looking like the pupil of an eye.

This was it.

He was going to die, right here, in a pulloff in Wyoming. He wondered if it was going to hurt. It probably would, at least for a while. But then, being dead, that wouldn't hurt. It would be nothing. He wondered who'd claim his body.

Thoughts scrolled through Chris's mind in seconds, and then they were gone, replaced by a sudden, animal desperation to survive at all costs. He weighed his options. Was there a way to get away without being shot in the back, the way Chase Ballengee had died?

Drolezki gave a little motion with his gun.

"Into the car," he said.

"You're not going to kill me?" Chris said, and was immediately embarrassed at how terrified he sounded.

"Not for the time being," Drolezki said. He flicked the gun at Chris again. "Later, you might find yourself wishing I had put a bullet between your eyes here. Now, get in the fucking car."

Chris got up. His knees felt wobbly, weak, and the dry wind turned sweaty patches on his shirt to chilly, clammy spots that clung to his skin. He looked over at Chase's car. Baxter was watching him through the passenger side window, his earnest and rather silly face full of canine worry.

"What about my dog?" he asked. He found he couldn't say anything more, his voice catching in his throat.

Drolezki stared at Chris for a moment. "Leave him," he said, in an uninflected voice. "Believe me, he's better off here. Someone'll find him."

"But..." Chris started, and stumbled again, stopped.

"No. Into the car. Now. Or it ends here, like it did with your friend." Drolezki nodded toward the inert figure of Chase, still lying where he'd fallen beside his car.

Chris got into the car, the same white sedan that he'd seen, ages ago it seemed, sitting in his driveway on the last day of school. Drolezki climbed into the driver's seat, pressed the button to lock the doors, and holstered his pistol. Evidently, he didn't think much of Chris's ability to defend himself. The agent looked completely at ease, entirely in charge of the situation.

"What about Chase? And Hargis?" Chris asked, as Drolezki started the engine. "You can't leave two dead bodies lying there."

Drolezki didn't meet his eyes. "We have people whose

job is to clean up the loose ends. They'll be here shortly. If anyone sees the bodies before then, well, they'll call the police, and the Wyoming state cops will have another couple of random, puzzling murders on their books for the people on *Cold Justice* to talk about."

He reached under the seat, pulled out a set of handcuffs, and cuffed Chris's right hand to the door handle. "In case you were thinking about doing anything stupid. For what it's worth, it's hard to survive jumping out of a moving car, despite what the movies'd have you believe. You hit the pavement doing sixty-five miles per hour, you turn into ground beef."

Drolezki pulled back out onto I-90. Chris turned, and the last thing he saw as they left the Ranchester Turnaround was Baxter's face, filled with puzzled incomprehension, watching them drive away.

Chris looked out the window as the shadowy crags of the Rocky Mountain foothills flickered by the car.

They got me. His mental voice sounded breathless and a little incredulous. *They finally got me. I never thought Drolezki was one of* Them. *I suspected Hargis, at first, but I never thought about Drolezki. He seemed like a comical sidekick.*

Ten minutes later, a blue sign saying "Welcome to Montana" loomed up in the glare from the headlights. It was shaped like the state outline, with a circle in the center showing a pair of snow-topped mountain peaks.

"Where are you taking me?" Chris said.

"You don't need to know that."

"Is Elisa still alive?"

"For the time being."

"Why didn't you kill us, like you killed the others?"

Drolezki glared. "I'm not going to spend this entire drive answering questions. Most of them I probably won't be able to answer."

Chris looked at him for a moment through narrowed eyes. "Who are you?" he suddenly asked.

A corner of the agent's mouth twitched. "Mark Drolezki. FBI."

"How long have you had that identity?"

Drolezki snorted derisively and didn't answer.

"Then at least tell me this much," Chris persisted. "All along, you've been trying to find the two of us so you can kill us. The last of the seven. And now, you have the chance. You could have shot me, like you did Chase and Hargis. And you've got Elisa, too. Why not kill us and be done with it?"

"You're making an assumption when you say that we killed the others."

"Oh, come on," Chris said. "Like there's any other explanation."

"Suit yourself."

"You were trying to kill me before, though. Those bullets in the motel parking lot in Missouri weren't meant as warning shots."

Drolezki gave a harsh sigh. "Let's just say my orders have changed."

"Why?"

"*Stop* with the goddamned questions."

"Look," Chris shouted. "You hold all the cards. I'm handcuffed in your car, being taken God knows where. You can kill me any time you like. Same, I'd guess, as Elisa. So at least tell me what's going on. I figure that in a day, maybe two, I'll be dead anyway, so what possible harm can it do?"

Drolezki looked over at Chris, as if he were evaluating him. "I never would have guessed that you'd give us this much trouble," he said. "I figured it was just a matter of waiting till you were taken care of, one way or the other. You gave us a good run, though. I gotta admit."

"So answer my questions."

Another sigh. "As much as I can, okay. I guess you're right, I can't see it changing the outcome any."

That was easier than he thought it would be. He'd figured Drolezki would just tell him to shut up.

"Why are you keeping Elisa and me alive?" he asked.

"There were hints in the emails you exchanged. We want to see how much you know, and find out who you talked to."

"Before you kill us both and take care of anyone we might have talked to that could cause problems later."

"More or less."

"What if I don't cooperate? What if I refuse to talk?"

"Not recommended," Drolezki said flatly.

Chris suppressed a shudder at how matter-of-fact he made that phrase sound, despite what it implied. Time to change the subject. "Who is Iktomi7979?"

Drolezki's brows drew together into a thunderous scowl. "Very funny," he growled. "Next question."

Chris frowned. That was a peculiar response. It seemed pretty certain, however, that persisting on that topic wouldn't accomplish anything. "Okay," he said, "why did you kill Chase Ballengee?"

To Chris's surprise, Drolezki's expression immediately lightened. This was evidently a question he'd anticipated and didn't mind answering. He shrugged. "Collateral damage. Given that he'd traveled with you, we'd probably have had to get rid of him eventually anyway. My supervisors don't like loose ends. Loose ends have a way of coming unraveled eventually."

"And Chase was a loose end."

"Yes."

"He looked like he recognized you. Right before you shot him."

Drolezki gave Chris a hard look. "Can't see how that would be possible."

"What about Hargis? Hargis didn't know about you?"

"Didn't know I was working for the other side?" Drolezki laughed. "No. Hargis was a good soldier and assumed that everyone around him at the Bureau was, too. I had a couple of close calls with him. But I finally realized that he did what all people from his cut do. They decide what people are, and after that there's no changing it. Hargis wasn't hard to fool, because once he came to a decision about who a person was, it would have taken an act of Congress to change it. He was so loyal, he couldn't imagine disloyalty in the people around him."

"Didn't mind betraying him yourself, though?" Chris looked at Drolezki, waiting to see if his question had pushed him too far, whether he'd snap at him angrily, or possibly refuse to talk further.

All he did was continue smiling. And he said, "There's more at stake here than Hargis was worth. I waited until I had no choice but to blow my cover. After that, Hargis was expendable."

"Expendable," Chris repeated.

"Yes."

"Like Elisa and me."

"You two don't even rank on that scale. If you weren't wanted for questioning, you'd already be dead."

Chris looked back out the window. It was completely dark now. Only the headlights of the occasional oncoming car cut into the blackness, with a harsh white glare that illuminated nothing.

"I suppose you were the one who poisoned the beer in my fridge and killed Adam Parrish."

"Nope. Sorry. I had nothing to do with that."

"But you would have been happy if I'd been the one who was killed."

"It'd have been a shitload less work," Drolezki said.

"So Adam was expendable, too."

"Of course."

Chris looked at him in silence for a moment. "You sonofabitch," he finally said, in a low, intense voice. "You aren't even human."

Drolezki didn't meet Chris's stare. He simply kept driving, looking through the windshield at the interstate winding away west in front of them. "You might want to save your bluster for my superiors," he finally said, chuckling a little. "Compared to them, I'm a pushover."

· · · ·

Despite knowing that he was almost certainly being taken to his death, Chris was able to sleep. Somewhere in the black Montana night, he slipped into a doze, then into a deep, dreamless sleep. When he finally awoke, some hours later, he blinked groggily, not able at first to make sense of his surroundings until the pain in his wrist reminded him that he was still handcuffed in Drolezki's car. It was dark, but behind them there was a trace of pearl gray in the eastern sky. The dashboard clock's red numerals told him that it was a little before five in the morning.

He looked over at Drolezki, who was still sitting in the same position as he had been earlier, one hand resting on the steering wheel. His round face showed no sign of fatigue.

"Don't you need to sleep?" Chris asked, his voice sounding slurred and indistinct.

Drolezki snorted. "You offering to drive?"

"No. I figured you'd have pulled over and taken a nap by now."

"No need. We have ways to avoid having to sleep. It's convenient."

"Not sleeping makes you crazy," Chris said. "It only takes a few days' worth of missed sleep to make you start hallucinating. I'm a biology teacher, remember? We know these things."

"Thanks for the concern, but as far as the biology you think you know, you might want to forget all of it. Most of it is wrong."

"How do you know that?"

Drolezki didn't respond.

"What happened to 'it doesn't matter, because you're gonna die anyway.'"

"I already told you. I wasn't sent to answer your questions. I was sent either to dispose of you or else bring you back. So shut up and let me drive."

Chris looked around him at the gradually lightening landscape sliding past the window. He saw rugged peaks

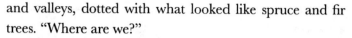

and valleys, dotted with what looked like spruce and fir trees. "Where are we?"

"You don't give up, do you? We just cleared Coeur d'Alene, Idaho. We'll be crossing into Washington before sunrise."

Chris shuddered. He'd always intended to go back to Washington after he left. He'd had friends there, many of whom had given him a standing invitation to visit. When he was hired to teach biology at Guildford High School, he had considered many times heading back out for a visit over the summer, but at first the cost of airline tickets was an impediment, and after a few years, other priorities replaced returning to the Pacific Northwest.

Now he was going back, under circumstances he'd never have imagined. He would have liked to see Deirdre, Glen, Gavin, and the rest one more time. Shoot the breeze, have a beer. Instead, they were all dead.

And soon he would be, too.

He wondered if *They* would track down all of the people Chris had interacted with along the way. The Harpers, Thomas T. Champion, the boy in the tollbooth, maybe even Luanne at the Super 8 Motel in Erie, Pennsylvania. Loose ends. Would all of them be eradicated, erased, found dead in bed one morning or killed in a hit-and-run? Taken out simply because they'd had the ill fortune to cross paths with Chris?

This got Chris thinking about his college friends again,

how they'd all teased Gavin about his interest in conspiracy theories. Gavin had been right, it appeared, and none of them had known it at the time except for him. There had been one evening, over drinks in a pub on campus. Lewis had been there, Chris remembered, as had Deirdre and Mary. Elisa hadn't been, he was certain of that, although where she had been that evening was lost in the haze of memory. As far as Glen, he couldn't recall if he had been there or not. Glen was so quiet that his presence sometimes went unnoticed until he said something, usually something perceptive and interesting, but if he didn't speak up it was easy to forget he was there.

Deirdre, he remembered, had been talking excitedly about flying to California for spring break.

• • • •

"I haven't felt comfortable on a plane since that Korean Air jetliner went down," Mary said. *She was sitting, leaning back in her chair with a lazy grace, a glass of red wine in one elegantly-manicured hand.*

Lewis snorted. "Right, Deirdre, you'll be safe as long as you don't fly from Seattle to California via Soviet air space."

All of them had laughed, even Mary, although her laugh sounded a little cool.

"You believe what the Soviets are claiming?" Deirdre asked, aiming the question mostly at Lewis. "That it was on a spy mission?"

"That's bullshit," Lewis said. "You don't send a fully-loaded passenger jet on a spy mission. One of their fly-boys got trigger-happy, and then they had to cover their asses afterwards."

"Actually, don't you think that would be the best way to spy?" Gavin asked. "It's like you said. Who would suspect a passenger jet would be on a spy mission? You send 'em over restricted space, equip the jet with a camera operated remotely. You don't need anyone more than the pilot and copilot to be in on it."

"Another conspiracy, Gavin?" Mary asked and rolled her eyes a little. "How many is this, now?"

There was more laughter, but Gavin, predictably, rose to the bait without a moment's hesitation. "No, really!" he said, opening his eyes wide. "You don't know what kind of things the government is up to. We don't even know one percent of what they do. And what's more, even a lot of the people working for them don't know. The people in control, the power brokers behind the whole thing, they know. They're the only ones. So they take their plans and divide them up into little pieces, give out the little tasks to the underlings, who then carry them out. One person, disguised as a tourist, takes pictures of restricted sites with a miniaturized camera. Another one gets a job in the civil service, and intercepts data coming in via mail, or telegraph, or whatever. Another one might pose as a custodian and plant bugs in diplomatic offices. None of 'em sees the big picture. Only the ones at the top do, and they report to no one."

"Not even the president?" Mary said, smiling down into her glass of wine.

Gavin made a scoffing noise. "You think Reagan is in charge?

He's a puppet, like most heads of state. You never get to see the ones on top. You probably wouldn't even recognize their names, recognize their faces."

"I did hear," Chris said, *"that Nixon was supposed to be on that flight, but changed his mind at the last minute."*

"See?" Gavin shouted. Beside him, Deirdre winced and took a sip of her beer. *"You think that kind of thing is a coincidence? Someone tipped him off."*

"Why would they tip Nixon off?" Lewis asked. *"I'd think the powers-that-be would be just as happy to be rid of that scheming sonofabitch."*

"No," Gavin answered. *"Killing an ex-president? That'd be too big a misstep. Even the Soviets knew that."*

"The Soviets?" Deirdre said, shaking her head in confusion. *"Why would they care? Like they have any regard for what we want or don't want."*

"That's where you're wrong," Gavin said. *"The Soviets and the people in government here in the U.S. are all pawns. The ones in charge, hiding in their posh mansions in Samoa or Bali or Jamaica, maneuver the elected officials around like pieces on a chessboard. Reagan and Andropov and the rest of 'em might even think they're in charge. I don't know. But what's certain is they're not. They aren't the ones making the decisions."*

"And the rest of us?" Lewis said, gesturing around him at the other people at the table, at the other patrons at the bar, chatting and drinking and laughing*

"Us?" Gavin said, his normally genial expression darkening *"As*

long as we stay out of the way, we're okay. It's like the way you don't make a point of killing a fly while you're outside. But if it gets into your house, starts to buzz around your ears, you swat it, any time you like, for any reason or for no reason at all. That's how they see us."

"Flies?" Mary said.

"Pretty much. Like the people on the airplane. They got in the way."

"That's horrid," Deirdre downed what was left of her beer and setting down the glass with a clunk.

"It is," Gavin said, nodding. "That's exactly what it is. Horrid. Because if one of us got in the way, it wouldn't be murder, the way it would be if you or I killed someone. It would just be..." He faltered, stopped.

"An unfortunate necessity?" Chris volunteered.

"Yes," Gavin looked up. "Exactly that. Collateral damage."

• • • •

Chris looked over at Drolezki, still driving with the same relaxed economy of motion. That's how he sees me, Chris thought. He used those very words to describe Chase Ballengee. Collateral damage. Chase just got in the way.

By now, the sky was shining with the early light of morning, although the sun had still not risen. Chris saw a sign ahead that said, *Rest Stop 1 Mile.*

"Hey, Drolezki," he said.

"Yeah?"

"I need to pee."

Drolezki looked over at him, shrugged, and then with a quick motion, flipped on the turn signal. "Okay, but listen. I let you out of this car, you keep in mind I'm a quick enough shot to put you on the ground before you take ten steps. If there are other people hanging around at that rest stop, I will not hesitate to do the same to any of them that try to intervene. You're not getting away from me, not unless it's on a one-way trip to the Pearly Gates."

"Understood," Chris said quietly.

"That means you walk, calmly, slowly, and you don't try to get help. You don't talk to anyone. You go in, take a piss, whatever you need to do, you come back out." He angled his car onto the off ramp, then pulled into the parking lot, and slid into a space. He turned off the engine, and looked Chris right in the eye.

Chris wondered how he could ever have characterized Drolezki as boyish-looking. He'd never encountered such complete arrogance before. He knew he was above the law.

Chris remembered Gavin saying, "As long as we stay out of their way, we're okay. They let us be." He held up his left hand, as his right was still cuffed to the door handle, and said, "Fine. Whatever. I'll play nice. I don't want anyone else dying because of me."

"That's the way." Drolezki pulled a key out of his pocket, and then reached over and unlocked the handcuff. Chris massaged his wrist, and then unlocked and opened the door.

It was going to be another beautiful, warm day. The sky was a brilliant sapphire blue, with only a few streaks of white clouds. He stretched, his back cracking pleasantly, and then walked off toward the men's room. Drolezki followed, his eyes scanning the area, appearing not to be aware of Chris at all as he ambled along behind him. But Chris knew that the agent had been telling the truth. That if he showed any sign of trying to escape, he'd be dead in under five seconds.

Chris half expected that Drolezki would follow him into the men's room. Instead, he sat down on a bench alongside the rest stop building and stretched his long, muscular legs out in front of him. Chris wondered if Drolezki took a pill that made him not have to pee, either. No sleep, no peeing, maybe no eating, drinking, or sex. He could be a robot. He certainly didn't seem very human.

He went into the men's room, and walked up to a urinal. A teenage boy was washing his hands and exited, leaving Chris alone.

He had just finished, and was rezipping, when an elderly man with a tan fedora and a rather ridiculous pair of plaid Bermuda shorts stepped up to the urinal next to him, and said, "Beautiful day."

"Yeah," Chris said, wondering if the man knew about the guy rule that you don't talk to someone who's standing at a urinal.

"Should stay nice," the old man said. "Long as you keep your eyes on the prize."

Chris's eyes widened, and he looked over at the man. "What prize?" Chris said, his voice a pinched whisper.

The old man turned toward him, and gave him a solemn wink. "Staying alive, of course. That's what counts, right? Half the battle, that. Staying alive."

"Yes," Chris said, and feeling like an automaton, he walked over to the sink to wash his hands. He glanced back at the old guy, who was still standing at the urinal, and was whistling softly to himself.

Had he actually heard the old man say that? Or was he losing his mind?

No. There were people on his side, he knew that. He didn't know how they were keeping track of him, or how far they'd go to help him, but he wasn't imagining it. The hobo in Missouri had been shot in the back for helping Chris to escape. There were others, scattered along the way. The boy in the tollbooth, Luella the hotel clerk who warned him about the guys who were after me, maybe even Thomas T. Champion and the Harpers and Chase Ballengee. Maybe they were all in on it, all trying to help him, all trying to keep him from becoming another casualty.

And not being alone made all the difference.

Chris walked out of the men's room to where Drolezki sat, and said, "Okay."

Drolezki smirked at him. "Smart guy. You follow orders well, once you know there's no way out."

Chris didn't answer and kept his face impassive with an effort.

For now, you arrogant sonofabitch. For now. But don't let your guard down, because I'll be watching. Because half the battle may be staying alive, but the other half is winning it.

CHAPTER 17

D rolezki gestured toward him to get back into the car. Chris noticed again how relaxed his captor seemed to be. He didn't do much more than give a cursory glance around to make sure no one was watching as he climbed into the driver's seat, leaned across the seat, and snapped the cuff closed around Chris's right wrist. Drolezki was completely in charge of the situation. Hopefully no one got in his way. No more deaths of innocent people because of all of this.

Other than himself, of course.

"Now I gotta take a piss," Drolezki said. "Don't even think of trying to call out for help while I'm gone."

"What happened to me being a smart guy who follows orders?"

Drolezki gave Chris a predatory grin. "I'm a smart guy, too, and I don't like to tempt fate. Don't try it."

He got out, shut the door, and strode back across the parking lot, back toward the men's room.

Chris hoped the old man was gone. He wondered if Drolezki had overheard what the guy had said. Doubtful. He would have mentioned it.

And at least this proved that Drolezki wasn't a robot. Robots don't need to pee.

He returned a short time later, got back into the car, and tossed something into Chris's lap—a vacuum-sealed package of cheese and crackers. Drolezki had an identical one, as well as two bottles of water, which he stuck into the cup holders between the front seats.

"The best cuisine the vending machines have to offer," he said. "Better than nothing, though, right?"

Then he started the car and put it in gear, pulled his snack open, and was already munching loudly on the crackers by the time he was back on the highway.

"Thanks," Chris said, opening his crackers and cheese and taking a bite. He hadn't realized until that moment how hungry he was. His last meal had been half a BLT in a diner twelve hours earlier.

"Don't want you to starve before we have a chance to ask you a couple of questions," Drolezki commented.

"No," Chris said in an uninflected voice. "It'd be a pity if I died before you had a chance to kill me."

Drolezki looked over at him, and frowned a little. "Look, bud," he said, after a moment, "it's nothing personal."

"No?" Chris said. "Well, I hope you understand that it's pretty personal to me. Getting murdered kind of is the ultimate in personal, you know?"

"That's one way of looking at it."

"It's the only way I have, at the moment. You'd feel the same way if you were the one looking down the barrel of a gun."

Drolezki shrugged. "There's more at stake than one life."

"You said that before," Chris said, and suddenly, his captor's unassailable coolness made anger surge inside him. He felt a swell that reddened his cheeks and set his heart pounding. "You said that about Adam's death, and Chase's, and the deaths of my other friends," he said. "So, one life? Two? Three? Ten? A hundred? When does it cross the line? When does life become worth something? How many lives does it take before you'd say it was too high a cost? I don't know what government agency you're working for, or another country's government, or no government at all. You may be one of the Illuminati, like Gavin thought, or just one of a group of power-hungry assholes who've somehow figured out how to do whatever they want to with no consequences. In the end, it doesn't matter who you're working for, because people like you are all alike. They can always find something for which they are willing to destroy the lives and happiness of others, and ultimately, they always lose in the end. I'm not going to beg for my life. Not now, not when I get to wherever you're taking me, not when you torture me to find out what I supposedly know. Because there's one thing I do know, and it may be the only relevant thing. There is *nothing* more important than respecting human life and freedom. So hear this, Drolezki, and you can pass this message as far up the chain as you want. You can do what you want to me, but I swear that at every step, I will do everything I can to thwart you. Put simply, you and your puppet masters can kiss my ass."

Drolezki looked over at him for a moment, his eyebrows rising a little on his broad forehead. Chris stared back at him, and their eyes met. Drolezki's gaze was impassive, unaffected, even a little amused. Whether through nature or long practice, he wouldn't, or perhaps couldn't, let himself be affected emotionally by what Chris said. The words struck like waves against a cliff face, and were equally easily thrown back. The corner of his mouth twitched a little as he said, "I see now why you evaded us for this long."

Chris looked down. Whatever fury he'd felt was gone as suddenly as it had arisen, and his anger turned to sickness and cold fear, like ashes in his belly. "I wish it was that," he said. "I'm not brave. Just lucky. Deirdre and Lewis and Gavin were always the brave ones, the ones who were willing to speak their minds no matter what the consequences." He leaned back in his seat, and closed his eyes. "And they're all dead."

· · · ·

They crossed into Washington State at a little after 6:30 a.m. The sun was shining as they descended from the last tumbled slopes of the western Rockies onto the flat, arid plain east of Spokane. Drolezki showed no particular inclination to talk, and in any case, there didn't seem to be much more to say. Chris's outburst of bravado felt like a coda, the words of a condemned man addressing the crowd from the gallows, standing on the trapdoor with the rope already around his throat, knowing that he'd never again feel the wind on his face, that the clock was ticking minutes to seconds to nothing.

Chris noticed his captor swallowing a small white tablet with the last mouthful of water in his water bottle after they passed the exits for the town of Sprague, and he briefly wondered if it was some kind of stimulant. An explanation, perhaps, for how Drolezki could keep driving for hours on end without a break. Chris felt emotionally and physically exhausted, with a week's growth of beard, still wearing the same clothes he'd had on when he'd fled Guildford after his house was destroyed. Drolezki, other than a few extra rumples in his nicely-tailored pants and dress shirt, looked as fresh and alert as he had the day they'd met.

Chris dozed as they crossed through mile after mile of wheat fields, cattle ranches, and sagebrush-dotted scrubland, rousing only to change positions before sliding off again into a light sleep. Drolezki drove on, never once showing any sign of fatigue. The towns of Ritzville, Moses Lake, George, Vantage, and Kittitas all passed in a dimly-registered haze, each one marked only by exit signs and a temporary increase in the traffic.

Chris opened his eyes and yawned, and looked at the dashboard clock. Just shy of eleven. The terrain had folded into gentle hills, still mostly occupied by farms, but there were stands of conifers here and there—lodgepole pine and white fir. The Cascades loomed ahead, their outlines hazy dim shapes in the distance.

Chris's heart gave a sudden uncomfortable gallop. The Cascades. Where it began. If they hadn't found that cave thirty years ago, would they all still be alive, leading their individual lives, completely ignorant of the existence of these people who are above the government, and possibly behind it as well? Chris would be having a nice, quiet summer, just him and Baxter and two months of relaxation and warm weather before another school year and another crop of kids to teach. But now he was going to be erased, and the knowledge he'd discovered would die with him. The people back in Guildford would never find out anything other than that he disappeared, wandered off somewhere and died. That's how they kept secrets. If you were not an initiate, and you found out about them, you were dead.

It was as they passed a sign that said, *Ellensburg, 10 Miles*, that Drolezki's cell rang. He reached into his trouser pocket, pulled it out, and gave it a casual swipe with his finger.

"Drolezki," he said.

There was a pause.

"Yes. I've got him. He's secured. . . .I should be there by two at the latest. I texted J. D. … He didn't tell you?" Another pause, and Drolezki chuckled. "No, that's taken care of. They cleaned up the mess, right?"

Chris looked over at Drolezki and frowned. A mess to clean up? Was he talking about the bodies of Chase and Hargis, left on the ground at the turnaround in Wyoming?

"No, no witnesses, unless you count the dog." A pause, and Drolezki snorted into the phone. "No, I didn't take the dog, like I have time for that… What the hell? No, I didn't off the dog. What, do you think the dog was gonna call the police? Wasn't worth a bullet or the time it would've taken. I left him in the car."

Drolezki frowned, his forehead creasing in perplexity. "No," he said, and the bantering tone was gone. "I'm sure. It was just Hargis and Ballengee. There wasn't anyone else there. I didn't have a lot of time to waste, and couldn't risk being seen by someone… I don't know… You checked Wyoming State Police scanners?… Piss off, it wouldn't be the first time you forgot something simple like that… Did you talk to whoever they sent out from Sheridan to take care of it?… Yeah, it was just Hargis and Ballengee. Ballengee was by the front passenger side of the car, face down. Hargis fell face down, too, but nearer to the shelter, maybe fifteen feet from the rear passenger side, give or take." Then his voice rose in anger. "No, I didn't, why the fuck would I do that?" Now there was a longer pause, and Drolezki turned his head toward Chris until their eyes met. Drolezki's expression was hard, dangerous. "No, I can't think of another explanation, either. Maybe it's time I have another little conversation with our guest, here." Silence, and then he made a scoffing noise. "Don't give me that 'it's just a dog,' crap. It's a loose end. They fucking hate loose ends, and so I fucking hate loose ends. Would you want to walk in and get asked the question, and not have an answer?" He snorted again, and looked away from Chris, back toward the road. "I didn't think so. I'll be in touch when I get closer."

He hung up the phone, slid it back into his pocket, and frowned thoughtfully for a moment. He seemed to be choosing his words carefully. "You got any idea why your dog wouldn't be in the car when our sanitation guys got there?"

"Sanitation?" Chris said, his voice registering a combination of incredulity and disgust.

"Answer the goddamned question," Drolezki said, his voice quiet, menacing.

"No. I have no idea. Why would I have an idea? You made me leave my dog behind. I've been along on this joyride ever since."

Without warning, Drolezki slammed his foot on the brakes. Chris's seatbelt snapped tight, and he jerked forward against it. The car screeched over onto the shoulder. As soon as it came to a complete stop, Drolezki swiveled around, and his left hand shot out and grabbed Chris's throat. Chris's head was pressed against the headrest, and his eyes were wide with equal measures of fear and defiance.

"I asked you a fucking question," Drolezki said, speaking nearly in a whisper, his face very close to Chris's. "And I want the answer, not some smartass response. Now, I'm going to put this clearly to you. After we left, our sanitation guys got there, maybe a quarter of an hour later, to take care of Hargis and Ballengee. They were still where we left them. Both very dead. The car was still there, too. But no dog. So in the fifteen minutes between when we left and when our men arrived, someone stopped, took your dog out of Ballengee's car, shut the door, and drove away.

Which means that there is a great big fucking loose end out there. Maybe someone who knew where you were, because the dog was bugged, and they didn't want us to find out that was how they were keeping track of you. Maybe the dog was important for some other reason. Or maybe it was some bleeding-heart PETA type who didn't want the dog left in a car. But if it was that, it's pretty funny that they didn't care enough about the two dead bodies lying right there to report it to the police, isn't it? Because there's been no report to anyone. Nada. So, I think you're being tailed, somehow, and whoever is tailing you thought it'd be clever to rescue your dog. Now, you wouldn't happen to know who that might be, would you?"

Chris didn't answer. The pressure around his windpipe increased, ever so slightly. He choked out, "Let me go, you stupid gorilla," and grabbed Drolezki's arm with his left hand. But his strength was no match for his captor's. Drolezki tightened his grip a little more, and he gagged. "No, I don't know," he said, his voice a thin wheeze. "I have no clue. I don't have the slightest idea about any of this."

Drolezki looked into Chris's eyes for a moment, and then with an exasperated grunt, he dropped his hand from around Chris's throat.

"If you are lying to me, I will see to it that you do not have an easy exit," Drolezki said.

"Why the hell is it so important to find out where my dog is?" Chris said, massaging his throat.

Drolezki put the car in gear again and pressed the accelerator, pulling them back out onto the interstate. "It's not the dog. I don't give a shit about the dog. But there's something going on here, and I don't understand it. And I don't like what I don't understand."

"You don't like it when you aren't calling the shots," Chris said, and coughed, clearing his throat.

"Fuckin'-A, I don't." One corner of his mouth twitched a little. "Doesn't matter. Maybe it was some local who saw the dog and took him and didn't want to get involved with a couple of dead bodies. In any case, if you're lying to me, we'll have it out of you eventually."

"Torture won't work," Chris said, hoping his voice sounded braver than he felt.

"Oh, we have way better methods than torture." He looked over at Chris. His expression was relaxed again, as if his outburst of rage had never happened. "I'm going to remember the gorilla comment. You've got something coming for that one, before I let them finish you off. Think about that, smart guy."

•   •   •   •

Up one slope, down a little, and up a steeper one, as the rolling hills broke into ragged waves of rock and the interstate climbed the foothills toward the grand peaks now clear against the western horizon. Chris saw the exit for Cle Elum and Teanaway. It was the road, he knew, to the trailhead that would lead to Lake Ingalls and the rocky cliff faces where, somewhere, the mysterious cave had been located, and perhaps still was. The pines of the lower elevations were replaced by subalpine fir and alpine larch. The highway angled north, skirting the azure waters of Keechelus Lake, its still surface mirroring the cloudless sky.

There was a sign that said, *Snoqualmie Pass, Elevation 3,022 Feet,* and almost as if they'd passed some kind of invisible boundary, the vegetation changed to Douglas firs and silver firs and the other familiar trees of the humid, misty western Cascades, and they passed underneath a pall of clouds and fog. Drizzle began to strike the windshield, and Drolezki turned on the wipers, swearing a little under his breath at the "Goddamned Seattle rain." Chris shivered. The Northwest was welcoming him back, it seemed, in mourning.

"Okay," Drolezki said, "that's our sign that it's time for lights out."

"What does that mean?"

"You're gonna take a little nap. The powers-that-be don't want you being brought in awake. You can't know where you are."

"Not much faith in your ability to kill me when you're done with me, I guess?" Chris said. "What's the likelihood I'll ever get a chance to report my whereabouts?"

Drolezki wouldn't be baited again. "I don't make these decisions. There's not much chance you're gonna get away, no, so you're right not to let this get your hopes up. But 'not much' isn't 'zero,' and they don't want to risk it." He gave a gesture with his right hand. "Open up the glove box. Inside you'll find a pill bottle."

Chris pulled the latch, and the compartment opened. Along with the usual things—the owner's manual, a tire pressure gauge, a package of chewing gum—there was a yellow prescription bottle with no label. At the bottom were two innocuous-looking white tablets.

"You got some water left?"

Chris nodded.

"Take 'em both. Then take a nice, long snooze. It'll be your last chance to sleep for a while, may as well enjoy it."

"And if I don't?"

Drolezki shrugged. "I pull over, and put a bullet in your head. Your call. It'll be a shame, really, that you somehow got free of the handcuff and attacked me while I was driving. Didn't have a choice, you know."

"What about questioning me for my valuable information?"

"Unavoidable loss, which I will regret greatly. Now take the pills, and cuddle up and relax. We'll be at grandma's house before you know it."

Chris opened up the bottle, and shook the tablets out into his hand. They looked like aspirin.

"Good boy. Nighty-night." The car descended a long slope, the first of many that would carry them down out of the mountains and into the lowlands of Puget Sound. Drolezki shook his head as an eighteen-wheeler passed him, splattering his windshield with muddy spray. "I don't know why you people like living here," he said. "The climate has permanent post-nasal drip."

"It's sunny sometimes."

"Yeah. Every other Tuesday in July. Otherwise it rains. I'm surprised you don't mildew. Now take the fucking pills."

This is where it comes down to it. This is where I start fighting back. He said his orders changed, that I'm wanted now, alive. Maybe he will kill me, but I'm banking on the fact that he won't. In either case, I'll be damned if I'll peacefully drink the KoolAid.

Chris pushed the window button, and before Drolezki could react, he'd thrown the pills out into the slipstream. The cool rain splattered his hand, and he felt strangely like laughing.

"Ball's in your court, Drolezki," he said, and then added, "you ugly gorilla."

Drolezki's face flushed dark red, and he heeled over the steering wheel again, and braked to a stop on the shoulder of the interstate. "You stupid sonofabitch," he said, through clenched teeth, and drew his gun out of its holster, aimed the barrel at Chris's forehead.

"I told you," Chris said, calmly. "I'm not going to do anything you say voluntarily. You may have ways to compel me, but I'm going to go down fighting, to the last breath.

Now, go ahead and follow through on your threat. Put a bullet in my brain. I wonder what your superiors will have to say about that? A middle-aged schoolteacher got so violent that you couldn't subdue him any other way than shooting him, even though you'd been ordered to bring him in alive? I don't think they'll be happy with you."

Drolezki's eyes narrowed, and he swore under his breath. Then, in a single motion, he turned the gun around in his hand, and brought the weight of it down on Chris's head. The world exploded into fireworks, then everything went dark.

CHAPTER 18

The first thing Chris noticed was that he was incredibly comfortable. After many days of unremitting anxiety, sometimes spiking upwards into genuine terror, he felt relaxed, warm, safe, despite a throbbing ache on the left side of his head. Even that pain, though, didn't register much. It was simply a curiosity, something to be noted, shrugged at, and forgotten. He considered his predicament, the likelihood of his impending execution, the plight of Elisa, the deaths of Chase and his college friends, and found, to his perplexity, that he couldn't work up any real distress over any of it.

Drolezki must have drugged him after he was knocked

out. Chris felt like he was not only hit with a sedative, but an anti-anxiety med as well. He knew he should feel upset right now, but he couldn't. He was aware that he would be afraid later. Right now, though, all he could feel was content.

He opened his eyes. He was lying flat on his back on a surprisingly soft cot, underneath a completely ordinary-looking blanket. He stifled a drowsy chuckle at the thought that he was half expecting his captors to have high-tech space blankets. The lights were on, but dim, and he could see a sparsely-furnished room, with a chair, a small table, and two doors, both closed.

There were no windows.

He lay there for a few more minutes, then found he wasn't sleepy any more. He sat up, and the throbbing in his head increased for a moment, then subsided. He reached up and touched the spot. His hair was crusted with dried blood. He was still dressed in his travel-worn shirt and jeans, but his wallet was gone. Even that fact couldn't disturb his feeling of well-being, or stay in his conscious mind for long.

He swung his legs out of bed. Only then did he notice he was barefoot, but his shoes were found in short order, sitting next to the foot of the cot, with his socks draped on top. He stood, staggered a little, and then regained his balance after a moment when he held onto the frame of the cot, not sure if his knees would support his weight. Finding that he was stable and capable of walking, he crossed the floor to one of the doors and tried the knob.

Locked.

The other one, though, led to a bathroom. He went to the sink, splashed some water on his face, which made him feel more awake if not substantially more alert, and took care of his other bodily needs. Then he exited back into the room with the cot and sat down on it.

"What now?" he said, aloud. "Do I pound on the door and let them know that I'm awake? Or wait for them to figure it out? I'm in no rush to be killed, honestly." He lay back down, and cupped his hands behind his head.

It was perhaps twenty minutes later that he heard the clicking of a lock mechanism, and the door opened to let Drolezki in. There was something indefinably different about his captor's manner. Before, in the car, he had been in charge, beholden to no one. Here, there was a subtle caution in the way he moved.

"Get up," he said.

Chris yawned, and sat up. "I knew you wouldn't kill me."

Drolezki scowled. "Don't get cocky. It's only delaying the inevitable."

"You drugged me after you socked me in the head with your gun, didn't you? If you'd slipped some of that stuff into my drink three weeks ago, I probably wouldn't have given you all of this trouble."

"We didn't think you were very important back then. Put your shoes on."

Chris thought for a moment about refusing, but decided that not complying would probably get him hit over the head again. He pulled on a sock, then his shoe, and laced it up. "Time to meet the hangman?" he asked, tying the other. He still couldn't work up any real fear about this. It was the drug, of course. Better living through chemistry. He found himself hoping that if he was going to die, that this feeling stayed with him until the end. Death wouldn't be so bad without the fear.

"Something like that," Drolezki said.

"How is it, being the hangman's flunky? Bet you get off watching the innocent folks walking calmly to their deaths."

Drolezki's cheeks flushed, and he said nothing.

"I'll assume that means yes," Chris said, standing up. "Take me to your leader, Koko."

Drolezki gave an angry snort, grabbed Chris's upper arm with his left hand, and propelled him toward the door. His right hand rested on his gun, still in its holster. They exited the room into a long corridor, unadorned, with a tile floor and off-white walls. It had the sterile look of a hospital or a scientific research facility, but no signs, nothing but a maze of hallways and unmarked doors and occasionally a small alcove with a bench or a chair or a water fountain.

"Big place," Chris said.

Drolezki didn't respond.

They entered an elevator. There were no floor numbers, but there was a keypad. Drolezki punched in a six- or seven-digit code, and the elevator started upwards. After a moment, it stopped, and opened onto another empty hallway, which they proceeded down, just as they had the first one.

They passed no one, heard no sounds. No windows, no signs, nothing that could mark a path, give Chris an idea of the way out if he somehow were to escape.

For the first time since he awakened, Chris felt a pang of fear, but it still seemed distant, padded, indistinct. The drug was wearing off. At least that meant that he'd be able to react faster, and fight harder, if necessary.

They came to a somewhat larger door, with another keypad. Again, his captor entered a code, and there was a soft click as a lock turned. He pulled the door open, and Chris walked into a room that looked like a cross between a medical laboratory and an executive office. There were spotless tiles, a large picture window overlooking woods, and several obviously expensive chairs, but to one side sat a rather formidable examining table, and a tray with several syringes and an array of other, less recognizable instruments.

A silver-haired elderly man was seated in one of the chairs. He looked up at Drolezki and gave him a grandfatherly smile.

"Ah, Mr. Drolezki," he said, in a voice that was tinged with faint traces of a British accent. "I'm so glad you have finally arrived. You are a bit later than I had been given to understand."

"We had to wait until the sedative wore off," Drolezki said.

Chris looked over at him. Drolezki's voice was subdued, hesitant. Here was someone who outranked the agent, probably by several orders of magnitude. Gone was all of his swaggering toughness. He looked like a school kid who had been sent to the principal for swearing in class.

"It is of no consequence," the elderly man said. "Do not trouble yourself about it." Drolezki looked at him, uncertain, for a moment, and then turned away toward the door. "Oh, Mr. Drolezki," the elderly man said, as if it were an afterthought. "One more thing, before you go."

Drolezki turned back, his face full of apprehension. "Yes?" he said.

"There is the matter of the dog, Mr. Drolezki. Mr. Corgan told me about the matter of the dog. That was sloppy, Mr. Drolezki."

"I didn't think the dog mattered."

"You should know by now. Everything matters."

"But a dog…"

"Had the dog been neutralized, it would be, as they say, a done deal. Did we not make it clear that any possible link to Mr. Franzia had to be neutralized?"

"Well, yes, but, there were other people he met, and nothing was being done... and a dog... I didn't think..."

"No, Mr. Drolezki. That is correct. You didn't think." The elderly man picked up a small remote that was on the table next to him and touched a button.

Drolezki let out a long, drilling shriek. Chris goggled at him. The muscular, tough man who had brought him, singlehanded, from Wyoming to Washington, was clawing at his face, his back arched, legs rigid. It went on for what seemed like minutes. Chris turned toward the man, who was still sitting there, watching Drolezki with a bland smile.

"Goddammit, stop!" Chris said. "Stop it!"

The man shrugged. "As you wish. Interesting that you show such concern for a man who would kill you without hesitation if I gave the order." He pressed another button, and Drolezki dropped to his knees, sobbing. "Hard to fathom such misplaced compassion. But then, he spared your dog, so perhaps you owe him that much."

Drolezki gradually got control of himself, and looked up at the elderly man, a combination of fear and hatred and submission in his eyes. He reached up and dragged one sleeve across his streaming eyes.

"Now," the man said, his voice still gentle and urbane. "You may go. You may consider your error paid for, in full. We will speak no more of it."

Drolezki struggled to his feet and made his way to the door, stumbling a little.

The door shut behind him, and Chris was alone with the elderly man, who was still wearing a faint smile.

"What did you do to him?" Chris said. He knew the euphoria wouldn't last. He was afraid now.

"Nothing that will do any lasting harm, unless perhaps to his emotional state," the man said. "Simple stimulation of the trigeminal nerve, via an implant. Trigeminal neuralgia is, they say, the most painful condition in the world, to the point that people who suffer from it naturally call it 'suicide syndrome.' Being able to induce it artificially, and turn it off at will, is useful in giving reminders."

"Drolezki needed a reminder?"

"I find that most people do, on occasion," he said. "A short one, every so often, serves to focus the mind amazingly well. But now, Mr. Franzia, there is no need to discuss such unpleasantness. Please. Sit down. Make yourself comfortable. Would you like something to drink?"

Chris sat in one of the chairs and shook his head.

"As you wish. I trust you know why you are here."

"Some of it. Apparently I know something I'm not supposed to know, and once you find out what it is, you're going to have me executed."

The man frowned. "Tsk, tsk, tsk," he said. "Crudely put. But accurate, at least in the essentials, unfortunately."

"What exactly do you think I know that is so important?"

"That is what I intend to find out. You gave my people quite a merry chase, you know." His eyes twinkled. "It might have been easier had you acquiesced and died quietly. But then, of course, I would not have had the pleasure of your acquaintance, and that would have been a pity."

"What about Elisa?"

"Ms. Reed? She is here, as well. I expect you would like to see her, but I am afraid that that will be impossible, although I very much regret it."

"But if we're both going to be killed, what's the harm?"

The man raised one eyebrow. "A tearful kiss farewell, you mean? How marvelously romantic. I was given to understand the two of you had never consummated a relationship."

Chris snorted laughter and was immediately surprised at himself for reacting that way, but suddenly the entire thing seemed ridiculous. The fact that these people had gone to great effort, and probably great expense, to track down a harmless middle-aged schoolteacher from upstate New York, and now he was sitting in some kind of high-tech torture chamber in western Washington talking about whether he and Elisa had ever slept together.

"No," he said, still chuckling, "we never had sex, if that's what you're saying. But yeah, if it comes to that. I would like to kiss her. Just once, if that's all I've got."

The man's smile faded a little. "I see no point in it," he said. "But I suppose you're right. There is no harm. And even condemned men are allowed one last visit with their loved ones."

"Very kind of you," Chris said, his voice heavy with sarcasm.

"You will find that we are no kinder, nor more brutal, than most people."

"I wonder if Drolezki would agree with that, after your 'little reminder?'"

The man frowned. "Mr. Drolezki understands that there are great things at stake."

"Yeah, Drolezki kept telling me about all these great things at stake. What great things?"

"Now, now, Mr. Franzia, patience. I am asking the questions, please. Why don't we start with your recounting whatever you recall about your field trips, with your college friends, up into the Cascade Mountains, back when you were at the University of Washington."

"So I was right. That is what this is all about."

"Yes. In part, at least. What do you recall of those expeditions into the mountains?"

"Can you tell me first why on earth I should answer any of your questions?" Chris shot back.

"Oh, certainly. That is an understandable question, given the circumstances. The easiest answer is that I can kill you any time I desire to. If you cooperate, I can make that death quieter and easier than any man has a right to expect. A gentle drop into blissful darkness and rest. If you do not, I can make it more painful than anything you can imagine. You saw what Mr. Drolezki endured? Perhaps that gives you some understanding of what we are capable of, technologically." He smiled a little. "You will beg for death, plead for it, before you find it. I can stretch out what Mr. Drolezki just experienced into hours, days, make it subside only to make it intensify, until finally your mind breaks. It is a choice between cooperation and a swift, easy release, and defiance and an excruciating and protracted journey toward death. Do you find my answer sufficient?"

Chris cocked an eyebrow at him. "So, without all of the flowery verbiage... tell you what I know, or you'll beat it out of me, and either way I'll end up dying, so I might as well cooperate."

"Again, crudely put, but essentially correct. Now, why don't you tell me what you remember about the class you took at the University of Washington, and the field trips you went on, and we can avoid discussing further unpleasantries."

Chris knew he had to choose his battles. Play along, for now, and look for any possible way out.

"Fine. You win," he said, holding up both hands, palms out, in a sign of surrender. "The Field Biology class? It was just a class. We went up more than once, sometimes to low-elevation sites, sometimes high ones. We took a couple of trips up to Teanaway Pass and Lake Ingalls. Camped, did bird banding and general wildlife surveys."

"You went up with a professor and perhaps two dozen other students?"

"Yes. Plus two assistants, I think."

"And while you were up there, near Lake Ingalls, I believe you and six of your classmates discovered something intriguing."

"A cave," Chris said. "A cave in a hillside."

"Ah!" the man said, both eyebrows rising. "So you do recall that, then."

"No. Not at all. Elisa told me about it. In an email. She said I was there, and I have no reason to think she was remembering wrong, but I have no memory of it at all. It's as if it never happened."

"Think carefully, Mr. Franzia. If you were there, the memories are somewhere in your brain. Memories can be suppressed, but not, apparently, erased. It was an error to assume the contrary. I want you to cast your mind back to the last trip you took with your class, up and over Teanaway Pass. You and your six friends went away one afternoon and discovered a cave. You were gone for hours. In fact, your professor was considering going out with one of the assistants to look for the seven of you when you came back under your own power. You have no memory of this?"

"No," Chris said. "None. I mean, Elisa described it to me…"

"No!" the man said, more sharply than Chris had yet heard him speak. "Do not conflate your memory with what you've been told. I am not interested in hearing you tell me what Ms. Reed remembers. We will have that out of her directly. I want to hear what is in your mind alone."

"But nothing is," Chris said. "I really, honestly, don't remember anything." He felt himself close to laughing again and tried to keep himself from smiling. "It really is kind of absurd, isn't it? All of this fuss to find out I don't know anything of value."

The man's voice dropped, became silky, dangerous. "Oh, I don't think that is necessarily the case," he said. "As I said, it is seldom memories are truly forgotten. They are usually accessible, with a little bit of assistance." He gestured toward Chris with a well-manicured hand. "Might I ask you to remove your shirt, Mr. Franzia?"

Chris felt a cold sweat break out on his skin. "Why?" he said. "Is this when the torture begins?"

He expected the man to get angry, but he just smiled. "Torture? Floggings and such things? We have progressed beyond such barbarism, even though the public spectacle of times past could be looked upon as a useful means of convincing the general populace to cooperate. No, I intend you no harm, and little in the way of pain, I assure you. Now please do as I say. I suspect you are aware I could summon help with a touch of a button, and my assistants would be much less gentle in removing your shirt than you might be comfortable with. So please, Mr. Franzia."

Chris's jump toward the old man was as sudden as a trap springing. He had never been in a fistfight before. He had always been a genial person, right back to childhood, and had made friends easily and seldom angered anyone. His own strength and reflexes surprised him. His greater body weight knocked the man's chair over backwards, and Chris landed on top of him, one knee solidly in his enemy's solar plexus. There was a wheezing gasp as the old man's breath came out in a rush, and then Chris's fist made solid contact with the old man's mouth.

It was probably hopeless from the beginning; he realized that afterwards. The door was locked, for one thing, so there would have been no way out even if he had had the chance. But seconds after his punch struck home, another door burst open, and two broad-chested men in orderlies' scrubs rushed in. Chris was lifted bodily from the floor, and his arms pinned behind him.

The old man stood, stiffly, and wiped a thin thread of blood from the corner of his mouth.

"Foolish," he said, in a tight, breathless voice. "A foolish and pointless act. Perhaps understandable, given your situation, but still, it will be paid for."

He nodded at Chris's captors, and Chris's shirt was pulled backwards. Buttons popped and flew, pattering down onto the tiles like hail. The torn remains of his shirt were tossed onto the floor. Then Chris was dragged back toward the examination table, forced onto it, and his arms and legs secured with straps.

"Thank you, gentlemen," the old man said, his voice

regaining some of its previous cultured urbanity. "You may leave us. Please let the doctor know we'll be ready presently."

The two men left through the same door, without uttering a word.

Those men are barely human.

More like automatons.

The elderly man approached the table. Chris struggled against the straps but to no avail.

"Please, Mr. Franzia," the old man said. "These straps are quite impossible to break, even for someone with far greater physical strength than you have. You are exhausting yourself for nothing."

"Fuck you," Chris snarled.

The man shrugged. "As you wish. If it amuses you, by all means keep struggling. You will simply end with bruised and cut skin on your arms, for no good reason."

Chris subsided, but still stared up at the imperturbable face of the old man with an expression of fierce hostility. "Before you kill me, I just want to know one thing," he said. "Just one."

"If it is a question I can answer," the old man said, "I suppose you have the right to that, at least."

"You people somehow cracked our code," he said. "Elisa and I came up with a code we thought there was no way anyone could break. You probably tracked me using some kind of bug. Somehow you put one on me, or my dog, and followed me around that way. I thought I'd lost you in Nebraska, but then somehow, you captured Elisa and used her as bait to get me. So before you start to interrogate me, or torture me, or whatever you're planning on doing, just tell me, how did you find Elisa? Because the code was something no one else who is still alive would have known about."

The man looked down at him with a beatific smile. "Yes, that was clever, I must admit," he said. "Ms. Reed was smart to come up with such a system. I think I will let someone else explain, however."

"Why?" Chris said, and gave an angry snort of laughter. "Watching me strapped down shirtless to an examining table giving you too much of a boner to think straight?"

The man chuckled again, shook his head. "Such noble defiance, and such a flair for drama," he said. He reached for the remote, and Chris winced, expecting to feel a flare of searing pain, but instead there was a click from a speaker, and the man said, "We are ready for you. If you would join us, please?"

A female voice said, "Be right there."

"We have found that our interrogations are best supervised by a qualified doctor," the man said. "Although I will be asking the questions, she will be responsible for the physiological side of things."

There was a soft click as a lock turned, and the same door opened that the orderlies had used earlier. A woman wearing a white lab jacket came in, a stethoscope around her neck. She had straight brown hair in a no-nonsense cut, and modern-looking plastic-framed glasses.

"Well," she said, in an amused voice. "Chris Franzia. Long time, no see, old buddy."

Chris stared, his mouth hanging open a little.

Deirdre Ross.

CHAPTER 19

There was a moment during which Chris froze in place, his mind wiped clean by incredulity. The question of whether the whole thing had been a dream drifted through his brain, but he had no certain answer to that, so he simply stared at Deirdre's smiling face for what seemed like minutes.

"Aren't you even going to say hi?" she said, lifting one eyebrow in an ironic gesture that was so characteristic of his old college friend his paralysis vanished, replaced by a desperate curiosity.

"You're—you're alive?" he stammered. "So—all the others... Gavin and the rest...?"

"No," Deirdre said, in a matter-of-fact tone. "They're all dead. Mine is the only miraculous resurrection you'll get to witness, I'm afraid."

"But how?"

She shrugged. "It never occurred to you that it was a little peculiar that they never found my body? It happens sometimes with drowning victims, I suppose, but still. How likely was it that I took off all my clothes, jumped into Lake Quinault for a nice skinnydip, and no trace?"

"I thought that because the others had died..." He trailed off, lapsed into a stare again.

She looked over at the elderly man. "You were right, then. I didn't think that story would fool anyone, but I seem to have been wrong."

The man gave a gracious nod of the head, but said nothing.

"You're helping them?" Chris said. "You helped them kill all of our friends?"

"Nope," she said. "Can't lay the blame for that at my feet. But there's no need to go into that now."

"How did you avoid getting killed yourself?"

Deirdre once again looked at the old man, an unspoken question in her eyes.

"Allow him five minutes to ask questions, and then we must proceed," he said. "Satisfying his curiosity on a few points will serve to clear his mind for questioning. Your giving him certain answers wouldn't affect our goals, except insofar as our main line of inquiry goes, and you know not to address those topics."

Deirdre nodded, and then turned back to Chris. "I was lucky," she said. "I left for work one morning, but had to turn back because I realized I'd forgotten my cell. I went into my apartment and found a guy in the process of poisoning the milk in my fridge. I'm a fourth degree black belt in karate." She grinned. "Once I'd broken his arm in three places, he decided to quit struggling. To make a long story short, he spilled his guts about what was going on."

"Pain causes people to make unfortunate choices, sometimes," the old man said, frowning disapprovingly.

"Bet you gave him a bit of a reminder," Chris said, a bitter tone in his voice.

"Oh, he was not one of our operatives, you may be sure of that."

Chris stared at the man, his expression a study in perplexity. "You mean…"

"He was working for the other side," Deirdre said.

"But he was trying to poison you."

"Indeed." The elderly man gave Deirdre a chilly little smile. "I believe that Mr. Franzia is about to have the other shoe drop."

Deirdre snickered. "He never was very quick on the uptake."

"You're…" Chris swallowed. "You're not the ones

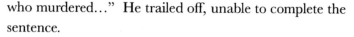

who murdered…" He trailed off, unable to complete the sentence.

"Correct. We are not the ones who killed your friends."

"Who did, then?"

"The ones who are behind what you stumbled upon in that cave."

"But then Deirdre… how did you end up here?"

Deirdre picked up the thread of the tale, looking as relaxed as if she had been telling them what she'd had for breakfast. "So anyway, after the wannabe poisoner was out of commission and tied to one of my kitchen chairs, I used his cellphone to get a hold of his boss. He told me how to unlock the phone as soon as I threatened to break his other arm, and if that didn't work, to surgically remove his genitals with a steak knife."

"Sweet talk was always your specialty," Chris said.

"Damn skippy. So the boss picked up, thinking it was her flunky reporting in. She was a little surprised to hear my voice. I told her I knew what was going on, that they wouldn't get another chance to kill me because I was going to disappear. My first plan was to go into hiding, but before I could get my shit together I got a call. One from my friend, here."

The elderly man gave her a courteous nod.

"He and his people found out what I'd done. I'm not certain how. But they made me what I believe is called 'an offer I couldn't refuse.'"

"Dr. Ross appeared to be an ideal ally," the man said. "Let us say that the way she handled the situation impressed us. We could guarantee her protection from further attempts on her life. For our part, the value of her medical expertise was immediately obvious. And we gave her our word that she would be entirely safe, as long as her allegiance to us was unequivocal."

"And you trust these people are telling you the truth?" Chris said, almost in a shout.

Deirdre shrugged. "I made sure that I had a guarantee of safety. Once I made up my mind, which didn't take long, I high-tailed it down to a bank that I will not reveal the location of, took out a safe-deposit box, and wrote out enough damning evidence to blow the whole thing open. Including a list of all of the contact numbers on Mr. Broken-Wing's cellphone, and a detailed description of the deal I'd been offered by my friend here. Then I gave instructions to a friend, who will also remain anonymous, that the box should be opened, and the contents given to the FBI, should I ever be killed, unless no body was found."

"Then you arranged your disappearance," Chris said.

"Yes."

"And here you are."

"And here I am," she said. "Safe and sound. They kept their end of the bargain, and I kept mine."

Another genteel nod from the elderly man.

I hope she realizes she'd better not slip up. I wouldn't want to be in her situation. It's playing with tigers. If they ever figure out how to get to her safe-deposit box, she'll be dead within the hour.

"And so you were the one who figured out Elisa's code," Chris said.

"Of course," Deirdre said cheerfully. "Good thing I was here. You were right that no one else but us knew the key. It was a good idea and would have worked had I actually been drowned."

"And now," the elderly man said, "we proceed. I recognize the pleasantries must be observed, but there is critical information my superiors need. Dr. Ross?"

"Whatever you say, chief," she said, then looked down at Chris. "Sorry, old buddy. Kind of sucks that it's come to this, you know?" She went to the other side of the room and came back pushing a small metal cart that carried an electronic device with a variety of dials and plugs. To the side was a horseshoe-shaped loop of metal, trailing a pair of wires. From the inside curve of the loop were regularly-spaced posts, each ending in a small metal disk.

Chris gave a frightened moan and began to struggle again, pulling away from her. He remembered how they had tortured Drolezki. He wouldn't be able to stand pain that severe. He'd tell them anything, he knew that.

"Oh, c'mon, just hold still," Deirdre said. "This won't hurt a bit." She retrieved a handful of wires from one of the lower shelves of the cart and began to plug them, one by one, into sockets on the machine. The wires ended with electrodes surrounded by sticky pads, and despite his thrashing she deftly placed them on Chris's skin—two on either side of his neck, two right above his nipples, two on his abdomen. She then turned to the machine, flipped a switch, and slowly turned a dial.

There was a fluttering sensation at the contact points, and Chris felt the fight drain from him. He had never been so scared in his life, but his ability to react to it physically, to fight back, slipped from him. His body, which had been taut as a guitar string, went completely slack, and he watched Deirdre, unable to do anything to thwart her.

The halo of metal was placed around his forehead and secured to the table. She twisted the posts until the disks they carried were securely in contact with his scalp. She worked calmly, unhurriedly. He heard the click of another switch, and then another. He could no longer turn his head to see what she was doing. His last thought was that he would have preferred a good old-fashioned flogging over this.

Then there was a hum emanating from somewhere inside his skull. It was like an internal itch. It was profoundly annoying. A heat slowly spread throughout his body, accompanied by a tension in his belly that was mildly uncomfortable but not really painful. He heard Deirdre's voice saying, "Okay, you can interrogate him. I'll keep track of his brain wave output and adjust the settings as needed, and you control everything else, as we've done in the past. I'll let you know if I need you to stop."

"Very good," came the man's voice, and then he heard a question being asked. The man had evidently moved close to Chris's left ear. He could feel the man's breath on his face, and a shiver ran through his frame.

"What do you remember from the cave?" he said.

Chris blinked. The itch became more intense. "Why should I cooperate with you?" he asked, and immediately the itching sensation doubled, tripled. He squeezed his eyelids shut, tried to lift his hands to rub them over his face, but the straps stopped him. If, indeed, the lethargy would have allowed him to move them that far. His arms felt like they weighed a thousand pounds each.

"Because I can reward you for answering," the man's voice said, like a gentle breeze in Chris's ear.

"I can't remember," Chris said. "I told you that earlier."

"Perhaps you might assist him, Dr. Ross?"

Chris felt a vibration from the disks against his scalp, and there was a visual sensation, like blue lightning radiating outward from him, illuminating everything in the room. Suddenly and astonishingly, he found he could remember. Whatever the halo was doing to his mind, it had jarred free his memories, and the images came flooding back, as clear as if they had happened moments before. Chris's eyes widened.

"So, I believe that you can remember, actually, can't you? As I told you, nothing is ever truly forgotten. Now answer the question. What did you see in the cave?"

"Fuck off," Chris said, but his voice sounded tired, powerless.

Instantly the crawling sensation inside him went from irritating to maddening to actual pain. He struggled feebly against the straps, heard his own voice crying out. "Stop," he shouted. "Stop it! Make it stop!"

"As you wish," the man said, and the intensity dropped back to an annoying internal itch. "Now answer me. What did you see in the cave?"

Chris's chest rose and fell in an irregular, jittery rhythm, but he didn't speak.

"Do you need another bit of urging?" the man asked in a menacing voice. "You may want to know that what you just experienced is perhaps five percent of what this machine is capable of. And the reward, should you cooperate, could be equally intense."

Chris knew he couldn't face the pain. His only chance was to stall—give him little pieces—and hope it would be enough to satisfy his curiosity. The rational part of his mind knew this wasn't true, but the thought of avoiding the torture again overrode it.

"We went into an opening in the hillside," he said, his voice quiet, monotone. Instantly the itching subsided, replaced by a pleasant warmth radiating from his solar plexus.

He gave a small sigh.

"We know that much," the man said. "Once you went in, what did you see?"

Chris closed his eyes. His forehead creased. "A long, dark tunnel," he said. "We thought… Glen thought it was too dangerous, that we shouldn't keep going. Lewis was worried, too, about drop-offs, holes in the floor. But we kept going, and it opened out. Then we realized we could see. It wasn't quite as dark. Elisa said she was scared, wanted to turn back. She was holding my arm…" He smiled at the memory. "Why do you want to know all of this? Don't you already know what was down there?"

"If we knew, we'd hardly be going to the trouble of asking you, would we?" the man breathed. The itch came back, slowly ramping up, still tolerable but unpleasant. Like bugs crawling inside his skull, inside his stomach, under his skin. "We know some. We need to find out more. And what you might have told others. Continue."

"We kept going," Chris said. The itching diminished again, the warmth returning. Manipulating the pleasure and pain circuitry of his brain. He knew enough neuroscience to understand it. Still, it was hard to resist, even knowing what they were doing. Even knowing he should not respond. Chris hoped he'd have the strength to refuse to answer if it was something important, but he simultaneously realized that he didn't. If they turned up the gain on the discomfort enough, he would cooperate. His mind might rebel, but his body would do what it was told, like a rat in a cage pushing a lever to activate the reward centers of the brain, doing it over and over, to the exclusion of everything else, until finally it died.

"We saw there was light ahead. It looked like artificial light. So we kept going. There were lights in the ceiling. Glen said he was scared, wanted to go back, but he didn't want to go back down the tunnel alone. Mary was terrified, but curious. She loved novelty, loved anything out of the ordinary and exciting, so she made a big act of being scared but was near the front of the group of us. And we came into a big, hollowed-out room, brightly lit." Chris paused.

"And what did you see there?" the man prompted.

Chris frowned at the image in front of his closed eyes, and then he opened them wide, but he could still see it, as if it was there with him. For a moment, he was mute with sheer incredulity. How could something this momentous have been buried for thirty years? Here was the answer to the link between him and his six friends, why all of them had been obsessed with outer space. Here was the link, however it had been suppressed.

"It's a spacecraft," Chris said. "A huge spacecraft."

"Ah," the man said.

"It's not made by humans."

"No," the man breathed in Chris's ear. "No, indeed it was not."

There was a sudden, sharp increase in the warmth in Chris's belly. He was being rewarded for cooperating. The warmth spread across him, rippling like waves across the bare skin on his chest, then down, down into his groin. He felt his penis stiffening.

"What did you see then?" the man asked.

Chris gave an inarticulate moan of pleasure, and the warmth spiked again.

"Answer me," the man said. "Or I'll make it stop. I'll bring back the discomfort. Be quick."

"It's damaged," Chris said. "It looks like it crash-landed. Mary went up and touched it. There doesn't seem to be anyone there, but it must have been brought underground... somehow... Glen said the cave was a lava tube. There was no way tthe spacecraft had gotten there on its own."

"No, he was right about that. What happened then?"

"Gavin has a camera. He's going to take some photographs." He paused, swallowed, and suddenly he realized that what he was seeing was only in his mind, that it was all something that had happened thirty years ago. Between the pleasure, and the vividness of his memories, he had felt for a moment like he was actually back there, standing in that cool, dimly-lit cave, Elisa still with her hand still on his arm, all of them staring at the wrecked vehicle of an alien race. "Gavin was excited. He took his camera out, and fiddled with it, then started snapping pictures. When the flash went off, someone must have seen it, because people came in. We got caught. They took us away, deeper into the cave complex. We were interrogated."

"Tell me what you were asked, and what you answered."

"We told them we had found the cave by accident. And we told them where the cave mouth was. They didn't know about that. Not until the seven of us stumbled in."

"How could they not have known that?" the man asked, his voice taking on a harsh edge.

"It's a huge cave complex," Chris said. His eyes were still closed, but he could see it clearly. "And the tunnel by which we came in was narrow. We heard them say the opening in the hillside must have only recently been exposed by erosion, and they would fill it in, to prevent any other hikers from finding it."

"Ah. I see. A sensible precaution. What happened to you next, after you were caught?"

"They separated us. I was taken into a small room by two men. One was a young guy, not much older than I was. Athletic-looking, tough, with red hair. The other was an older, heavy-set swarthy man who seemed to be in charge. There was… it looked like alien technology. They punished me when I refused to answer."

A faint laugh. "Just so," the man said. "The same is true here. Cooperation is rewarded, refusal is punished. It is a remarkably simple system. That much both ourselves and our enemies have realized."

"There was some kind of lab. They had all sorts of devices laid out on tables. It looked like the same material the ship was made of. I don't know what they were for."

"They didn't discuss any of them with you, I presume."

"No."

"A pity. But I feared as much. It was too much to hope for that you'd have details about what they'd recovered."

"But you know some of it, don't you?"

"Some. Not enough. We would like all of it. One day soon, perhaps."

But Chris was pulled back into memories, and his eyes opened wide. "They were going to kill us," he said.

"Yes. I would imagine so."

"But then they changed their minds. They said they'd wipe our memories, instead. Seven college kids disappearing would raise too much suspicion. There'd be search parties. So they put a gun up against my head..."

"Not a gun, I am certain, although it may have looked like one."

Chris swallowed again. "I thought they were going to kill me. I felt a cold piece of metal touch my forehead. Then there was a shock, like touching an electric fence. My ears were ringing."

"And they led you out, back to the cave mouth."

"Yes."

"Do you remember anything else?"

Chris didn't answer for a moment. The itch returned, a prickling beneath his navel, behind his eyes. His erection dwindled, and he squeezed his eyes closed.

"What you're doing to me now," he said, and it was an effort to talk. Much easier to cooperate, to let them stroke his pleasure centers, to relax into it. Much harder to fight back... But after a moment, he said, "What you're doing to me now. It's alien technology, isn't it? This halo, and the way it's making me feel things..."

"Oh, indeed it is," the man said, and the prickling intensified. "But you're not answering the question. Do you remember anything else?"

"From the cave?"

"Anything else connected to what you saw."

"No," Chris said. "Nothing. I really can't think of anything else."

The intensity of the discomfort rose, just slightly, like a warning. "One more thing, Mr. Franzia," the old man said. His voice made it sound like an afterthought. "Who is Iktomi7979?"

"Who?" Chris said, frowning. Again, only a hint of an increase, like insects crawling in his abdomen, making the skin on his belly flutter.

"Oh, don't play coy, Mr. Franzia," the man breathed in his ear. "You know perfectly well who I'm talking about."

"I…" Chris began, and licked his lips again, stopped. What could he say about this without betraying Elisa? Or was she right now in a different room, also strapped to a table, and undergoing the same interrogation? The idea filled him with rage. That he might die, even that he might be tortured to death, he could accept. That they would be doing the same to Elisa was intolerable.

"I have no idea what the fuck you're talking about," Chris said.

"Oh, I think you do." The intensity spiked, crossed into actual pain. Chris gave a muffled groan, then clamped his mouth and eyes shut. "I think you know exactly who I'm talking about. Ms. Reed mentioned him in her email to you. He knew Mr. McCormick. That much was clear from the outset. But we have strong reason to believe that he knew all of you, Mr. Franzia. He knew every one of the seven. And we need to know his identity. So I will repeat my question again… who is Iktomi7979?"

"I don't know."

The pain became a burning, searing sensation, like he was being torn apart by red-hot pincers. He strained against the straps, muscles burning with exertion. Didn't they do that, for real, back in the Dark Ages? Heat metal spikes in the fire, drive them into the feet, into the belly, into the eyes. Chris's mind fought to convince his body that the pain wasn't real.

Again the question. Patient, calm, uninflected.

"I don't know!" Chris said, through clenched teeth.

This time Chris cried out. His back arched until only his head, secured by the metal halo, and his heels were touching the examining table.

"Who is Iktomi7979?"

"Fuck you! I don't *know!*" Chris screamed, and that was when the pain passed the point where he could think, respond. He was balanced there, on the pinnacle of agony beyond anything he had ever experienced, for what seemed like an eternity…

… and then it was gone. Nothing, the simple absence of pain, seemed like bliss by comparison. His body slumped back onto the table, his skin dripping sweat, his chest rising and falling spasmodically. His eyes were rolling upwards in his head; he thought he might faint, or vomit, but successfully resisted both.

"Mr. Franzia," the man said, still from a point near his left ear, "you realize, of course, that we can repeat that as many times as necessary, to ensure your cooperation. Because there is nothing being physically damaged in your body. You are in no particular danger of dying from the procedure, although you might wish you would. So, shall we begin again?

"Who is Iktomi7979?"

Chris lost count of the number of times they repeated the cycle of torture. His shrieks echoed from the walls at the peaks to be replaced by jittering breaths, sometimes actual sobs, when the pain stopped. Once, during one of the respites, he gasped out the words, "Kill me and get it over with."

"Oh, we will," the man said. "Once you answer my question."

And up the escalating ladder of agony he went again. He couldn't take any more. And then he thought of Elisa, undergoing the same treatment, and the fury rose in him, made the pain bearable, made him able to resist.

But resist what? Chris didn't know who Iktomi7979 was.

Or did he?

The torture swelled in him, like burning acid inside his torso, and he lost everything but the awareness of pain.

After more cycles than Chris could remember, he lay, shivering and twitching on the table, his whole body soaked with sweat. He heard Deirdre's ask, "What if he really doesn't know?"

The man spoke, his voice tight with barely-controlled fury, "He must know. The emails we intercepted, that led us to McCormick. They implied a close connection."

"Well, I was part of that circle of friends too, remember? And I didn't know. It's possible that Chris doesn't, either."

A hand came down on a table with a bang. "We must find out. It is evident that Iktomi7979 knows who we are, what we are attempting, enough of it to cause serious problems. The other communications we have intercepted from the individual using that handle were damning."

"I know. We've been through this before."

"Someone else besides McCormick must know his identity."

"Maybe, but I don't think it's Chris." Chris heard a note of compassion entering Deirdre's voice. "Putting him through more of this won't make any difference. You already had the intensity up to eighty percent. If that didn't make him spill what he knows, he doesn't know what you're after."

A muffled snort of anger. "Then he's useless. He knows nothing of value. We should have simply had Drolezki execute him." The man's voice neared Chris's ear again. "Mr. Franzia, can you hear me and respond?"

There was a pause, and then Chris said, his voice hoarse and weak, "I told you. I told you I didn't know."

"Yes, well, you also told us that you weren't going to cooperate, so we are perhaps to be forgiven for thinking you might need a little urging."

"A little urging?" Chris said, licking his lips and then coughing. His head ached, and the points of contact between the halo and his scalp felt like enormous swollen bruises.

"We have found such methods necessary in the past," the man said.

"You enjoy this, don't you?"

"Mr. Franzia, really…"

"Bet you love these torture sessions," Chris said, his voice rising. "People like you always do. You probably videotape it and jack off at night watching it. You knew from the beginning I didn't know anything, didn't you? Deirdre apparently didn't know what was in the cave, or who Iktomi is, so why do you think I would? The whole thing was only a game, a way to pay me back for putting you people to so much trouble. For not just dying quietly like the others did. You're not even human. And you, Deirdre?" He struggled to see her. "You used to be a good person. Now you're assisting these people? I'm going to die now, I know it, and I'm okay with that, because if you folks are in charge of things, I'd rather be dead. But watch your back, Dr. Ross. Trust no one. If they find your weak spot, you'll be where I am before you know it. Just remember you chose to align yourself with the worst people in the world. I hope they're paying you well…"

Chris heard the old man say, rough anger in his voice, "Shut him up." Then there was a sensation like a soundless explosion in his head, and his consciousness went out like someone flipping a switch.

Chris opened his eyes an uncertain amount of time later, disoriented, confused, with vertigo and a splitting headache. He was lying flat on his back. He blinked once, twice, and his vision cleared enough to see that he was once again in the first room, the one he'd awakened in earlier that day.

If it was the same day. There was no way to tell.

A familiar voice spoke, and Chris once again had the sense that he was dreaming.

"Oh, God, Chris, I thought you might never wake up."

He turned his head, activating a thousand new aches and pains, to see Elisa Reed, her kind face pinched with anxiety, walking toward him. She looked much like he re-membered—small, with green eyes, long chestnut-brown hair held back by a clasp, round wire-frame glasses. She had some gray in her hair, and laugh lines around her eyes, but the thirty years since they'd last seen each other had been kind.

She knelt by the bed, stroked his cheek with one cool hand, and said, "How are you feeling?"

"Like I was put through a meat grinder," Chris said. His voice was hoarse.

She slid her arms beneath him, rested her head against his chest. He passed one arm around her, then the other, still feeling terribly weak. "They tortured you," she said.

"Yes."

She was silent for a moment, and Chris felt a tear strike his bare skin and roll downward, leaving a cool trail behind it. But when she spoke, her voice was steady. "You didn't tell them what they wanted."

"No. Mostly because I didn't know the answer."

"Good." Her voice took on a hard edge. "I'm glad."

"But, Elisa, if I had known… I think I would have told them anything, anything to get the torture to stop." Chris felt close to helpless tears himself.

"It's over. It's over now." She pressed her face to him, held him in a tight embrace. He closed his eyes and re-laxed into it.

"They didn't… hurt you?" he asked, a few minutes later.

"Not much. They used some kind of mind-reading device on me. At least that's what I think it was. It felt like mental lightning, but it didn't hurt. No worse than a carpet shock, at least."

"Did they tell you they weren't the ones who killed Gavin and Glen and the rest?"

"Yes. Do you believe them?"

"I don't know what to believe. But even if they aren't the ones who killed our college friends, they're not good guys. Good guys don't torture people."

"No. No, they don't."

He sighed. "They were getting even with me. They're playground bullies who have figured out how to get away with it." He cleared his throat. The headache and the vertigo were subsiding. "How long have I been here?"

"They brought you in, unconscious, a while ago. Deirdre was with them. Did you know… know that she…" She trailed off, leaving the question unspoken.

"Yes, I know she's alive. She was there while they were torturing me. She was helping them."

"Goddamn her!" Elisa burst out. "How could she? We were friends. How could you do that to a friend?"

"All I can say is that we misjudged her. A lot. I always thought she had a ruthless streak, even back then. She's not just aggressive. She's mercenary. Amoral."

"She was the one who persuaded them to let us spend some time together. At least she did that much."

"How much time do we have?"

A pause. "She said no more than an hour." Another tear, and her arms tightened around him. "We're going to be terminated."

"Figures," Chris said, but he felt his heart race at the thought.

Another pause. "It's not fair. It's not fair at all."

"No. You're right, it isn't. Nothing is, really. Fair is a concept that doesn't mean much. Why would we expect the universe to be fair, anyway? Look around you. Some things end well, others end badly, and there doesn't seem to be any reason for any of it. If the Christians are right, and God does have a plan, then all I can say is that he's hiding it well, because it sure as hell looks like chaos to me."

"We could have had something together, you know."

He rubbed his hand across her back. "I know."

"I thought about you sometimes, in those thirty years. Especially after Tim and I broke up. That was twelve years ago. I wondered where you were, and if you had a wife or a girlfriend. I thought about calling you. I used to fantasize about it. That we'd have this long-distance romance, and then you'd come to visit me, sweep me off my feet." He could feel her smiling, against the skin on his chest. "But I never did it. Inertia, you know? You stay at rest because you're already at rest, and that's that."

"Oh, I know all about inertia," Chris said.

"It's the same reason why I never changed my name

back. Tim and me, we never really fought. We drifted apart. Maybe we never had much in common to begin with, I don't know. It would have been different had we really hated each other. I think I would have changed my name back. But I'd grown used to being Elisa Reed, so it was just as easy to stay Elisa Reed. Never doing anything different. Never taking a chance on a new life."

"If you'd gone back to being Elisa Howard, they'd probably have found you quicker, like they did the others. Caught up with you and killed you."

"Well, they did, anyway. Here we are, remember?"

"I remember. But at least we've got a few minutes together."

"That's true." She took a deep breath. "Did they tell you how they're going to do it? Execute us?"

"No. The guy who was running the torture machine on me, he said he could make me die easily or painfully, and which it was going to be depended on how well I co-operated. I didn't cooperate very well. Maybe they'll think they've already put me through enough."

"I think I could take anything except being hanged. That has always struck me as the most horrible thing I can think of."

"Being burned at the stake probably isn't any fun, either."

Elisa laughed softly. "Can you believe we're talking about this? I'd have thought I'd be running around in circles screaming. I've read stories about people facing the death penalty. Have you heard about Sir Thomas More?"

"I know the name."

"He was a staunch Catholic, back in the time of Henry VIII. Bad idea, that turned out to be. More wouldn't convert, so Henry had him beheaded. So there he is, walking up the stairs to the block. The headsman is there, with his axe, waiting. And More stumbles a little. So he says to the guard, 'See me safely up onto the scaffold, sir. On the voyage downwards, I'll fend for myself.'"

Chris laughed. "That takes balls, joking around with the guys who are about to kill you."

"Probably the best way to exit," Elisa said. "If it's inevitable, may as well keep some dignity."

"I didn't keep much dignity when they had me hooked up to that pain machine," Chris said. "I think I used some pretty inappropriate language, mostly aimed at the guy who was turning the dials, not to mention screaming myself hoarse."

"Nothing wrong with defiance, either," Elisa said. "After all, that's what gallows humor is. Spitting in the face of Death. You can kill me, but you can't break my spirit."

Chris's arms tightened around her. "I wish this wasn't about to end."

"Me, too. But at least we have this moment. The moment is all we ever have, really."

Chris smiled. He knew what he wanted to ask, but he

was scared to do it. It was like being in the tenth grade all over again. The difference this time was that he was about to die. So he said, "Can I kiss you?"

She lifted her head, and looked at him. She was smiling herself, but her eyes were glossy with tears. "Of course."

He sat up, and reached out and touched her face. Then he leaned toward her, and their lips met. She slipped her arms around him. The electricity of the kiss set every nerve in his body tingling, with a deep, pure sweetness that was nothing like the false induced pleasure he'd felt when his brain had been stimulated by the halo.

This is what it's like, being alive. This feeling. At least he got to experience it once before he died.

They separated, and he said, gently, "I wish this could have ended differently."

"Me, too."

"But we gave them a good run, you know. If it hadn't been for Deirdre, we might have made it."

Perhaps ten minutes passed. There seemed to be nothing more to say, so they just held each other. Lying there, feeling Elisa pressed up against him, he came to a decision. When they came to get him, he was going to echo what Thomas More had done. Keep his dignity. If this is what it had come to, they might kill him, but he'd go without crying or begging. Maybe no one would see it but the executioner, but even so, it was better than giving them the satisfaction of seeing him fall apart.

Elisa spoke before Chris did, but she spoke what he was thinking.

"I think it's been over an hour."

"I doubt they'd forget about us," he said. "I don't want to sound pessimistic, but it's probably not the time to get our hopes up, yet."

Her arm tightened around his middle. "I've never given up hope."

He chuckled. "You were always like that. I remember you had a hellacious home life and you still always made the best of things."

"It wasn't always easy."

"I'm sure. My parents were great. I can't imagine what you went through."

"My stepdad was a beast. Abusive. And he made inappropriate comments to me, and about me to my half-brothers. Jay and Dennis, they made me stay away because they were afraid for me. I have no idea how my mom put up with it; but she apparently loved him, however weird that seems to me. He died twenty years ago." She paused. "My mother wanted me to come back, when he was dying. To see him one last time. So I did. Seeing him there, in that hospital bed… I had built him up into this monster, all those years, until he was larger than life. I was really afraid, walking into the room, but then I got there, and I thought, 'That's all he is?' He was this shriveled little old man lying there, a wisp of a thing, like a dry husk that a breeze would blow away. I know some of it was the cancer, but I thought, 'This is what I've been terrified of, all this time?' And since then, I've always remembered that. What you're afraid of tends to be very much less than what you think it is. Maybe that's what death will be like. Maybe we humans have built it up into this horrible thing, and then when we're there, we'll laugh, and say, 'Wow. This is what I feared? If only I'd known.'"

Chris kissed the top of her head. "I think I love you," he said.

She smiled. "You only think so?"

"I didn't want to be too forward."

Elisa laughed, a genuine, joyful laugh. "Still as gentle and kind as you always were," she said. "Well, Chris Franzia, I think I love you, too."

The lights flickered suddenly. There was a sound like a static crackle. Chris looked up, feeling the hairs on the back of his arm prickling. The overhead lighting came from recessed fixtures with circular panels of translucent glass. It looked fluorescent, but it was hard to be certain. There was another flicker, another crackle, and the lights went out. The room was plunged into complete darkness.

Then there was the soft click as the lock on the door unbolted, and a slight creak as the door opened just a crack. There was a faint sliver of light from the hallway.

Chris tensed. Was this it? Were they about to be led to their deaths?

But a minute passed, then two. Nothing more happened.

Chris stood, and Elisa let her arm slip from around him. He walked slowly toward the door, and then pulled it open.

There was no one there.

"What's happening?" Elisa said, as she came up behind him. She put one hand on his shoulder.

"I don't know. I wonder if the power failure caused the locks to malfunction. They're all electronic. They're operated by keypads."

"That'd be a dumb design. Don't you think they're smarter than that? Fancy electronic locks that malfunction and release everyone they're holding prisoner whenever the power stutters a little?" She pointed out into the hall. "And there's obviously a backup generator. There are emergency lights in the hallway."

Chris peered out into the long hall, first in one direction, then in the other. It was hard to see very far. Even with the lights positioned along the floor every ten feet or so, he could only discern a little way.

"Do you know the way out?" Elisa asked.

He shook his head. "I was brought in drugged. I have no idea where the exit is. I think we're below ground, if this is the same hallway I was in when I first got here."

"Well, we still should try to get away. We won't get another opportunity. Anything is better than staying here."

That seemed like good advice. He reached out and

took her hand, and together they walked down the hallway, past door after door. About a hundred feet on, it took a right angle turn, and there they got their first real shock.

There was a blonde woman lying on the ground, dead, with a single bullet hole in the middle of her forehead.

"Jesus," Elisa breathed.

"Do you recognize her?"

She shook her head. "I've never seen her before."

They walked on. A second dead body, this one a young Asian man, was slumped in an alcove. He, too had been shot, but he'd evidently tried to defend himself. There was a gun lying on the floor next to him, and across the hall there were two bullet holes in the wall.

Chris picked up the fallen gun, holding it a little gingerly. He looked down at it, his face an unreadable mix of emotions.

"Could you use that on someone?" Elisa said.

"If I run into that old man who tortured me," he said grimly, "I think I could. And it's better than being unarmed."

She squeezed his hand, and a little further on, they came to a door with a window. In that entire long hallway, it was the first window they'd seen. There was no exit sign, or in fact a sign of any kind, but through the window they saw stairs. Chris dropped Elisa's hand to pull open the door, and peered inside, cautiously looking up and down the staircase. He held the gun at chest level, feeling the ridged metal of the trigger against his index finger.

But there was no one there.

"Come on," he said, and she followed, taking his hand again. The door shut with a loud clunk behind him, making him jump a little.

"Shit," he hissed, under his breath. "What the hell is going on? Where is everyone?"

"That's not a bad thing," Elisa said.

"No, but it's creeping me right the hell out. I don't like what I can't understand." Drolezki had said that, Chris recalled. We like to have explanations, we humans.

They walked up the staircase, their footfalls echoing against the tile walls. They went one floor up, only to find another long hallway, then up another, and another. The light three floors up seemed brighter and more natural, so they opened the door into yet another hall.

Just outside of the door from the stairwell, there were eight bodies, all dead of gunshot wounds. The linoleum floor was slick with their blood. Chris tried not to look at them, especially into their eyes, now staring into nowhere. Hands were stretched out on the floor like reaching claws. Several more guns were there, fallen where they'd been dropped.

"Should you take a gun?" Chris said, but Elisa shook her head, shuddered, and gripped his hand more tightly.

The furthest body in the group, lying face up with his chest covered with blood, turned out to be Drolezki.

Chris stopped, and looked down into Drolezki's face, and a shiver ran through him.

"Glad they got you, you sonofabitch," he said. Elisa looked at Chris questioningly. "The guy who caught me and brought me here," he explained, and they started walking again.

"What happened here?" she asked. "How can they all be dead?"

"No idea. But whatever went down, went down fast. I can't imagine people like this being caught unawares. This is almost scarier, somehow."

"Why?"

"Because it implies that however powerful and destructive these people were, there's something worse."

"At least they seem to be on our side. The enemy of my enemy is my friend."

They passed two more bodies. Chris found himself already getting used to seeing dead bodies, and found the idea repugnant. It was like what happened in war. And it happened amazingly fast.

"Have you seen the people who interrogated you?"

She shook her head. "It was a middle-aged woman. African American, with thick glasses. She had an assistant, a young guy, kind of nondescript. Mousy-looking. But they could be anywhere. I had no idea how huge this place is."

"How badly did they hurt you?"

"Not much. They were very clinical. It was uncomfortable but bearable. Certainly not the kind of torture you went through."

"I'm glad. When the pain was happening I kept thinking about them doing the same thing to you, and it made me absolutely furious. I was so angry that I couldn't be afraid, and couldn't give too much attention to what they were doing to me."

"Just hearing that makes me want to cry."

"Don't. It's over. Whatever happened here, I just know it's over. Maybe we're jumping out of the frying pan and into the fire, but this part of it... this place is finished. It's a tomb."

And that was when a hand grabbed Chris's ankle.

Chris gave an inarticulate shout and a reflexive kick, and stumbled backwards, almost losing his balance. Elisa was frozen in place, her eyes huge.

The hand belonged to an elderly woman, whose face and hand were covered with blood. She wore eyeglasses, but one lens had a jagged crack and a piece missing. Despite Chris's kick, she held onto his pants leg, and looked up at him with a fierce expression, baring her teeth like an animal.

"You've done all this, you two," she hissed at him. "It's your fault. But you can't stop us. You're scheduled to be terminated."

Chris brought up the gun, and before he could stop himself, he'd fired off three shots. One of them ricocheted off the floor, and he heard a sharp crack as it shattered one of the tiles on the wall.

The other two struck the woman in the back. She gave a spasmodic shudder, and a hoarse rattle, and then her hand relaxed.

Chris stood there, his breath coming in whining gasps, trying to stop his heart from pounding. Inside his skull, like a voice in an echo chamber, came the words, "I just killed someone," repeated again and again.

He looked down. There was a bloody handprint on the leg of his jeans. He reeled backwards, dropping the gun with a clatter, and then fell to his knees and retched, but brought up nothing but acrid saliva.

The dry heaves struck him over and over. For a time all he could do was huddle on all fours, gagging, as the image of the woman's bloodied, desperate face stared back at him. Elisa knelt next to him, her cool hands on the naked skin of his back, centering him, bringing him back to the present. The feeling passed, leaving only a sick, helpless shivering. And she said quietly, "Chris, it's okay. Come on. You'll be okay. You had to do it. But we've got to get out of here."

He looked up at her and nodded, but couldn't manage words. With her hand on his arm, steadying him, he struggled to his feet, wiped his mouth with the back of his hand. He staggered a little at the first step, then scolded himself for being weak. He cleared his throat, and managed a faint smile at her.

"I'll be all right," he said.

"I know."

She kept her hand protectively on his upper arm as they went forward down the hall. It was like the cave all over again, only the other way around. Here, Elisa was the strong one.

Five minutes later they heard sounds ahead of them. Other than the woman that Chris had killed, the only sounds they'd heard since leaving confinement. Running footsteps, an angry shout, followed by the unmistakable sound of gunfire.

Chris and Elisa both flattened themselves against the wall. There was nowhere to hide. They were in a long hallway with only a few doors, none of which were nearby, and which were likely to be locked in any case. But a little further up was a turn to the right. It seemed to be the direction from which the sounds had come.

Chris motioned for Elisa to stay where she was, and edged his way forward. There was now only silence from ahead. He got to the angle of the wall and cautiously peered around it. He could see a huddled form, probably another corpse, a little way ahead.

Then suddenly three men wearing black riot gear, including helmets and visors, crossed the hallway. They moved quickly and silently and didn't turn his way. Chris gave a gasp, then winced, hoping he hadn't been heard.

They must be the people who had destroyed the base.

If so, were they on Chris's side? Had the old man been lying about who had killed Gavin and Glen and the others? Either way, jumping out in front of armed men on a search-and-destroy mission seemed inadvisable. It'd suck if they were trying to help him, but shot him only to discover their mistake afterwards.

He slipped back to where Elisa was still standing.

"There are some men up ahead," he whispered. "Armed. They must be the ones who did all this. They weren't coming this way. They crossed the hall and kept going, I think."

"Is it safe to keep going?"

"Probably not. But I don't know what else to do."

They got to the turn in the hall, and once again peered around the corner. Other than the dead body, it was completely empty.

Only a minute later they turned another right-angle bend and ahead of them was the unmistakable pale glow of daylight. Two more bodies lay prone, one against the wall, the other sprawled face down in the middle of the floor. Chris gave them wide berth, but they showed no signs of life. And then past them, beyond all hope or guessing, what they most wanted to see…

An exit.

They broke into a run, and Chris's bare shoulder punched the doorframe, flung it outward. A cool gust of wind, carrying a spray of drizzle, slapped them in the face.

"Hey," someone shouted.

They slowly turned together, Chris's hand still clasping Elisa's.

A car was driving slowly toward them. It was a gray sedan. Behind it was a small fleet of other vehicles. Leaning out of the driver's side window of the sedan was a handsome young man with a tanned face and sun-streaked brown hair that Chris had last seen in a tollbooth on the Indiana state line. He gave them a broad grin.

"We thought we were going to have to go inside and search the whole building for you two," he said. "Get in."

CHAPTER 21

"A ren't you cold?" the boy asked in a conversational tone. His name was Keller Davis, and he himself was dressed in a long-sleeved t-shirt and a sleeveless fleece, driving with one hand casually draped on the top of the steering wheel, the wipers swishing back and forth across the windshield like a metronome.

"I lost my shirt in there," Chris said. "They didn't give me another one."

"Yeah, we know about that," Keller said, flashing another grin at Chris. "That's how we were tracking you, you know. A bug on your shirt, powered by your body warmth.

But when you took your shirt off, we didn't know where in the building you were."

"My shirt was bugged?" Chris said, a little incredulously.

"Yeah. That's why we found your shirt, even though you were no longer in it. It was in bad shape, unfortunately. I'm guessing you didn't take it off voluntarily."

"Very much the opposite."

"That sucks. I can turn up the heater if you want."

Elisa had her arm around Chris's shoulders, and he leaned into her a little. "No, that's okay," he said. "I'm fine. But if I can get another shirt at some point...?"

"Oh, sure. I called ahead. I'm sure they'll have one for you."

"They? Who are they?"

"The people I'm taking you to see. The ones who engineered your daring rescue. Sorry you had to get out of the building under your own power, but it's a big place, and like I said, we didn't know where exactly you were. When we realized that it would have taken too long to find you, we hacked into their security system and disabled the locks. We sent some of our people in to try and find you, and then hoped for the best." He grinned. "You got out before you got found, which is pretty amazing, considering. I don't know if you got the grand tour of it while you were there, but it's mostly underground. From the outside, it looks like a little office building, nestled amongst the trees. An insurance agency, or something." Another grin. "Impressive place. It's like an iceberg."

Chris looked out of the window. It was still drizzling, and the road wound its way through craggy hills covered with Douglas fir and thick undergrowths of salal and salmonberry. He saw a turnoff that said, *Skykomish 10 miles*, which told him that he was somewhere northeast of Seattle, but not much more than that.

Chris had no intention of ever coming near this place again. If he got out of this alive, he vowed to never set foot within a hundred-mile radius of that place. He shivered a little, and Elisa pulled him close.

"So," she said, in a light tone. "These people you're taking us to see. Are they also eager to torture us for information and then kill us? Because if so, you might want to know that the people we got away from didn't get much in the way of useful information for all of their time and effort."

Keller laughed. "No, I don't think so," he said.

"You don't think so?"

"Well, I'm not in charge. But we wouldn't have kept you alive all of this time if we really wanted to kill you, would we?"

"I guess not," Elisa admitted. "But why did you keep us alive? What was in it for you?"

"I think I'll let my boss explain that. She has more information than I do. I'm a flunky, really. Odd jobs." Another flash of white teeth. "Like taking over for tollbooth operators when they get unexpectedly delayed while coming to work."

"I don't know if that's supposed to be reassuring, but at the moment, it's creeping me right the hell out," Chris said.

Keller laughed. "Well, it worked out in your favor, didn't it? Don't knock it."

The drive continued, winding northward along the western Cascade foothills. Chris suddenly felt exhausted. Not surprising, considering what he'd been through. Whatever more they had planned for them, he decided that he'd deal with it after he took a nap.

• • • •

He awoke some uncertain amount of time later when the car braked to a stop, its tires crunching on gravel. It was completely dark, and the drizzle had shifted into full-blown rain. There were lights on in a nearby building, partly hidden amongst the silhouettes of shrubbery. To Chris's eyes, still a little blurred from sleep, it looked strangely like the place he'd just left, and he had a sudden clenching fear that they'd driven in a circle.

But he realized that was ridiculous. If he was supposed to be killed by those people Deirdre Ross was working with, he would have been left there, not put through the charade of a fake rescue. This place had to be opposed to the people who were trying to hurt them. It was more like the equal-and-opposite of the people who tortured him. Yin and yang, light and dark, black and white, good and evil.

"Sorry, you're gonna have to make a run for the door," Keller said, giving Chris an apologetic smile. "It's freakin' cold for July, but you know, that's western Washington for you. We can get you some warmer clothes once we're inside."

"No problem," Chris said, and opened the door. The smell of wet vegetation struck him, along with a wind-blown spray of rain, and he got out, following the boy at a jog toward a brightly-lit front door, as the chilly drops stung his skin.

Keller held the door for Elisa and Chris, then followed them through. Chris shivered a little, and the boy said, "Did you get a sweatshirt?" to a tall, lanky man wearing a neat white shirt and dark tie who was standing inside a reception booth against the far wall.

"Yes," the man said, and held out a brand new University of Washington Huskies t-shirt and sweatshirt. Chris took them and donned them, and then said, "Thanks. Much better."

"Catch your death out there," the lanky man said with a smile.

Chris said, "Yeah."

"Got you some food, too," the man said, handing Elisa a pair of plastic-wrapped sandwiches. "Tuna fish. Hope neither of you is vegetarian."

"Wouldn't stand on principle at this point even if we were," Elisa said, and handed a sandwich to Chris, then unwrapped the other and took a grateful bite.

Keller said, "This way," and gestured toward a hallway that led off toward a series of doors.

This place really was the counterpart of where they'd just left. What if they were walking blindly into the hands of people who were worse? But however much his logical mind sounded the alarm, his emotions couldn't respond. It'd have to be whatever it was. He couldn't run any more.

Keller stopped in front of one of the last doors in the hall, opened it, and said, "Step right in. I'm leaving you in good hands. Glad you made it here safely."

Elisa went into the room. Chris followed, and they stepped from the tile hallway floor into a plushly carpeted office, with tasteful furnishings and a large teak desk. More welcoming, at least, than the tile-floored laboratory/torture chamber in the other place.

Sitting behind the desk, her hands folded primly in front of her, was an elderly woman, smiling at them in a maternal fashion.

Chris goggled at her. "You?"

"I don't expect you thought you'd ever see me again. Peru, Indiana, wasn't it? I gave your doggie a biscuit."

"And..." Realization dawned, and he reached up and touched his shoulder. "You're the one who bugged my shirt."

She nodded. "Excellent memory, Mr. Franzia. A

friendly pat on the shoulder is all it takes if you are skilled in such things. There were three bugs, actually. All powerful, high-tech, waterproof, virtually indestructible, and able to keep running indefinitely if kept warm. We try not to put all of our eggs in one basket. The one on your vehicle was not my doing. We'd placed it there weeks earlier. When you abandoned your car in Missouri, we lost that means of locating you. The other two, however, I placed. One of them, on your dog's collar, you found and removed immediately. A smart bit of work, that was, and putting it in another car was clever. It put us off your trail only for a few hours, though, because the one on your shirt remained with you. We used it to track you all the way across the country." She stood, and reached out a hand, and shook Elisa's hand, and then Chris's. "In any case, welcome. We're very glad you're here. My name is Mrs. Dorothy Hargroder."

"That's not your real name, is it?" Chris said.

She laughed. "Such a suspicious nature. But well-earned, I would say. No. It is not. That is who I am here and now, so it will do." She gestured toward Chris. "In any case, first things first. Before we discuss several matters of great importance to all of us, there is something even more urgent." She stood, walked to a closed door in the far wall, and opened it, revealing a small utility room with a throw rug and two plastic bowls on the floor.

Baxter cannoned out the door, nearly bowling her

over, and leapt at Chris with an enthusiasm only a dog can muster.

After a moment, Chris looked up, tears in his eyes, and said, "How…?"

Mrs. Hargroder gave him a grandmotherly smile. "Those who help us are rewarded for it."

Chris stared at her, his eyes narrowing. A sudden chill tempered his excitement at seeing his dog, beyond all hope, still alive. That's what the old man said. Reward and punishment. "What did I do to help you?"

"You led us to the enemy headquarters, of course. In their eagerness to interrogate you, they did not make you strip completely when you were caught. Sloppy of them. We have been trying to find their central office for a long time. We knew for years that it was somewhere near Seattle. But 'somewhere near Seattle' is a big, big place, and until now, they have been exceedingly careful. The tracking device on your shirt allowed our technicians to pinpoint its location."

"And you came in and killed them all."

Her expression tightened, by an infinitesimal degree. "Surely, Mr. Franzia, you are not about to go all tenderhearted about our eradicating men and women who would have been delighted to torture you and your friend to death."

"But who were they?" he asked. "They're like the Illuminati, right? Gavin was right about all of his conspiracy theories?"

"In a way," she said. "It's not that the conspiracy theorists are wrong, really. The world is full of conspiracies. The mistake most conspiracy theorists make is in assuming only the bad guys can successfully engage in one."

"And you're the good guys?" Elisa interjected.

"At the moment, it appears we are," Mrs. Hargroder said. "Given that had we not stormed the compound, as it were, the two of you would almost certainly be dead by now."

"They told us they weren't the ones who killed Gavin and Glen and the others. Is that the truth?"

Mrs. Hargroder looked at Chris for a moment without speaking. "There are some parts of this it would not be in your best interest for us to explain."

Chris stared at her in dawning comprehension. "You're the ones who killed them, aren't you?"

Mrs. Hargroder did not answer him.

"You did. You killed them. The others were telling the truth, about that, at least. But why did you start to help us?"

Elisa shook her head, and said in a bleak voice, "That's easy, Chris. We were bait. Once they'd failed in their attempts to kill us, and realized we were fleeing right into their enemies' arms, it was more prudent to let us live and get the whole prize."

"That is a narrow view," Mrs. Hargroder said, displeasure showing in her face. "I have expressed to you my gratitude for your assistance. I would have thought you would be somewhat grateful in return for ours. Without it, you would by now have been tortured to death."

"Maybe," Chris said. "But even so, you're the same. Both of you are trying to accomplish the same thing, aren't you? Controlling people. Influencing governments. You're at the same game. You're enemies not because you're philosophically in opposition, but because you're in competition."

"Mr. Franzia, I hardly think…"

"No, wait. You've killed five people, and tried to kill us, and then when that didn't work you used us as pawns to find their headquarters. If you were any different from the people you call your enemies, you would have warned us right away, protected us. Not killed people because of what they might know, then let us run across the country directly into a situation where we were tortured and interrogated and might have died."

"You must understand, Mr. Franzia," Mrs. Hargroder said. "We did not do these things because we wanted to, because we're some kind of evil geniuses bent on harming others for fun. It is at its base about the welfare of humanity, and about keeping dangerous technology out of the hands of people who, despite your doubt on this point, are capable and willing to do far worse than we are. What you and your friends knew was simply too dangerous. Mr. Mc-Cormick, especially, had become a serious liability."

"Liability?" Chris snarled. "This is not some kind of

game. We're talking about people's lives. Not just Gavin and the rest. Chase Ballengee…"

"Mr. Ballengee knew the risks he was undertaking," Mrs. Hargroder interrupted, in a stern voice.

"Oh. So he was one of you, too? What about Thomas T. Champion? What about the Harpers? What about the bum who they shot in the motel parking lot in St. Joseph, Missouri? What about the woman at the hotel in Pennsylvania, who warned me about the guys who had asked about me? Are they all working for you? Were they all just trying to keep me alive so I could perform a service?"

"I am not going to confirm or deny anything regarding people you may have met. You need to understand, Mr. Franzia. Great things are at stake, here."

"Yeah," Chris said, his voice rising angrily. "That's what the other side said, too. Great things. More important than human lives. Let me tell you, once you decide that accomplishing a purpose is more important than a human life, there is nothing to separate your acts from those of your enemies. Not one fucking thing." He stood up. "Elisa, if you agree with anything I said, we should leave now."

"Yes," Elisa said, and stood up, putting her hand in Chris's. "Yes, we should go."

"Wait," Mrs. Hargroder said, and they stopped. Chris turned until his gaze locked on the old woman's. "You cannot leave," she said.

"What, now you're going to hold us prisoner?" Chris said. "What happened to gratitude?"

"Sit down and stop being a fool," she said.

Chris remained standing. "What you have to say, I can hear it just as well standing up," he said. "But make it fast, because in five minutes, Elisa and I are walking right the hell out of here and taking our chances with whatever's out there. Unless you change your mind and decide to kill us. Because I am done with this, and this whole ridiculous war." He looked over at Elisa. "Disagree?"

She shook her head. "I'm with you. One hundred per-cent." And then both of them looked over at Mrs. Har-groder, waiting for her to explain.

"You have two options," she said. All of the grandmo-therly benevolence was gone. She looked like she was con-trolling her anger with an effort. "You can, as you say, walk out. I won't stop you, although of course I cannot let you go without your being blindfolded and transported a dis-tance away from this place. Our enemy was set back, but not vanquished, and we cannot afford to let them know our location. If you wish, we will drop you off anywhere within a hundred-mile radius. I will say, though, that if you choose to leave now, I would put your chances of survival for more than a week at near zero. Perhaps you do not realize the scale of the search you led our enemies on. There were hundreds of operatives looking for you, perhaps thousands. Your faces are, shall we say, rather well known amongst the

people who would enjoy nothing more than capturing both
of you, torturing you, and killing you."

"And our other option?" Chris said slowly.

"Simple. You put yourself under our protection. As I
said, we do owe you our gratitude. We are willing to guarantee your protection, insofar as it is within our ability to
do so. An ability, I might add, which is considerable."

"You never offered protection to Gavin," Chris responded.

"Your situation is different from Mr. McCormick's.
Your flight complicated matters, but its end result was to
place you in a situation where you did us a great service.
We are willing to repay that service with our protection of
your lives."

"Under what conditions?" Elisa said.

"The conditions are few, but are non-negotiable. We
can provide new identities and all of the appropriate doc-
umentation. We will set you up with a place to live, and a
modest but reasonable income, for life. During that time,
we will have you under our continuous protection. Understand that should you accept our conditions, it will be as
important to us that you remain at liberty as it will be to
yourselves, considering what you could reveal about us if
you were captured."

"And? What's the price?"

"You relinquish all contact with your former life. It is
purely for your safety, you understand. Our enemies cer-

tainly know by now what happened at their headquarters, and who was responsible. They will be desperate to know if you survived, and, more importantly, if you were captured by our operatives. Therefore, you cannot—you must not—contact family or friends. No one can know that you survived the raid. Should you choose this option, then after a short time, we will see to it that there is an announcement of your deaths sent to the appropriate people in your home towns. The documents will give our enemies reason to believe that you were killed during the raid on their headquarters. Certainly a likely eventuality, given the circumstances."

"What about the fact that there won't be any bodies to bury?" Chris asked. "Kind of makes it difficult to issue a death certificate."

Mrs. Hargroder smiled. It wasn't a particularly nice smile. "Oh, my dear Mr. Franzia," she said. "There won't be any bodies left from the raid. The enemy headquarters is going to be completely destroyed. There will be nothing left for them to sift through. So in the absence of evidence to the contrary, it will be easy enough for them to be led to the conclusion that you died along with your captors."

"Convenient."

"Yes. But you must realize that once you start down that path, there can be no turning back. You must realize that your lives, and those of your loved ones, will only be safe if you follow this rule. If the enemy thinks you survived, that we have secreted you away, they will be enraged. It will make them even more desperate to find you. If they believe that they can do something to force you out of hiding, they will do it, by whatever means possible. It is only if they believe you are both dead will they give up. It is only then that you and your family and friends will be safe. And therefore, you must be dead. You must consider your old life to have died in that place from which we rescued you today."

"That's horrible," Elisa said.

"Horrors occur when people become caught up in matters that are outside of their purview," Mrs. Hargroder said, and there was a measure of sympathy in her voice. Or perhaps it was a ruse, as everything else had been.

Chris had been right to think that he could trust no one. There was no way to tell truth from lie. He felt he had lost his touchstone for reality.

Except he had Elisa. Elisa would have to be his touchstone now. His hand tightened on hers, and he felt a squeeze in response.

"What else?" he said.

"If you accept our offer, we will transport you to any location of your choice and set you up in your new home. After that, you simply live your lives. But be aware your communications will be monitored, indefinitely. Telephone calls, emails, and so on. You know too much now ever to be completely free. True freedom is only possible for the ignorant."

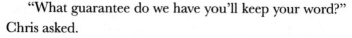
"What guarantee do we have you'll keep your word?" Chris asked.

"None," she said flatly. "I can give you nothing more than an assurance that if it had been our intent to kill you, we could have done so many times before now, and at much less inconvenience. You said we were the same as our enemy, but you're wrong in one very fundamental way. We are limited in what we are willing to do, by a sense of morality and, I might add, compassion. Our enemy sees no such limits."

"A morality that permits you to kill."

"Only when it is absolutely necessary."

"And a morality that allows you to use innocent people to serve your ends."

"When it is warranted, yes."

"So it's take our chances with the guys who intended to execute both of us, or live the rest of our lives in a cage," Chris said.

"Just so," she responded with a chilly smile. How could he ever have thought she looked maternal? There was a glitter in her eyes that was like a predator. Completely ruthless. Her expression reminded him of brilliant, pitiless Deirdre Ross, who had seen her attempted murder as an opportunity and seized that opportunity with both hands. She'd thrown her lot in with the other side and would have helped them torture him to death on that examining table rather than intervene and put herself at risk. He wondered if she'd died with the rest of them, or if she had somehow escaped the carnage.

If anyone could have survived, it would be Deirdre.

"Hobson's choice," Elisa said quietly.

"In reality, they all are," Mrs. Hargroder said, turning toward her. "We rarely see it at the time. You call our offer a cage. Perhaps that is true. But if it is a cage, it can be a lovely one. Together, I would presume?"

Chris looked at Elisa, a question in his eyes.

"Live together, or die together," she said to Chris. "Either way, I'm not leaving your side."

"But which do you want?" Chris said. "Do we agree to what these people are offering?"

She looked down. "It's terrible. What they're asking of us, no one should ever have to decide."

"No."

"But…" She stopped, and looked up into his eyes, and a clarity and strength met his gaze. "No," she said. "This ends here. We've been through enough. If she's telling the truth…"

"I am," Mrs. Hargroder said. "As I said, there would be no reason to go through this charade if we had intended to kill you. Frankly, it would be easier, and perhaps more prudent, to kill you and eliminate the chance of your breaking the rules. We are choosing not to do so."

"And also, in case you ever need to use us again," Chris said. "You'll have destroyed our past. You'll hold all the cards, and you're counting on the fact that we'd do it, for the same reasons we did this time. Desperation and hope."

But Mrs. Hargroder would not be goaded into anger again. "Come now, Mr. Franzia. Are you always so suspicious of gifts? The truth is that there is no reason for us to do this except for the fact that my superiors feel that you deserve some recompense for what you have done for us, however unwittingly it was done."

"Your superiors?" Chris said.

Mrs. Hargroder laughed. "Oh, you certainly can't tell me you think I am one of the leaders," she said. "No, sad to say, a little cog in a bigger wheel I am and shall remain, Mr. Franzia. Now, the time has come. Which will it be? The free choice of two free humans, which will almost certainly result in your untimely deaths? Or a long and peaceful, but limited, life under new identities, in a new place? I believe you understand your choices, and once chosen, you cannot go back. There is no particular reason to delay any further. Delay is only fruitful if there is the chance that time will provide you with additional information, or with greater clarity of mind. Neither is the case here." She smiled again, and tented her fingers together. "So, shall we cut to the chase, as they say? Which will it be, the Lady or the Tiger?"

EPILOGUE

Baxter gave a single warning woof at the knock on the door. Chris jumped. He wondered how long it was going to take him to stop panicking every time something unexpected happened. He was as safe now as he could be. He set down his newspaper, went to the door of the cottage, and opened it.

A slender young woman with waves of curly red hair and bright green eyes was standing there, a broad smile on her face and a box in her hand.

"Hi," Chris said.

The woman stuck out one hand, and shook his firmly. "Hi! I'm Rainey Carrington. I'm sort of your next door neighbor. I live down the road a little. I wanted to welcome you to Crooked Creek."

"Come in," Chris said, stepping aside. "I'm Dave. Dave Hamilton."

"Thanks. It's great to meet you, Dave." Rainey came inside, and handed Chris the box. "It's just a little welcome gift. I have an herbal tea business, and I put together a little sampler for you and… your…" She hesitated a little.

"Wife," Chris said. "Abigail." He turned a little, and said, "Abby? We have company."

Elisa came out from the kitchen a moment later, drying her hands on a tea towel. "Hi," she said, smiling.

Rainey shook her hand as well. "Rainey Carrington. I live right down the road. It's the next house down toward town, but on the other side of the road."

"The house with the beautiful flower gardens?"

"That's the one," she said with a broad grin. "I live there with my boyfriend, Tyler. He's a wildlife biologist. He's off doing field work right now. He should be back in two weeks or so."

"I've always wished I'd gone into research," Chris said. "I'm a retired biology teacher."

"Cool!" Rainey said enthusiastically. "Tyler's off in Cameroon at the moment."

"Wow," Chris said. "Cameroon. I don't even know if I could locate Cameroon on a map."

"Studying what?" Elisa said.

"Well… Wildlife," Rainey said, with a cryptic smile. "I think I'll let him tell you about it. He does some pretty unusual stuff."

"Can I get you a cup of tea or coffee?" Elisa said.

"Tea, please," Rainey said.

"It's just commercial stuff," Chris said. "Not nearly as good as what you make, I'm sure."

"No problem. I'm not a snob."

Elisa left to get cups of tea, and Chris motioned for Rainey to sit down on the couch. Baxter walked over to her, sniffed her curiously, and then sat down next to her and leaned heavily against her leg.

"Aren't you a good boy?" Rainey said and was rewarded with an enthusiastic wag. She looked up at Chris. "He probably smells our dog, Ahab." She skritched Baxter's ears, and he sighed heavily.

"This is Baxter."

"Hi, Baxter." Rainey smiled. "He's about a quarter of Ahab's size. He should have been named after the whale, not the ship's captain."

Chris laughed.

"So, what brought you to Crooked Creek?" she asked.

He had rehearsed the story so many times that he knew it by heart. It still seemed like a lie. Which it was. All of it was a lie, and Chris was living in the center of it. He wondered if eventually he'd tell it so many times, to other people and to himself, that he'd start believing it.

"I retired last June from teaching high school biology in Sacramento," he said. "Abby is a painter, so she can work anywhere. We got tired of the city and the heat and the cost of living, so we decided to find a quiet place to live. When we found this cottage for sale, it seemed ideal. I've always loved Oregon."

"I hope you don't find it too cold in the winter," she said. "We're kind of high up."

"Doesn't bother me a bit. My parents moved around a lot when I was a kid. I lived in central New Hampshire for a while. This is bound to be milder than what I remember from there."

"Definitely. Crooked Creek is a sweet little town. I think you'll like it. We have some characters around here, but they add to the interest."

Elisa came out of the kitchen carrying a tray with three steaming mugs of tea.

"Thanks, honey," Chris said. He stood, took one and passed it along to Rainey, and then took another for himself.

"So, I overheard you make herbal teas?" Elisa said, set the tray on the coffee table, and sat down on the couch next to Rainey.

"Yup. I do a lot of sales through mail order. We'll never get rich from it, but it helps to pay the bills. Tyler's off doing field work pretty often. I go with him when I can, but at least some of the time I have to stay home and mind the shop and take care of the pets."

Chris relaxed. His tension levels always rose when talking to strangers. After two months, he still felt it was at least even odds that he'd find himself suddenly facing the business end of a gun. However, this kind young woman, with the earnest face and the hand-sewn linen dress, she couldn't be one of *Them*, could she?

The conversation continued for a while, on topics from interesting local citizens of Crooked Creek to which parts of the nearby Three Sisters Wilderness Area they'd yet to explore. But finally Rainey said, with a smile, "I should be going. Once Tyler comes back, we'll have you over for dinner."

"That'd be wonderful," Elisa said.

They said their farewells, and Chris watched through the window as Rainey walked down the driveway. He followed her with his eyes until she went around a bend in the road and was lost to view.

"Should we throw away the tea?" Elisa said, standing next to the sofa, holding the box in her hand.

"Absolutely," Chris said.

"We can't distrust everyone, forever," she said.

"I thought that was the agreement."

Elisa looked down at the box of delicately-bottled tea mixes. "Do you ever wish we had just taken our chances?"

Chris sat down heavily in his rocking chair. "Of all the things we were told in that place, that's the one I think was

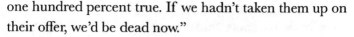

one hundred percent true. If we hadn't taken them up on their offer, we'd be dead now."

"At some point," she said, "you have to assume that things are going to be okay. You can't live balanced on that pinnacle of fear and suspicion indefinitely."

"No," Chris said, after a while. "No, I suppose you're right."

"I'm not saying that we should proclaim to the world our real names, and where we came from, or try to get in touch with people from our past lives," she said. "What we have here, Mrs. Hargroder was right about that, too. If it's a cage, it's a beautiful one. And we have each other."

"We do."

"So if this is all we have, we should let go of worrying about everything. Like everyone else in the world, we exist within our limits, love the people who are dear to us, and live as many years as we are given. Beyond that, what more can we do?"

Chris looked down. "There's just one thing that I can't let go."

Elisa set the box of tea down on the coffee table, came over to him, and knelt down, just as she had two months earlier, when he'd awakened in that horrible room to see her next to him. "What is that?"

"It makes no sense," Chris said. "The whole thing about Iktomi7979. The old man who tortured me kept asking me that. I still have dreams about it, hearing that question over and over. Who is Iktomi7979? He insisted I must know. Deirdre didn't know, and he accepted that, apparently. I thought, initially, they were hurting me to pay me back for eluding them for so long, for giving them so much trouble. But you did, too, and they didn't torture you."

"No. No, they didn't."

"And Mrs. Hargroder. It seems like her group would have been equally at risk from what Iktomi and Gavin were doing. Because that was it, wasn't it? You hit it, when we were talking to her. Both groups were trying to accomplish the same thing. They were at each other's throats not because they hated each other, but because they were in a race to accomplish the same thing—figuring out how to use alien devices, probably for things like mind control, and who knows what else."

"Yes," she said, and there was a tentative note in her voice.

"But Mrs. Hargroder didn't even ask us about Iktomi. She gave us tuna fish sandwiches and new identities, and once we agreed not to talk, and to follow her rules, she sent us off with a pat on the back, holding our new birth certificates and driver's licenses and so on. And there's only one way that all makes sense."

Elisa looked away. Outside the window, the fog descending on the Douglas firs as evening fell. "And what is that, Chris?" she asked. Her voice sounded distant, without inflection, without emotion.

"She knew who Iktomi is already. I hadn't given it away to their enemies, she figured that much. And it wouldn't have mattered if I had, because they killed them all. At that point, the last thing she wanted was my asking too many questions, or getting more ideas." He paused, looked down. "I guess she could have had me killed, too, but once I got away from New York, once I talked to people, interacted with people like Jim Hargis and Thomas T. Champion and the Harpers, it was too risky. Better to dupe me, get me to buy in, and then to offer me a carrot. Reward and punishment. Be a good boy and then go live your life in a cabin in the Cascades with the woman you've been in love with since college. But don't ever talk to anyone again, about anything." He shook his head. "They knew exactly what would tempt me."

"There's no way to find out if you're right."

He put his hand against her face, and gently but inexorably, turned her head until she was looking at him. "You know I'm right, though, don't you? You know. It wasn't just a lucky accident that you were safely hiding in your friend's house in Hoquiam when the the others were being killed, was it?"

She looked into his eyes for nearly a full minute before she spoke. "Chris, does it really matter if you're right or wrong?" she said, quietly. "It's over. You wanted out. You're out. And you can stay out." She took his hand. "We can both stay out. Forever. If there's one thing I've learned from all of this, it's that there's too much pain and death and intrigue and secrecy in the world. Some secrets are not worth knowing. Some secrets, when you discover them, turn out to be banal and foolish and pointless, and not worth the cost. There are some secrets I regret ever trying to find out." A single tear ran down her cheek, but her voice did not waver. "Let it be, Chris. You have a life, here, if you want it."

"Even if it means that I spend the rest of my life as Dave Hamilton, retired schoolteacher from Sacramento?"

"Yes. Even that. There are worse things. Far, far worse things."

"I suppose there are."

"I think Dave and Abby Hamilton could be pretty happy together, honestly. As long as they are willing to let Chris Franzia and Elisa Reed remain in their graves."

"And Iktomi?"

"Yes. Iktomi, too. They all belong to another world. Let it go, Chris."

He took her hand. "I used to have a sign up in my classroom, back in Guildford. It said, 'Per Scientiam Felicitas.' It's Latin. It means, 'Through knowledge, happiness.' It's simply not true, is it?" He shook his head. "It's simply not true."

There was a pause, and then Elisa said, "I remember my yoga teacher, back in St. Cloud, telling us about a Taoist precept. 'To become smart, learn one thing a day. To become wise, forget one thing a day.'" She smiled at him, and gave his hand a squeeze. "Perhaps that's closer to the truth than your classroom sign was."

"What deal did you make with them, Elisa? What part in all of this did you play?"

She looked at him searchingly, and it was a long time before she spoke. "I could tell you that. But would it really satisfy you? Everything that happened, everything we both did, led here. And to the end of our part in all of this. I would go back, do things differently, if I could, but that is an option we never have. All we can do is take the past, mistakes and all, and try to make the best of it. So if you ask me again, I will tell you. But are you sure that you want to know?"

The room was sliding into shadow as the sun approached the western horizon. Leave it. Take the carrot. Gavin got this started by looking for answers, and where did it get him? And how many people died because of it? Sometimes answers are not worth the price. He felt tears start up behind his eyes, but fought them back. Getting answers would not give him what he wanted most, which was to have the world go back to the way it was. Simple, straightforward, honest. And if he couldn't have that, what was the use of knowing what the truth was?

"Okay," he said, his voice weary. "You win."

She reached up and gave him a light kiss on the mouth. "I don't know if my yoga teacher was right," she said. "But maybe sometimes, happiness comes from knowing which questions not to ask."

KILL
switch

GORDON bonnet

about
the author

Gordon Bonnet has been writing fiction for decades. Encouraged when his story *Crazy Bird Bends His Beak* won critical acclaim in Mrs. Moore's 1st grade class at Central Elementary School in St. Albans, West Virginia, he embarked on a long love affair with the written word.

His interest in the paranormal goes back almost that far, although it has always been tempered by Gordon's scientific training. This has led to a strange duality; his work as a skeptic and debunker on the popular blog *Skeptophilia*, while simultaneously writing paranormal and speculative novels, novellas, and short stories. He blogs daily, but is never without a piece of fiction in progress—driven to continue, as he puts it, "because I want to find out how the story ends."

Gordon currently lives in upstate New York with his wife and two dogs.

CPSIA information can be obtained at www.ICGtesting.com
Printed in the USA
BVOW03s1618160415

396366BV00002B/2/P